QUINN

Recent Titles by Harriet Hudson from Severn House

INTO THE SUNLIGHT
NOT IN OUR STARS
SONGS OF SPRING
TO MY OWN DESIRE
WINTER ROSES

QUINN

Harriet Hudson

This first world edition published in Great Britain 2001 by
SEVERN HOUSE PUBLISHERS LTD of
9–15 High Street, Sutton, Surrey SM1 1DF.
This first world edition published in the USA 2002 by
SEVERN HOUSE PUBLISHERS INC of
595 Madison Avenue, New York, N.Y. 10022.

British Library Cataloguing in Publication Data

Hudson, Harriet
  Quinn
  I. Title
  823.9'14 [F]

ISBN 0-7278-5753-3

Typeset by Palimpsest Book Production Ltd.,
Polmont, Stirlingshire, Scotland.
Printed and bound in Great Britain by
MPG Books Ltd., Bodmin, Cornwall.

Acknowledgements

My thanks are due to my agent, Dorothy Lumley of the Dorian Literary Agency, who with her usual flair recognised the germ of a book in the few paragraphs of the storyline I had submitted.

I also owe much to my friends Mike Murray and Adrian Turner, whose logic and expert knowledge hauled me back from a plot heffalump pit, and to my sister, Marian Anderson, whose eagle eye for detail picks up unconsidered trifles I have strewn along the path.

H. H.

Part One

ELLIE

One

W ho says there's no such thing as being happy ever after? Just because it doesn't always happen, doesn't mean it never does.

Certainly on that September afternoon, I had no intention of ever moving down from Cloud Nine, where I'd just spent my honeymoon with Quinn. True, clouds can bring rain, but our Cloud Nine was a mere wisp of summer white on which we floated in the clear blue sky of our horizon. Received wisdom seems to be that nowadays we 'youngsters' – I'm twenty-six – don't know what love is. Show us a bed, and apparently that's all we're interested in. Call it what you like, but the red rose of love smells as sweet today as ever it did, and at that moment it was roses, roses all the way.

'Ellie!'

Even the sound of his voice sent a tremor of bliss through me, and when it was followed by the sight of his tall, comfortably sized person appearing at the dining room doorway, it was almost enough to make me leap on him to demand instant sex. (For all the roses, it didn't mean I wasn't interested in the basics.) It was just as well I had some restraint, for the movers had conveniently 'forgotten' to put the bed together, and there remained only a tiny area of floor free of boxes and a sofa too small to accommodate his six foot one, my five foot five, piles of important papers, and my – now *our* – cat Irving.

'Where's my easel?' Quinn demanded plaintively.

'No idea.' How could I know? We'd only moved into the

3

Charham Park Lodge an hour ago, and most of the time since then had been taken up with supplying tea and biscuits to the removal team, who had only just departed.

'Good.'

'Good?' I repeated cautiously as he grinned lazily in that way he has which seems like a physical touch. Even on honeymoon Quinn had refused to be parted too long from the tools of his illustrator's trade, and now that munificent fate had provided him with a studio of his very own in the Lodge garden, naturally I had expected them to receive a higher priority. Maybe his thoughts were running along the same lines as mine.

'I can put the bed together,' he leered, 'while you're hunting down the stuff that goes on it.'

'*We're* the stuff that goes on it,' I said happily, but nevertheless went to seek out one of the black bags full of sheets and duvets in the entrance hall while Quinn bounded with alacrity up the stairs.

Then I saw it.

It was lying oh-so-innocently on a packing case addressed to Mrs Quinn Connelly, where a removal man must have placed it, having picked it up from the doormat before staggering in with the wardrobes and tables.

'What's wrong?' Quinn was bounding down again at my yell of dismay.

'It's a letter from my aunt.' There was no mistaking her huge black scrawl.

'So? She sounds quite a character. Anyway, she found us this place, so in my book she's okay. I thought you told me you liked her.'

'I do.'

One of the problems with a rushed wedding to someone you've only known a month is that one doesn't get to learn much about one's partner's background until it's too late, and on a honeymoon there are far more interesting things to do than discuss family history. Now came the time of reckoning.

Our July wedding had been arranged at short notice and Aunt Columba had been filming in the States. Quinn therefore had not yet met her.

I was eyeing that letter as though it were a bomb. 'Her letters always mean trouble,' was all I could find to say. It sounded weak, even to me, but then I knew just what had happened that time a peremptory letter had arrived demanding that my parents and I join her in an idyllic remote Caribbean island. By the time we had struggled with aircraft, ships and finally rowing boats, the bird had flown. Indeed, it had never arrived. It had sped back to London to take part in a chat show. Or take the time a cable had arrived announcing she was destitute in Paris, omitting to mention she was in Paris, Texas, not France. From time immemorial my mother had viewed a letter from her sister as a catastrophe waiting to happen, and I suppose I simply picked up the habit.

'Would you like me to open it?' Quinn asked as I stood like a hypnotised rabbit in the glare of my aunt's oncoming headlights.

'Yes please.'

He tore it open and scanned quickly through it. 'No problem,' he decided. 'She just says she's coming down to Charham next week and would like to have dinner with us on Monday evening. Do you judge that as meaning big or little trouble?' he enquired politely.

I tried to make a joke of it. 'Nothing my aunt does is little. It'll be big.'

How right I was.

Family skeletons are the biggest secret one has. Even the most inoffensive, ideally happy childhood can produce an unexpected reaction from a future partner, for what is the norm for one family can be outrageously unconventional for another. It's all a matter of confidence, and I had confidence in the kernel of mine, my life with my parents. But beyond that glowing light, there were, as I suppose in most families, areas of darkness that for one reason or another I had never penetrated. Quinn was adopted, and though I wouldn't have changed my contented childhood for his early start in life, at least he is spared those black holes in which even a photograph in an album can acquire the mystery of a full-blown secret.

For instance, a photograph of a severe lady in late Victorian clothes in my father's family collection bears the legend 'The Militant Monster of Mottingham', but nothing lingers either on paper or in the memory of my living relatives to explain further. Why was this lady a monster? It remains a mystery as to whether this was a family joke, or stemmed from fervent radical politics, or something more. As a child, I stared at the bleak eyes, trying to puzzle out the answer, but it eluded me and probably always will.

Unfortunately, my aunt, Columba Flowerdew, is not the elusive sort, nor does this skeleton waste time lurking in a cupboard. She and my mother come from a prominent thespian clan which dates back to times when the theatre was far from respectable in society's eyes – at least as a profession to follow. It spanned the twentieth century, adapting to different times, and has burst triumphantly into the twenty-first as a multimedia favourite. My aunt is a well-known face on television, though she prefers straight theatre or film. Comedy of the Lady Bracknell variety is her speciality on stage and screen. In real life, she inclines more to high drama.

How my grandparents came to have two such dissimilar daughters beats me. My grandmother, who is going strong at eighty-nine, is sweet, if somewhat steely-natured, and her husband, the late William Flowerdew, was gentle and only too happy to be led by her. Their elder daughter, my Aunt Columba, however, inherited the charm and melodrama of William's father, Sir Claud Flowerdew, actor manager of Edwardian times, who died donkey's years before I was born. My mother Margaret is six years younger than Columba and takes after her father with a strong dash of her mother when roused. Any theatrical streak in her was quickly suppressed when, as a young dancer, she was swept off her feet by a young pop star in the heady days of the 1960s. By the time she regained them five years later, the boards had ceased to have any appeal. In due course she married my architect father, Gerald Peters, and began to sculpt. She's no Barbara Hepworth, but she does a neat line in prestigious garden figures, eschewing gnomes for historical personages. In their garden you can spot her rejects – Good Queen Bess lurking under the bushes minus one ear, or a noseless Mozart leering down at you from a bank.

Her marriage is a happy one – so far as one can tell – but there are secrets in her life too, or at least a secret sadness. By her bed stands a photograph of me as a toddler, and by it one of another child taken when he was two or three years old. It's of my half-brother Marcus, who died when he was three in 1969 – so Dad told me, as I have never dared to ask my mother. I'd been on the brink of doing so several times, but always pulled back in case it was too painful for her to talk about even now. Marcus's father was the pop star. My mother never spoke of her first husband, let alone Marcus, and so nor did I. Yet I wondered about him very often, puzzling at this evidence of a passion before her love for my father, a time when I did not exist, and the emotions of which lie buried in the quicksand of time. He would have been eight years older than I, not too great a gap to bond. After all, there are eight years between Quinn and myself. Brothers may be different – but I'd have liked the chance of finding out.

Aunt Columba falls into another category of family secret – idiosyncratic if not downright eccentric relations. It's hard to think of Columba as a secret, however. She and my father hammered out their considerable differences many years ago – such as who had first call on my mother's time. My father maintained it was my mother herself; Columba was prone to dispute this in practice, at least, if not in theory. They reached an amicable compromise of mutual respect and minimum meeting, since even Columba realised that she could claim no sister without a certain amount of tolerance of Father, and vice versa.

Columba and I, however, are a different ball game. Not least because I love her so much. Don't ask me why. I know why I love Mum and Dad over and above the requirements of filial duty, but Columba beats me. She's inconsiderate, warm-hearted, self-centred, understanding, illogical, generous, and impossible to deal with. And yet, remove her from my life, and a 200-watt light bulb would vanish too. Perhaps that's love?

'Oh, I'm so glad to see *you*,' Jane said as I walked cautiously into the office I had trustingly left in her hands for my three weeks of honeymoon.

She didn't look glad, but then she never does. Pessimism is her stock in trade, but as she is reasonably efficient and even more importantly reliable, she has a permanent place in my office so far as I'm concerned. 'Glad to see me' didn't sound promising though.

'What's gone wrong?' I asked.

'The Catchpole wedding's doubled in size,' came her doom-laden reply.

'Marquee on the lawn,' I said briskly. I believe in disposing of problems quickly where Jane's concerned.

'It will be in November.'

'Ah. Well, we'll sort it out.' I was confident of it. There is always a way, even if I have to seat them on the beams.

Charham Place is a Jacobean house, with a Victorian ballroom usefully tacked on. Stephen Marsh, the American owner, lives in the USA, only comes over on visits, and never interferes. Our trading name is Happy Ever After, and we play our part to achieve it. We offer the complete service, from advising on jokes for the best man's speech through every aspect of The Day itself, right through to touching up the wedding photos. I know every intimate stick of what the bride is wearing when she arrives, flushed with her first realisation that she is now a wife. We can even hold the ceremony here too.

'And Mr Marsh's flying in next weekend.' Jane was determined to reduce me to gloom if possible. 'He says he wants the red dining room for himself on Tuesday evening.'

'It's let for the Bromefield wedding, isn't it?'

'I told him that. He says we can unlet it.'

'Sure. I'll just explain to the couple that they can't get married after all.'

'They could have the ballroom.'

'So they could,' I sighed, 'but a party of eight might look a tad lost, don't you think?'

It was thanks to Aunt Columba that we're based here, for it was she who introduced us to Stephen. Relationships are funny things. There's Stephen, a rich, calm, delightful man of fifty-eight, hankering after madcap Aunt Columba, who hit sixty-two running last year and has no intention of stopping. Especially for poor old Stephen. You'd think he'd know better. He's been married and divorced twice, and yet here he is romantically hiring out his house for wedding receptions in the forlorn hope that it will host his own.

It was just my bad luck that Stephen had heard about Aunt Columba's impending visit. News travelled fast in the theatre, and Stephen, a billionaire on a scale that would make lottery roll-overs look insignificant, was an angel, a backer of what he fancied. Of course, what he fancied most was Columba.

There was a flaw in this visit though. If he didn't know about her visit next week, then her main reason for visiting us couldn't be Stephen. It often was, since she was very fond of him – and indeed, I suspect fondness takes their relationship quite a way. Yet, she will always say disarmingly, she wasn't ready to marry him and settle down. What, I thought with foreboding, was her reason for coming? Mere curiosity to meet Quinn? Hardly. She would have summoned us to her London penthouse.

By the pricking of my thumbs, I thought to myself, something *extremely* troublesome this way comes. Only I didn't dare put a name to the play I was misquoting. That would be bad luck, and I had all I needed at the moment.

'Safe haven, I've crawled into harbour,' I called out of the kitchen window in relief when I got home, and it was a satisfactorily short time before the studio disgorged Quinn to stroll up to the house and enquire what I might be shouting about this time.

'What is?'

'This is.' I snuggled into his welcoming arms. 'This house, this husband, this home.' We'd lived in my flat for three of the four weeks we'd known each other before we married, but it had never felt like home.

'You have to pay port charges here.'

'Sex?'

'You have a one-track mind, I'm glad to say. I meant dinner, actually.'

'We can try living on love.'

'Yes, but I can't work on it.'

'What happened to your bachelor skills of living?' How Quinn had escaped matrimony until the ripe age of thirty-four and a half was a constant wonder to me. I gathered from vague remarks that I wasn't the first woman he'd lived with, but since I had no desire to recap my own errors of judgement in this respect, I left it at that, and thanked kind fortune for wheeling him my way.

'You told me to forget them.'

'I meant woman skills – except for me,' I added quickly.

'Deuce,' he declared amiably. He's an amiable size too, is Quinn. Not too fat, not too thin, and all the comfort of a goodnight story. I make this comparison since Quinn is not only an illustrator of children's books, but a computer cartoon animator and general provider of wicked wit to the under-fourteens and all parents wishing to keep up with the current trend. Quinn is the credit on the 'Sadie O'Grady and Dirk Dog' cartoons which swept the awards last year and which brought him so much publicity he's had to farm out the trademark for T-shirts and mugs to a limited company run by an agent.

Quinn copes with publicity but prefers to retire to his studio to get on with the business of drawing and painting. His first love is book illustration. I suppose it appeals to the Peter Pan in him, an elusive quality that must have come from his Celtic roots. I can just see him swinging round Ireland, narrating stories to all and sundry. Our honeymoon was based on fairy-tale castles, beginning at St Michael's Mount, moving over to Mont St Michel, then down to the Dordogne and Perigord to admire castles hanging perilously in what seemed mid-air. The odd thing about Quinn is that head-in-the-clouds he might be, but his feet are more firmly on the ground in many ways than mine.

'Why do you need a safe harbour?' he asked an hour later in bed, just as I was beginning to think dinner might not be such a bad idea after all.

I briefly described my annoying problems at work, which had now happily receded.

'You know what they say,' he commented. 'The worst fears are those that never happen.'

'This one is happening next week.' I tried to explain just why it was so awkward, but it sounded feeble. I could see Quinn was dutifully doing his best to be a partner and battling with the issue of why the red dining room was so important to me.

'It's because Aunt Columba's mixed up in it,' I concluded dolefully. 'I could easily solve it otherwise.'

'Ellie,' – his arms tightened round me – 'whatever ghoulies and ghosties remained with you when you left your childhood behind can be expelled. You're not the same person now.'

'I've grown up, do you mean?'

'No. Grown *into*. We're one.' The most wonderful words
I'd ever heard. The feel of his arms around me, the memory of
the sex, and now a firm declaration of intent for the future.

'Does that extend to cooking dinner?' I asked hopefully.

'No, but it does extend to your blessed Aunt Columba.
But I'll wash up. How's that?'

'There's a dishwasher.'

'Do I ask you to lay a fire to cook with and rub sticks
together?'

Reluctantly ceding the point, I swung my feet down from
the bed. Immediately they touched down, back came the
spectre of Aunt Columba. We'd watched her in a sitcom
on TV last night, and Quinn had appraised her carefully as
a relation-in-law, joking about Lady Bracknells and handbags containing lost children at Victoria Station. How we
laughed.

'Is the aspic set yet? You could turn out the whatsits.'

'Ellie,' Quinn yelled, exasperated at last. 'Will you *stop*?
You're having your aunt to dinner, not the Queen.'

'I'll just put the pot-pourri in the bathroom.' I got a grip
on myself. It was just bridal nerves that said everything had
to conform to the glossy mag perfection. That's what I told
myself anyway.

Quinn regarded me grimly. 'You know what we agreed.
No fuss.'

'That's just like a man,' I found myself replying to my horror. How could I trot out that old cliché – even if it was true? I
excused myself on the grounds that I'd been in a quake at the
office all day, expecting my aunt to march in at any moment. I
don't know why this should be. Columba is the least critical of
women. She accepts you as you are. She has a sharp eye, mind
you, but it observes, not condemns. I suppose my keenness to
shine in her eyes is just because of this. I'm perhaps saying,
Here stand I, Eleanor Connelly, count me as worthy.

Stephen had flown in, and I'd invited him along this evening. Initially he had declined, nobly saying that it was a family occasion, and anyway Columba would be coming to dinner at Charham Place. He'd given way to me, as Stephen would, and switched from the red dining room to the blue for that occasion. That's what must have made him such a good businessman, separating the reasonable from the unreasonable quickly and decisively.

I should explain why the red and the blue dining rooms are so important. The red is an intimate family room of great taste combined with comfort. It is the room where legend has it the first owner managed to seduce the then Queen of England while the monarch was slumbering off the effects of the wine. It is a happy room.

The blue room, on the other hand, although most elegant and of the same size as the red room, is bleaker because of its predominant colour and its position facing north-west. It also has a legend attached to it: the second owner murdered his wife in it. There is a distinct chill here that has nothing to do with the lack of sun and everything to do with the fact that it's rumoured to be haunted. Naturally enough, Stephen was reluctant to entertain Columba, whom he hoped to make his wife, in any place where subconscious vibes might be suggesting she should get the hell out of it. I should explain that Columba has had her share of matrimonial adventures too – not to mention extra-marital – and therefore is an expert on vibes. The vibes Stephen wanted her to pick up were those of security, loving warmth, and so on, not cold formality.

When I saw the look on his face as I came to leave for the day, I could stand it no longer. 'You're coming tonight, Stephen. You're aspiring family, after all.'

He brightened up immediately. 'I'll be there at seven thirty. I've already ordered flowers.'

Oh yes, a very good businessman. Plan what you want to do, and it will happen.

Now it was seven o'clock and I was in a worse than

usual host's panic. We had divided the cooking between us, Quinn doing the main course, me doing everything else. All miraculously seemed ready. Only one thing was wrong. No Aunt Columba had yet appeared.

And then the telephone rang. Quinn went to answer it and came back with his coat on. 'Your aunt's at the station asking to be picked up. She doesn't want to bother Stephen, she says.'

'Unusually thoughtful of her,' I snarled, one eye on the clock.

Quinn saw it. 'I'll be back in an hour.'

'It takes five minutes to drive to the station.'

'Not Tonbridge it doesn't.'

My heart sank like a soufflé. How could she do it? Tonbridge is half an hour away at least. Quinn's *canetons aux petits pois* would be ruined. The door banged behind Quinn, and for once I shared Jane's pessimism. We were off, as no doubt we would continue, on a course set straight for disaster.

'My darling!'

At eight fifteen the door reopened and Columba hurtled in; I was swept into her Shalimar-perfumed embrace, and found myself almost crying in my pleasure at seeing her. Columba might be over sixty, but age is not the first thing that comes to mind when I see her shining brown bobbed hair, dark lively eyes, and five foot seven of spare, intense energy. The hair is not always so brownly demure, but the occasion called for it. Today she wore black velvet leggings and jacket, scarlet tunic, scarlet lipstick, and an old-fashioned black cap with a peak pulled down fetchingly over one eye.

'And darling Stephen too,' she cooed. Stephen, who had arrived promptly, was drawn into the embrace, still clutching his tribute of flowers.

'Now, this man of yours, Ellie,' Columba continued,

tearing off her jacket and tossing it casually somewhere in the general direction of Quinn. 'Quite delightful, my dear. I quite see why you married him.'

Quinn gave me a smirk as if to say, See? What were you worried about? – and indeed I began to wonder myself. The thing about Aunt Columba is that she means (at the time at least) everything she says, even if she shouldn't say it.

'Darling Stephen. The light has come into my life again,' she assured him.

He glowed, pressing the flowers into her arms. 'You'll still dine with me tomorrow, Columba?'

'Of course. The red dining room.'

Stephen glanced at me. 'The blue, but—'

'Oh no, Stephen. That's sweet of you, because you know how much I love the blue. But you like the red, and red it shall be.'

'It's already let, Columba.'

Columba turned to where I was waiting in trepidation. 'That's Ellie's department. Darling,' – she turned to me – 'I don't ask for myself, but don't you think Stephen should have the red room? He doesn't come here very often. Don't you worry, Stephen. I'll sweet-talk Ellie into it. Don't let her bully you.'

Already it was beginning to seem that surrender was the only possible solution. I stared at the drooping roses in my hands, which had been handed over to me to deal with. I knew just how they felt.

Yet it began so well. The tarragon eggs in aspic were delicious, the wine flowed, and even the *canetons aux petits pois* survived their incarceration. Columba was on her best behaviour, alternately enchanting and, to me at least, irritating as she chattered on from theatre to mutual friends, politics and television. Quinn seemed hooked, which was a relief – even if I knew from experience that this could only be temporary. I flew in and out with dishes, trying to keep abreast of the conversation to ward off problems. I longed to be in there, but I longed to be away in the kitchen, far from any Sword of Damocles that might yet fall.

And of course, fall it did – just when at last I began to relax. As I carried in the damson crumble, I heard Quinn ask innocently:

'Why did you come, Columba? Just to admire Ellie's good taste in husbands?'

'I have to admit,' Columba gurgled confidingly in her famous husky tones, 'that I had an ulterior motive.'

I clung to the dish with my now nerveless hands.

'And what is that?' Stephen asked mildly. 'Apart from your passion about dining in the red room.'

'I'm getting married and I thought you should be the first to know.'

The dish couldn't take this shock, and right on cue in the stunned silence it crashed to the floor. I watched the splodge of damson juice creeping over the beige carpet and hours seemed to pass, though it could only have been a second or two before Quinn was at my side.

'I'll get a cloth,' he said quietly.

As I looked at Stephen, unable to speak, I was foreseeing with an awful inevitability what was going to happen. He looked so happy, I thought I would cry.

'Thank you, Columba,' he replied quietly. 'I guess this isn't the place to discuss it, but tomorrow—'

A peal of throaty laughter, as Columba patted his hand and said fondly, 'Oh Stephen darling. You don't want to marry me. You know it wouldn't work. I'm marrying some-one else.'

I couldn't look at Stephen now, and it was left to Quinn to pick up the pieces, and I don't mean the crumble.

'Then why come here?' he asked angrily, busily scrubbing at the crimson stains.

Columba peered down at his bent figure. 'Darling, to see Ellie of course.'

Even then I did not understand. I was genuinely pleased she wanted to tell me first.

'We can discuss the business in your office tomorrow morning,' Columba continued. 'But we'll toast it tonight, shall we?'

Business? Tomorrow morning? This sounded bad. 'Where are you holding the wedding, Columba?' I asked carefully.

'At Charham Place, of course.' She looked amazed at the question. 'Where else? Stephen would be so hurt if I got married anywhere but here.'

Stephen himself began to cut off my protest, struggling now to hold on to his usual urbanity, but Columba forestalled him with a pleased smile. 'It's the least I could do for you, Stephen. I know it will give you pleasure.'

'No, it would not.' He banged his fist down in angry frustration. 'Don't you realise, you ghastly woman, that I love you? The only wedding you'll be having in my house will have me there as the groom.'

Columba looked surprised at the way things were developing.

'Very well,' she replied nobly. 'If you're quite sure. I'll find somewhere else.' Bright sparkles of tears indicated she was deeply hurt.

'Who is this poor sap you're marrying?' Stephen hurled at her.

'Why, it's Graham Padbury, of course. Whom else would I marry?'

Quinn, who had been trying to keep a low profile, now came roaring in. 'He can't be more than sixteen, Columba.'

Graham Padbury was the delinquent 'baddie' in the running sitcom, and thus the idol of the masses.

'He is, if it has any relevance, over forty. I don't believe age is any obstacle in a loving relationship.'

'Does he know yet?' Stephen asked, showing a more acute grasp of Columba's character than I'd given him credit for.

'Certainly he does,' Columba declared grandly. 'Shall we say two weeks' time, Ellie?'

'We shall not,' I found the strength to say. 'Firstly, I'm fully booked, and secondly, Stephen won't allow it. You heard him say so.'

Columba looked lovingly into his eyes. 'Dear Stephen. I understand why you're worried, but my marriage need not affect our . . . er – shut your ears, Ellie – little private arrangement.'

'Our little private arrangement, as you call it, is over, Columba.' Stephen rose to his feet, a muscle in his cheek quivering with suppressed emotion. What the emotion was, I could only guess: grief, shock, a strong desire to throttle his beloved, or a combination of all three. 'Thank you, Ellie, and Quinn, for what might have been a delightful evening, but I guess it's more sensible if I bow out now. As I shall from my backing of *Three's None*.'

From Columba's immediate farewell kiss to him, one might have thought he'd just offered to buy in to her new play, not pulled out. Quinn and I returned to the dining room in despair after he had left. I was racked with pity for Stephen, and fury at Columba for fulfilling even worse fears than I had dreamed of.

'You were right,' Quinn muttered as we prepared to face our guest. 'She's a monster.'

The big trouble had come, and a glance at Quinn's face told me he was thinking along the same lines.

Columba was engaged in opening another bottle of wine. 'I'm so sorry to put you through that, darlings,' she said, all smiles. 'Somehow I had to make Stephen see that I'm impossible to live with, quite unfit to be his wife. So I thought I'd show him how outrageous I can be. In fact, it's rather heroic of me. I adore him, but I don't want to marry him. Well, not for a while anyway. This way I'm playing fair. I'm giving him the chance to find someone else.' She looked at us, confident of our approval. 'I hope he doesn't, of course,' she added, 'but if he does, I don't mind sharing him.'

'You mean all this about marrying Graham Padbury was a put-up job?' Quinn asked incredulously as I gaped at her, speechless.

'Oh yes, I have been at my wits' end over how to convince Stephen. Now he'll believe it at last.'

'And what about us?' I choked.

'You?'

'It hasn't occurred to you that Stephen, in his unhappiness at what he thinks is losing you, might sell up and throw me out of my office and both of us out of the Lodge?'

The dismay on Columba's face was real. She just hadn't thought about it. 'I'll make sure he doesn't do that,' she promised.

'You'll talk to him?'

'Talk?' Columba considered this. 'Something like that.' (I realised the private arrangement was clearly going to remain in force.) 'But the red room, I think, darling,' she added.

'Anything, *anything*,' I instantly submitted. 'What about Graham?' I added. 'Are you really marrying him?'

Columba fixed me with a stony eye. 'Don't pry into my private life, darling.'

Quinn began to laugh, and after a while I joined in. 'Ellie said there'd be trouble. I didn't believe her then, Columba. I do now.'

'Did you, Ellie? I can't think why,' she replied complacently. 'Anyway, it's over.'

Fool that I was, I believed her, especially when I passed her in the entrance hall of Charham Place early on the Wednesday morning. She was coming out as I was going in to the office. Stephen, trotting behind her with her hold-all, had a smile as big as the Cheshire Cat's, so I guessed everything was all right. The trouble was over.

We saw Columba into the taxi. One of her elegantly trousered legs had manoeuvred its way in and was being

followed by the other when she remarked idly, 'Such a handsome man, Quinn.'

'Yes.'

'You're lucky, Ellie. I wish I'd found a gorgeous hunk like him. Margaret did, so why can't I?'

'Father isn't like Quinn. He never was.'

'No dear, not Gerald. I meant Margaret's first husband. The spitting image, darling, the spitting image.'

Two

I thought nothing of it at first. Why should I? Everyone looked like someone else. After all, my mother had met Quinn at our wedding and she hadn't fainted with shock at being faced with a younger version of her first husband. Nevertheless, by the time I got home I was aware that my undefined niggle was still present – probably because it was Columba who had put it there.

'How did the dinner go?' Quinn asked me during our own dinner, just as I thought the whole subject could be lulled into non-existence. 'Or didn't it? Did he fling her out into the snow telling her never to darken the red room again?'

'It seems' – I carefully helped myself to an orange – 'that he and Columba are on the best of terms again. Certainly they were when she left – this morning. Your studio's safe for the moment.'

'Good. So what happened? Why did Columba change her mind and go for stability rather than toyboys?'

'I've no proof she did, but Stephen reassured me he wasn't selling up and had no plans to do so. For all I know she's persuaded him to set up a ménage à trois. Maybe the glorious Graham is to be my manager.'

'Is that why you have a look on your face like Sadie O'Grady on a bad day?'

'Have I?' I was surprised he could read my face so well. I thought I'd inherited more of the Flowerdew talents than I apparently have. 'Columba remarked that you remind her of my mother's first husband.' I hadn't meant to tell him, but out it came.

Quinn looked puzzled, then he laughed. 'So you think that as your mother's marriage broke up, her daughter's life will automatically follow suit, because of a passing resemblance?' There was nothing forced about his amusement, and, put that way, my niggle seemed ridiculous. 'No way. What happened to him, incidentally?' he continued.

'I don't know. My mother never talks of him.'

'You said he was in the pop music world. What was his name?'

'Richard something.' I struggled to remember. 'Hart, I think.'

'Never heard of him. Unless by any chance he was the Mighty Rich?'

'*Who?*' The name meant nothing. It came of an era before my ears were flapping and my toes a-tapping. To the youngsters of the middle to late eighties, the sixties were ancient history, apart from the mega-giants.

'He was the lead singer and guitarist in a group called the Mighty Rich and the Coinmakers.'

'Ugh.'

'Bad pun or not, they made several hits – *Demolition Squad*, one called *Last Night* something, and I think *Love on the Rates* was theirs. The problem is there were so many good bands then, so many hits, that unless they kept up the turnover, they just vanished. The Mighty Rich himself was pretty good, I gather. Then he went solo, made a few more hits, and then disappeared out of the charts. So did the group.'

'I've no idea. It could be him, I suppose. Maybe that was the time of the divorce.'

'I wonder if your mother could be persuaded to talk about him. I'd be interested to know.'

'Why?'

Quinn shrugged. 'Idle curiosity, to which all these where-are-they-now? inquiries appeal.'

'I suppose there's no harm in just asking her whether he was the Mighty Rich.' I was doubtful though.

'I tell you what. I'll scour libraries and the Internet to track down a picture of Rich, and you can adjudicate as to whether he looks like me.'

'Good idea.' Inexpressible relief flooded over me – I suppose because it delayed the need to worry about it.

Not for long. I was peacefully browsing through some wedding magazines a few days later when a well-thumbed book was thrust under my nose. It contained a photograph of the Mighty Rich. Quinn plonked himself down beside me on the sofa and we both stared at it. There was a scruffy mid-twenties long-haired hopeful looking out at us as though he owned the world.

'Well? Is that me?'

'No, but it's hard to tell with the hair.'

'I knew you'd say that.' Carefully he closed most of the hair off.

'There's a similarity in the shape of the face, and maybe something about the eyes,' I offered hopefully. 'But he's skinny, and you're taller and—'

'Not skinny. Case not proven. I tell you what, why don't you ask Columba if he was the Mighty Rich? That could do no harm, surely?'

'You have to be joking.'

'Don't tell me – it would lead to trouble. Very well, *I'll* ask your mother. It's only a question of fact, after all. We got on very well at the wedding.'

'Don't!' I cried, and was instantly ashamed of doing so.

He was silent for a moment. 'Why not, Ellie? Can you explain?'

'It's opening doors to the past,' was all I could say. I couldn't even explain my niggle to myself. 'You never know what might crawl out of the tiniest crack.'

'That's pure Stephen King. All right, I won't say a word,

but you don't realise how lucky you are to be *able* to open a door.'

He said it lightly, but I saw his point. 'Did you ever try to find out who your real parents were?' I was hesitant in asking, not knowing how far to tread on delicate ground, especially since he might mistake my motive.

He didn't seem to. 'Yes. The Connellys scooped me out of an orphanage in France, but the orphanage was no longer going when I started investigating. So I tracked down the papers through the French authorities and found I'd been taken in as a waif and stray when I was three. Despite all the police investigations, I was never claimed or traced. I might just as well have been found in a handbag at Victoria Station, *à la* Lady Bracknell.'

'I'm sorry, Quinn.' It was an appalling story, to think he had grown up not only unable to find his real parents, but to then discover he had been deliberately abandoned.

'You needn't be, sweetheart. It made me all the more determined to make sure I found a woman like you.'

'Like me?' His soft words amazed me. What could I have in which he would see the answer to his years of what must have been inner loneliness. 'Roots, you mean.'

'No. A safe haven.'

He kissed me, long and hard, and my voice was unsteady when at last I asked, 'Despite the port charges?'

'What are they?'

'Aunt Columba.'

'I love any baggage you care to bring with you.'

'Because all you trail with *you* is clouds of glory?' I asked happily. 'Are you sure you're not one of the guardian angels like you see in old black and white films?'

'I can prove it.' His lips came down on mine, one arm satisfyingly warm round me, the other hand on my breast and then irresistibly lower. And for once there was no cat Irving on the sofa to show a disapproving eye.

Only afterwards as I was loading the dishwasher did it

occur to me to wonder why a French orphanage should have given Quinn to an Irish couple for adoption. Then I noticed the dishwasher was out of salt and forgot about doors to the past.

My parents live in Sussex on the outskirts of Ashdown Forest, and I was looking forward to showing the house to Quinn. I deliberately hadn't told him much about it. Kingsgate House had fascinated Conan Doyle when he lived in this area, and it was easy to imagine a deerstalkered, ulster-coated Sherlock Holmes marching up the drive. I never read any of his stories without providing them with a mental background of my parents' home. It had a touch of everything – Tudor brick and beams, mock gothic extravaganzas added by an eighteenth-century eccentric and Victorian bits and pieces tacked on wherever the fancy took the owner.

It was just the sort of house to appeal to Quinn, but a strange one for my father. I'd asked him once how he reconciled this mishmash of style with his own elegant clean-lined architectural designs. He'd thought for a moment, pushing his glasses up his nose – as he so often did while considering his work, as if they could help his mental sketching pen – and replied, 'It took a while.' It was only then he told me that it was here that my mother had lived with her first husband. 'I must admit I did a double take when I first saw it,' he confessed, 'but it grew on me. It was the contrast, I suppose. Even when I tripped over those wretched three steps between the different levels on the first floor, it helped me make a mental note to avoid that kind of thing in my own plans. One of the advantages of being an architect,' he added, 'is that you are aware that new houses are only bricks and mortar until someone lives in them to give them atmosphere. This house has had a lot of happiness over the years, especially after you came along.'

Quinn took to Kingsgate House right away, to my pleasure. I could see he was mentally reaching for pen and pad, even as he paused to admire the façade – if such a word can be applied to the ins and outs of the front of this house.

The door opened as we got out of the car, and my mother Margaret came running towards us with Dad behind her. I haven't said much about my parents so far, because it's hard to be objective about them. They're home, they're me, they're blessedly *there*. They look like two standard middle-aged parents to the outsider. They're much the same height, about five foot six, and their faces seem almost to have grown into one another, they seem so alike. My mother is the severer-looking of the two, my father the softer. But this Tweedledum and Tweedledee are deceptive. My mother's severity is a mask she adopted to protect herself against the Flowerdews, my father's softness a guile to seduce anything that challenges his bristling defensiveness of my mother.

Unfortunately, after lunch, at a time when we had all relaxed, highly pleased with one another, I regaled my parents with the story of Columba's visit, which had now receded to the level I could joke about.

'That woman's impossible,' Dad remarked in the tone of one who has come to terms with his fate.

'All the Flowerdews are, Gerald,' Mum said defensively. Well, she would, wouldn't she? 'It's not her fault.'

'*You're* not impossible.'

'Only to you. I'd have been quite impossible with any-one else.'

I couldn't imagine this, but I suppose it started me thinking again about her first marriage. From her comfortable middle age it was hard to imagine, as for any child, a stormy, passionate Margaret who could ever work herself up into asking for a divorce. But perhaps Dad could, for there was a silence between them that lacked the companionable quality of a few moments ago.

'That applies to us all,' Quinn remarked easily, to rescue the situation.

I was immensely grateful to him, and yet why was it so

important? I'm twenty-six, so her first marriage must have been over thirty years ago, and yet there appeared to be some feeling there. For the first time it occurred to me that this might be the reason it was never mentioned. I'd assumed the reason was that it was long forgotten, but now I wondered.

After lunch Quinn went off with Dad to discuss the architecture of castles in Spain, via a tour of the house, and I embarked on one of the garden with my mother.

It was then Mum asked, 'Happy, Ellie?'

'Very,' I said complacently. 'Marriage is easy, isn't it? Why does one get so many warnings about having to work at it? It makes it all sound boring, and that's the last thing life with Quinn is.'

'Yes.'

It was a very short answer from Mum, who is normally talkative, especially if there are events like honeymoons to be discussed.

'You do like him, don't you?' I asked, alarmed.

'Oh yes, darling. He's very charming. He doesn't have an accent, but I suppose he's Irish. His name is.'

I'd mentioned to Mum that Quinn was adopted, but hadn't had a chance to tell her about the French orphanage. Now didn't seem the right moment. 'He's lived here too long to have an accent.' The Connellys had moved to London when he was ten, and he'd been based here ever since.

There was still something odd hovering in the air. It was waiting to dive-bomb me like a mosquito. I hesitated. Stay out of it, everything warned me. You have to go on, urged the Pandora inside me. So naturally I opened Pandora's box – for which the key had kindly been provided by Columba – and out flew all the troubles of the world.

'Columba remarked,' I announced to Mozart's weathering bust, 'that Quinn looks like your first husband.'

'Really?' Surely Mum could not have invented that look of surprise. True, she is a Flowerdew, but it would have taken greater talent for the stage than I'd ever suspected in her.

'What happened to him? You never mention him.'

'Because I've no idea what did,' Mum answered me a little too patly. 'We were divorced, and he disappeared into the blue.'

'Is that possible?' I frowned, pushing my luck. 'Surely there'd be some news from him?'

'If you knew Richard you'd see why there wasn't. He was in the pop world – he probably got involved in a new mystic life in India in the seventies. He could be in a Buddhist monastery now, or performing in a Thai nightclub.'

'Or, I suppose,' I said unthinkingly, following my own train of reasoning, 'he may be dead.'

'Oh no,' Mum whipped straight back at me. 'Not Richard. He's alive all right.'

So there was indeed some feeling still left, if she could not bear the thought of his death, even though she'd heard nothing from him for years.

'Is he still singing in this country?'

'I've never seen his name.' My mother was clearly longing to get off the subject, but obstinately I could not leave it now. I had to *know*.

'Quinn was wondering if he was the Mighty Rich who had a burst of fame in the late sixties, then disappeared off the music scene.'

'As a matter of fact, he was.' Mum appeared preoccupied with plucking nasturtium seeds to pickle for ersatz capers, and it was difficult to see her face, especially since she kept it averted.

'What was he like? Why did—'

'We break up?' Mum interrupted, laughing, to my great relief.

'You never talk about him,' I muttered, shamefaced.

'Why should I? We were married for a few years, well over a quarter of a century ago. No bones were broken on either side, and we split up because we married too young. I was too much of an old sobersides for Richard and he was too

28

laid back for me. I became tired of the pop scene and wanted a permanent home. Richard didn't. End of story.'

'Quinn's laid back too,' I ventured brightly.

Mum looked exasperated. 'Just because Rich and I broke up, does *not* mean that you and Quinn will, Ellie. Don't start seeing heffalumps, or you'll fall flat on your face in the pit.'

She was right, and that was that. There was nothing more to be said, and I quickly admired King Canute, parked at the side of the lily pond.

For some reason, when we went back inside I used the bathroom upstairs, not the downstairs loo, and on my return journey glanced through the open door of my parents' bedroom. There was my five-year-old self clutching a posy of primroses, grinning out of the photograph. There at its side was my half-brother. *That* was the flaw in my mother's story. The child must have died about the same time as the break-up. *How* had he died? Of illness? An accident? Was there more to the divorce than she was revealing? I would never know, for I could not peer into her past, which was closed by her own will. Or could I? There was one way, and I marvelled that I had not thought of it before. I would ask my father.

In my pleasure at such an obvious solution, I wandered over to study the photograph. I picked it up in its frame and looked at my half-brother, who gazed back at me with chubby face and friendly trusting eyes. He had half my genes in him; we shared a mother. I began to feel a ridiculous sense of loss – this was the brother I might have grown up with.

Stop this, Ellie, you're going too far, I warned myself, and yet I went on. What year was this photograph taken? Maybe it had been snapped here in this garden. The frame was old and loose and as I picked it up it came apart in my hands. Before guiltily trying to put it back together, I looked to see what was written on the back of the photograph. There might be a loving message from his father or from my mother. There was no date, no message. There was nothing but a name: Marcus Quinn Hart.

Something seemed to turn over in my stomach. True, Quinn was a very common Irish name, at least as a surname, and not uncommon as a forename, but why had my mother never mentioned the coincidence? Easy, I supposed. She had buried the death of her child so deep she could not and would not resurrect it. That was the obvious answer, and yet it had not seemed to interest her that my husband had the same forename. It was true she had had plenty of time to adjust, and would hardly have told me about Marcus's sharing the name, because she never mentioned Marcus anyway. And yet . . .

I mulled it over the rest of the afternoon. It wasn't until we were on the point of leaving that I decided I had to know more about Marcus, and only Dad could tell me. An opportunity arose when Mum took Quinn to see the pond and her statues, and I plunged into my questions before I could think better of it.

'I was looking at that picture of my half-brother,' I told him.

'Oh yes. Why?'

'Something Quinn said to me. That I was lucky I could open doors to my past if I wanted to. My brother's name was Quinn, then? That's a coincidence.'

My father did not reply, but I wasn't going to give up.

'What happened to him, Dad?'

'He died.' Don't go there, Ellie, was the hidden message.

I went there. 'Yes, but of what?'

'Meningitis, I think.'

'That's terrible.' I was appalled at what Mum had been through. She and Richard had split up, and the boy had died shortly after. Or had it been the other way around?

Dad wasn't as good at covering up as my mother. He lacked the Flowerdew flair and was looking distinctly uncomfortable, I realised, as if he'd said more than he meant.

'Your mother did remark on the coincidence of the name,' he said almost angrily. 'It was Marcus's second name. Richard was born in Ireland to an Irish mother and he wanted her to be remembered so he gave Marcus her maiden name, which was also conveniently a forename. But look here, Ellie, not a word to your mother. I won't have her upset. Now you know the whole story, I hope you'll be satisfied.'

I wanted to believe that this was all there was to it, but I couldn't. There was nothing more I could do, however. I couldn't question my mother any more, nor my father. And certainly not Columba. If she did know more, she might tell me, but either way, she'd bomb straight in. I couldn't wish that on my parents.

We drove home almost in silence as I put two and two together and made several thousands in one ghastly scenario after another. Quinn glanced at me once or twice, and then, wise man that he is (in fact the name Quinn means wise) he left me to my own confused thoughts.

When we reached home it was a different matter. He poured us both a glass of wine, handed mine to me, and said casually, 'Your mother told me you'd asked about the Mighty Rich. I thought we agreed we wouldn't upset her. I gather my guess was right about who he was. Why's this so important to you, Ellie?'

'I don't know. I suppose it's just the coincidence of your looking like Rich.'

'I asked your mother about that. She doesn't think so.'

'So she says.'

He groaned.

'I looked at a photograph of the child that died,' I rushed on. 'His second name was Quinn. He'd be about your age, thirty-four or five, and you were adopted . . .' All my fantastical fears burst out of me.

Quinn looked at me in sheer bewilderment. 'I'm beginning

to think you're the innate storyteller of the two of us, Ellie. If you're thinking what I deduce you are, might I point out that I didn't die at three years old?'

I was in the deep end. Might as well go on. 'Yes, but suppose Marcus didn't die.'

'Then there's no earthly reason why your mother should have told you he did, is there?'

I thought this through. 'No.'

'You sound doubtful. Look here, if you were making a story of this, could you dream up *any* reason she and Gerald would have lied to you?'

'No.' My face cleared. 'Of course not.'

'So that's okay then.'

And it was. Until Columba took an uninvited hand.

'My dears,' her flowing script on the letter read, 'all this talk of darling Richard – Margaret's first husband – set me thinking. *So* like Quinn, and yet I had absolutely no photographs of him. That ghastly Greg (husband number one) took *all* my lovely albums simply to spite me. So I telephoned around and see what darling Felix sent me. Enjoy, darlings, enjoy.'

Enclosed were several photocopied pages of an article in a tabloid magazine of the seventies, headed: 'What Happened to the Mighty Rich and the Coinmakers?' Whoever wrote it – and I didn't recognise the name – had done some homework at least. It seemed to be part of a series on the transition of pop music from the sixties to the seventies, covering the disappearance of the big names – Buddy Holly, the Beatles, etc. – and some groups who rose to brief fame and then vanished from the charts.

The Mighty Rich and the Coinmakers was an interesting case. The group had split up in January 1969, Rich went solo, had one or two hits – and then nothing. No more was heard of him, even on the club circuits. The former members of the group had various explanations for the interviewers: Rich was dead, he was in South America, he had changed his name and so on. Even his wife, ran the article, did not know where he was.

Wife? The article was dated 1975 and Gerald was my mother's husband at that time. After all, I'm twenty-six. It could have been a mere slip, or Richard might have married again, but it still left a niggle, and I peered at the photographs. The best of them, however, was the one Quinn had already shown me; the others were of poor quality and told me no more.

I was reading the letter at work, since Columba had for some reason addressed it to my office, and not our home. I had hardly got over the new disquiet when Quinn rang. I'd better come home, he said. *Now.* Somehow the press had got interested in the Mighty Rich again, and my father was after my blood.

When I reached the Lodge, not only was Dad stomping around looking more agitated than I'd ever seen him, but Mum was there too, stony-faced. 'Why couldn't you have asked me first?' she asked me sadly.

'Asked you what?' I *had* asked her, hadn't I?

'I told you not to meddle,' Dad said crossly.

'Look, I didn't say a word to the press,' I cried. 'I haven't a clue how they got on to it. It's true Columba's just sent me a cutting from a friend of hers called Felix—'

'Columba?' I had lit the fuse and Mum burst into tears, while my father exploded:

'Felix Turner from the *Sunday World*? That bloody, *bloody* woman. I suppose she just rang him up and ordered him to send all he had on the Mighty Rich. It didn't occur to her that someone on a tabloid might well investigate just why Columba Flowerdew would be making such an enquiry over a quarter of a century later. Why won't she mind her own damned business?'

I agreed wholeheartedly with him.

'Lunch!' In the midst of this bedlam, Quinn appeared as if this were merely a friendly family visit. This was a working day, and I wouldn't have blamed him if he'd just disappeared into his studio. Instead he'd taken time away from Sadie O'Grady and the illustrations for a new children's book to produce some trout fillets, bread and cheese, a tuna rice salad and cider. He was too good to be true, I marvelled thankfully, fearful that at any moment I might wake up from this dream of a marriage.

I managed to soothe Mum down. 'Everything looks better after a meal. That's what you used to tell me.'

'Columba doesn't,' Dad growled.

Even if it were rather a silent meal, at least it was a breathing space, and gave us all time to look at the question dispassionately.

'I'm going to have to tell them, Gerald,' Mum announced firmly at the end of it. 'If I don't, the press will ferret it out somehow, and I'd rather they heard it from me.'

My heart plummeted. I'd almost convinced myself there was nothing to tell. But of course there was, and what's more, Quinn and I were only deemed worthy of this knowledge because we'd find out anyway. Hurt feelings vanished, however, as with set face my mother told us her story. She plunged into it, and it came out in a steady monotone, as though it were well rehearsed.

'I was very young – only nineteen – when I married Richard, and I was wildly in love with him. He wasn't much older than me, and being a Flowerdew I was used to the unconventional, so the pop scene didn't seem too formidable a change. I went on loving Richard too, and I'm sure he did me, but it grew impossible to live with one another. We had Marcus when I was twenty-one, and from the first we quarrelled over him. I wanted him to have a steady background; Richard was set on widening his horizons at the first possible moment. He'd take him to gigs, fill him with dreams, and disappear with him for days at a time.

'Then one day in '69 Richard left on a gig, taking Marcus

with him while my back was turned, and they never came back. No word, no letter. I never saw either of them again. I tried everything, of course – friends in the pop world, police, hospital. Even the Salvation Army. Nothing.'

'But' – I was completely bewildered – 'you must have heard from Richard when Marcus died.'

There was a silence, and then I knew.

'You mean he didn't die?' I whispered painfully.

So that was why Mum so desperately wished Richard to be alive, because it meant Marcus was probably alive too. I couldn't even begin to imagine the nightmare that she had lived through.

'I believe both of them are still alive,' she continued steadily. 'If it wasn't for Gerald, I couldn't have borne it. As it was, we had to wait the statutory five years before I could get a divorce, even though Gerald came to live with me in '72. It went through late in '75. I took Gerald's name by deed poll before we were married so that you were legitimately Ellie Peters. I told everyone that Marcus had died. Columba believed it, because she was touring abroad at the time. At least, I thought she did, but I wouldn't put it past her to have smelled a rat and I suppose she's smelling it again now.'

'Thanks to you, Ellie.' Dad glared at me.

'Now wait a minute.' Quinn rose magnificently to my defence. 'It was Columba who started all this.'

'Ellie should have learned by now that the only way to deal with Columba is to ignore her. Ellie encouraged her.' Dad wasn't angry, he was merely resigned, which was almost worse, and I sat there miserably knowing he was right.

'How did you bear it?' Quinn asked Mum compassionately.

'There was Ellie,' she replied, 'and there was Gerald. Otherwise I could not have done so. I told myself God had been good to me to grant me a second life.'

But still the photograph remained at her bedside, I thought.

35

'Where was the gig?' I asked, trying to ignore the lump in my throat.

'In Richmond, though knowing Richard he could easily have gone straight on to another one from there. He'd often do two or three at a time. It was the time of all the big pop festivals, and the young of three continents were on the move.'

'Have you ever tried to advertise for them since?'

'Oh yes. But Marcus would surely know about me by now. He'd have asked questions. There's never been a whisper from Richard or Quinn.'

I did a double take. 'You mean Marcus,' I said quickly.

'Yes, I'm sorry. Marcus was his first name, but he took a fancy to his second name, probably because it was easier to say. So we fell into the habit too. It actually gave me a lot of pleasure, Quinn, when Ellie first told me your name.' She turned back to me. 'I couldn't tell you, of course, but it was like a little piece of Marcus had returned to me. Stupid, isn't it?'

'And he really doesn't resemble Richard?' I couldn't help it. I had to seek my own peace of mind.

Quinn groaned. 'Despite the fact that one in twenty Irish people was called Quinn at one time, Ellie has some wild idea that I'm really your son.'

'Oh, darling,' – Mum turned to me before I could protest – 'do you think I didn't wonder that myself the moment you mentioned his name? Reason isn't always at the forefront of reactions. Oh, Ellie, you needn't worry. Quinn may have a slight superficial facial resemblance to Richard, but he *isn't* Marcus. I'm positive Marcus has been brought up by Richard. Irresponsible though Richard was, he would never have abandoned him. He was devoted to him.'

'Quinn was adopted,' I faltered, 'from a French orphanage. Suppose Richard handed Quinn over to it?'

'It's out of the question. He *wouldn't* do it. Why should he?' Mum asked. 'Firstly, he adored Marcus, and even if looking after him palled, then there's no earthly reason he couldn't have sent him back to me. I deliberately stayed here in the same house, waiting, though I'd married again.'

For a moment I was happy, completely reassured. My mother was right. I was being illogical. Then a terrible thought struck me. 'Suppose Richard was killed,' I asked doggedly. 'Then Marcus could have been put in an orphanage.'

'My dear girl, we weren't living in Victorian times. Wherever they were, the authorities would have easily been able to trace me, even if I couldn't find them. For a start, I was advertising like crazy everywhere.'

'Even India?' I managed to squeak out. 'A lot of pop stars went there.'

'Even India,' Margaret replied more gently than I deserved. 'The pop world had its own communication network. I'd have heard.'

'Oh.' Pandora's box snapped shut again, all the troubles safely packed back inside.

Or so I thought.

Three

Pandora's box wouldn't stay shut, of course. During the day it graciously condescended to close while I worked, but at night the lid flew open, and all my niggles marched back into my stomach, churning themselves around on an endless treadmill.

At my side Quinn slept peacefully on, while I tossed and turned. If Marcus Quinn were still alive . . . Increasingly bizarre fancies presented themselves to my brain as truth.

I carried on as normal at the Lodge outside working hours, though Quinn cast me some of his thoughtful looks every now and then, making me work all the harder at playing happy young wife. This wasn't too difficult with Quinn playing opposite me. His hours of work were erratic, but nevertheless we managed to strike up one or two tentative friendships in the village of Charham, and to explore the countryside around us, which was now beginning to take on the warm glow of autumn colours. There was wild life aplenty in the fertile Weald of Kent, even though Quinn saw it somewhat differently from me.

'What are you staring at?' I asked him once. We were walking in a meadow by a bubbling stream, with a sloping hillside coming down to the far river bank.

He jumped at the sound of my voice, obviously completely absorbed in his own world. 'Really want to know?'

'Yes.'

'I was peopling it – if that's the right word – with Rab-Hits.'

'Rabbits? Like *Watership Down*?' I asked sagely. It was almost dusk, and white bob-tails could be seen everywhere.

'No. Rab-*Hits*. Never heard of them? They're like hit men, but they're the police force protecting the rabbit population.'

'Against what? Foxes or farmers?'

'Both, and cows, sheep, kids, poachers. A bunny's life is fraught with danger. It's time someone drew attention to it.'

'And just how do these hit rabbits carry out their job?'

'They're specially trained. They walk on two legs, and have armoured ears and whiskers – James Bond style, you know. The whiskers shoot out a laser beam; the ears are killer spears.'

He began the very next day, first with pad and pen, then with his computer. When I got home there were no signs he'd been scavenging for lunch in the kitchen, and I thought he'd miss dinner too. He did arrive eventually, with a little smirk on his face.

There was no such smirk on mine, since for the sixth night in succession I had awoken at two a.m., so that my brain could solve all the problems of the world. All save mine, however. I went to bed telling myself it was crazy to think that Quinn was my half-brother, but a few hours later a little voice inside my head would wake me up, whispering, How do you *know* he isn't, Ellie? Maybe we get on so well just because we're siblings.

And we did get on well. Too well, in fact, for I failed to see the breaker rolling right towards me while I was busy splashing around with Quinn in the shallows.

'How are the Rab-Hits?' I asked brightly at lunch the following day. He doesn't always emerge for lunch – it depends whether he's flirting with his Muse or not – but this day he did.

'Pen on pad stage. Not bad.'

He hesitated, and cast me a look which I interpreted as: are you really interested? I was, and I showed it. 'Tell me,' I prompted.

'I've got the horned helmets and whiskers – it's the body I can't get right. Do I go for soft and cuddly or lean and mean?'

I thought about this. 'Arguments on both sides. I suppose you couldn't have both – make the hit men lean and mean, offset not only with your soft and cuddly rabbits but a sort of civil service, or bat-rabs, acting as spies.' My burst of invention came to a halt.

A silence. Then: 'You know, I could think along those lines.'

'And what about their gangsters' molls?' I continued with a new brainwave.

'Ah. They would have to be fairly lean and mean too for the look of the thing.'

'Unless a Rab-Hit falls for a cuddly bunny chick from a nice upper-class family.'

He laughed. 'I'll book the wedding at Happy Ever After. How was yesterday's wedding? I forgot to ask you last night.'

'Just as well. I nearly threw in my hand. The bridegroom was ogling the bridesmaid, the bride's father was too drunk to make his speech and a few nameless horrors were executed on the gardens. I was glad Stephen's not in residence.'

'What do you do if you get a booking from someone you don't like the look of?'

'Cheat.' I proceeded to explain my methods of disposing of trouble, from downright lies – such as fully booked – to various ways of making them deduce for themselves that we were not quite what they were looking for. Unblinkingly, Jane on one occasion pushed a menu of the beef-burger variety beneath the toffee-nose of one whiny young swell and with the same aplomb spent five minutes extolling the virtues of our caterer's fusion cookery to a known toughie. (Unfortunately she sold him on it, but that's another story.)

Quinn nodded approvingly. 'Anything on today?'

I answered this and that finished work as a topic. I opened

my mouth to speak about something else – and my mind went blank.

I could think of nothing to say.

My mind scrabbled desperately, but every subject I thought of seemed to lead back to the family, to the past. That great future we were to explore together became a frightening desert, with no established landmarks in our marriage by which to regain my bearings.

I caught Quinn's eye, and for a moment thought he must be in the same situation. And perhaps he was, for all he said was, 'I don't think much of this pizza.'

It had happened once, fear compounded fear that it would happen again, and it did. Finally I woke up one morning with a crystal-clear message for myself. If ever I was to sleep soundly again, I needed to prove once and for all that my beloved Quinn was not Marcus Quinn Hart.

The message did not include suggestions on how this was to be achieved. That was left to me.

It seemed to me there were two plans of attack for this battle. I could try to find out who my Quinn really was, and secondly, I could track down what had happened to the Mighty Rich. Marcus, if still alive, would be out in the big wide world by now – probably married with ten kids – but presumably he would still be in touch with his father.

'Okay, attack,' I muttered to the muesli.

'Now that's an idea.' Quinn has remarkably attuned ears. 'How about animated muesli, fighting off the great shreddies and cornflakes?'

'Do you ever stop turning things into something else?'

'Do you?' was his mild retort, which floored me. Wasn't that exactly what I was doing? I was looking for bogeys where they did not exist. Is that what he meant? I didn't dare ask him in case I blurted out that my fears had not been put to rest, but were all too active. It was a no man's land I feared to cross.

Instead I took the lofty approach. 'I turn basic ingredients into superb cuisine.'

'You do,' he agreed charmingly, and we retreated to our separate – and silent – positions.

During my often theoretical lunch break, I wandered into the grounds of Charham Place and tried to think logically about my next step. There were major snags on both fronts. I couldn't ask Quinn any more about his background, since in his mind the question of his likeness to Richard was settled, and I couldn't ask my parents any more about Marcus. I couldn't even begin to consider the reactions if I suggested a DNA test. The stark truth was that I was on my own.

Where could Private Investigator Eleanor Connelly begin? With the telephone directories of the major cities of the world? Useless. Since no one appeared to have heard of him since 1969, Richard must surely have changed his name and therefore Marcus's too would be different. The same applied to other obvious sources – death and marriage certificates, census records – everything, so far as I could see.

Okay, take the other front: Quinn himself. His passport, for instance. What would that tell me? Precious little, I discovered after a sneak raid. There was nothing new to me in it save that he was an Irish citizen. Even the date of his birth must be debatable, as his parentage was never traced. It was highly unlikely that a child of his age would know the precise date of his birth. I didn't even know where the orphanage had been, though that must be known to someone. Quinn's adopted parents, for example, are still alive, though my heart quailed at the prospect of Quinn finding out I'd contacted them. Perhaps I'd suggest lunch. I put this into effect immediately.

'Shall we ask your parents down this weekend?' I asked Quinn as nonchalantly as I could. Although they were in their early seventies, they lived in Surrey, so it wasn't too long a journey.

He glanced up from the crossword. He loves them; his

convoluted thinking is admirably suited to them. I get bored even with the quickie, let alone having the patience to tease out the 'grown-up' puzzles.

'Why not? Give them a ring now if you like. Sunday lunch.'

Highly pleased at my success I did so, and it was duly fixed.

Meanwhile I read and reread the article Columba had sent us about the Mighty Rich and the Coinmakers. The journalist had managed to track down the three other members of the band, and there was a photograph of each of them taken at the time they were interviewed. The other photographs, however, were taken in their time of fame in the late sixties, and I studied the most prominent of them for some time. It was a posed group shot, with the Mighty Rich in the middle, surrounded by his flock.

Colin Atley on the drums, thin, nervous-looking, perhaps even sly. Bryan Whatley on the bass, a younger more hopeful figure than the overplump version in the seventies' photo. Michael Patterson, second guitar, tall, with a shock of long bedraggled blond hair. Behind the group to one side was a curious figure, somewhat apart, with a trilby hat, suit, long scarf and a monocle. I looked at the caption: William Gossage, manager. What, I wondered, had happened to him? Maybe he was still in the business. But then my eye was drawn back to the Mighty Rich, slender, arrogant, staring out at the world which he did not doubt was his own special oyster.

If Rich had stayed with Mum, he would have been my father, I thought. The 'me' inside Eleanor Connelly would have been completely different. I considered this. I had quite enough of the artistic temperament through my mother's Flowerdew genes. With Rich as my father, I would have gained a whole lot more. Unfortunately, the music in my soul would have been a plus outweighed by the loss of Dad's common sense and stability. Not that I seemed to be making the most of these qualities at the moment. On the whole, though, I was sure I had the best of the bargain.

And most surely Quinn would agree. He's so Johnny Head-in-the-Air himself, he couldn't be doing with a wife of the same ilk. I began to see myself as a tethered balloon in this marriage. My hot air (as I was forced to admit I could often spout) was firmly rooted to Quinn, thanks to Dad. It was my role, I told myself sanctimoniously, to keep the wheels of everyday life oiled so that the Great Artist could work undisturbed in his ivory tower, free of mundane matters.

Unfortunately, mundane matters at the moment included discovering whether or not we were half-brother and sister – and *before* I came off the pill. How could we have the family we both wanted (at least I presumed Quinn did – it suddenly occurred to me we'd never discussed it in our short courtship) with this still hanging over us like a Sword of Damocles? True, it was a very small sword in terms of probability but nevertheless it was there – for me, at least.

All means at my disposal had to be used, I decided. That photograph caught my eye again, and the smile on Rich's face turned into a supercilious smirk, daring me to discover the truth.

I'd accept his challenge. I grasped the rose at the thorny end. The Quinn side of things I had to tackle myself, but for the Mighty Rich I needed contacts in the showbiz world. I groaned. That path seemed to lead inexorably to one person.

I searched desperately for an alternative. Stephen leapt to mind, but he was back in the States. Then out of the blue came an answer – or so it seemed at the time. Royalties. Just because Rich had disappeared and was presumed dead, they didn't stop coming in on his solos or on his share of the Coinmakers. Wasn't there an organisation that took care of such things?

There was. I tracked down the Performing Arts Society with eager questions on where Rich's royalties now went.

Was I a relation? No, but my mother was once, I told them. Quite rightly, owing to the Data Protection Act, their lips remained sealed. End of trail.

It was obvious that along the road to my destination there was a hitchhiker I could not afford to ignore: Columba.

In fact Columba was more of a petrol station than a hitchhiker. She was going to have to give me a lot of fuel in return for this capitulation (as I saw it) on my part. I rang the doorbell of her North Kensington flat with some trepidation. How to go far enough, but not so far that Columba seized the bit between her teeth and roared off on her own?

There was no reply. Typical. I wasn't calling by chance; I'd played hookey from work claiming a potential client to see in London, and had telephoned my aunt to ensure she'd be in.

'Darling!'

Columba was extricating herself amid several huge boxes and bags from a taxi. The leggings had disappeared in favour of the Grande Dame today: chic lilac two-piece, tottery heels, Hermes scarf and a captive taxi driver. With his help I struggled up to the first floor flat with the luggage while she stood at her front door imperiously waving us on. Her now slave-for-life disappeared with a large tip in due course; bone china teacups and Earl Grey tea appeared and Columba chattered on with scurrilous gossip culled from the TV studios and theatre green rooms until I declared my purpose.

'I want to know—' I began.

'Of course you do, darling.'

'About—'

'Dear Richard. I would too in your place.' She donned the same look of earnestness I recalled seeing in a TV adaptation of *Lady Windermere's Fan*.

'Everyone thinks I've been convinced that Quinn is not Marcus.' I was both relieved and exasperated that Columba guessed exactly what I was here for. 'But I'm still worrying that the likeness between them, and the fact they share the same forename, may be no coincidence.'

Earnestness changed to concern. Was it real? Who knew with Columba? In her case, the stage and real life were one.

'Oh, my dear. And Quinn is such a darling.'

'I can't question Mum any more, and you *mustn't* breathe a word to her. Or to my father. And' – I heard my voice rising as I realised the extent of my own recklessness in coming to see Columba – 'most certainly not to Quinn.'

She was hurt. 'You know you can always rely on me, Ellie.'

I refrained from comment. 'So I've come to you for two reasons.'

'Name them,' announced the Grande Dame.

'The first is that I have to try to trace Richard Hart. Mother is sure he is still alive and' – here was the tricky bit, since this was most definitely breaking a confidence – 'therefore so in all probability is Marcus.'

Any director would have been proud of her. Columba stood up, paced to the window, stared into the calm serenity of the street outside, turned to me, leaned back against the window ledge, arms clasped behind her, head flung back as though assimilating the full shock of what I was saying, and murmured simply:

'I always suspected it.'

The arms emerged gravely, indicating a reluctance on her part to enter into a combat arena in which I knew full well she was panting to take part.

'Mum told me,' I said carefully, stepping into it myself, 'that Richard disappeared in 1969, presumably after the Coinmakers had split up and he had gone solo. According to Mum, he took Marcus – as he often did – to a gig, and just failed to return. You were away in the States at the time, so when did you enter the story?'

Columba returned to my side, sat gracefully down, and stared earnestly into my eyes. 'I *can* help you, Ellie. Fortunately, I keep scrapbooks – solely for my fans, of course.'

And the eventual biography, I thought meanly.

She rose again, swooped into an adjoining room and re-emerged clutching a large scarlet-bound scrapbook. 'Here,' she announced eagerly, placing it reverently on the table. There were two volumes for 1969, so it must have been an exciting time. 'Let me see. Oh, how could I have forgotten? That was the time I was filming the great soap *Philadelphia Main Line*. How could I have forgotten it?'

How could anyone? It ran forever, it seemed, on screens all around the world. It was *Dallas* and *Dynasty* all over again, set in high society with all its scandals, luxuries and secrets.

'That was the year I married. What an excitement. And then down to Virginia for filming. Did I ever tell you how rude Frankie Sinatra was, and of course I was married to him at the time—'

'Frank Sinatra?' I asked incredulously. This was a new one.

'No, no. My darling . . . er' – she searched her memory – 'Alex. Only briefly, of course. Such a sweetheart.' (It hadn't prevented her from pushing for a very handsome divorce settlement, according to my mother.)

There, staring at me on the page, was a younger but instantly recognisable mini-skirted Columba on the singer's arm.

'I must have returned in December that year,' Columba said. 'No, it was the following spring. Such fun at Christmas. Skiing in Aspen. I think that's when my marriage began to go sour. He was the sweetest instructor. It wasn't until I returned that Margaret told me that Richard and she had split up, that Richard had disappeared, and that poor Marcus had died of meningitis. I suppose she couldn't face telling me the truth.'

'Didn't you think it strange she didn't write to you or telephone with such terrible news?'

Columba considered this. 'No,' she said at last. 'I was very busy, of course. Margaret knows how much I dislike being interrupted in the middle of filming. But of course she should have told me, the silly girl.'

'Are you filming now?' I asked innocently.

'As it happens, yes. A TV adaptation of Reade's *The Cloister and the Hearth*. Such fun, my dear. A delightful man playing Denys. I positively thrill each time he says in that deep voice: *Courage, mon ami. Le diable est mort.*' Columba's own voice dropped accordingly. 'But for you, Ellie, my door is always open. As it would have been for Margaret had she contacted me. I would even have flown back home to be with her. A sister *should*. But she told me nothing. She bore his death *alone*.' A dramatic pause which I punctured.

'He didn't die.'

'Very well,' Columba said crossly. 'She bore his *loss* alone, hid from me that her child had been kidnapped, hid from me that—'

I sighed. 'So what did she say when you finally met her again?'

'Very little, save the fact that Marcus was dead, and that he had been cremated. I realised how deeply she was grieving and did not question her further. I have great delicacy in such matters.'

I struggled to ignore this challenge. 'Didn't you even ask where Richard was?'

'Why should I? The divorce would be going through.'

'But it wasn't.'

'No,' Columba conceded, 'but I didn't know that. It's true some time later I remembered she explained there was a delay because Richard had disappeared, but I thought it was resolved, since in '73 she married your father.'

'She didn't,' I reminded her. 'She married him at Christmas '75.' I had wrung this information out of a very reluctant father.

'But I'm sure I was there in '73.' Columba was indignant. 'I wore the sweetest little flower posy hat.' She stared at me, and her voice switched from posy tones to a broken croak. 'Oh, you *poor* child. You mustn't take it to heart.'

'Take what?'

'Your illegitimacy.' The hushed voice would have done justice to a nineteenth-century melodrama.

'We're living in the twenty-first century now,' I pointed out. 'I won't be cast out by my husband for bringing disgrace on his tribe.'

'It doesn't seem,' Columba said, obviously disappointed, 'that I can help you after all.' She looked genuinely woebegone and I rushed to console her.

'So you don't have any brilliant ideas as to where Richard might be hiding himself?'

'No. He and I trod different boards in life.'

By which she meant they didn't get on, I presumed. Well, it had been a forlorn chance. 'But I still need you, Columba. There's my second reason for coming. I need contacts.'

This word was always a touchstone, and it didn't fail this time. She brightened immediately. 'Explain, expound, *tell* me,' she ordered, her ego almost visibly expanding once more.

'Mum told me she advertised everywhere for Richard, so there's no point going over the formal ground again – police, hospitals, coroner's reports, and so on—'

'Why are you doing this, Ellie?' Columba interrupted. 'To find Marcus for your mother, or to satisfy yourself that Quinn isn't your brother?'

'Both.'

She nodded, satisfied, and listened – quietly, for her – as I told her about my abortive attempt with the Performing Arts Society and how I needed to track the other band members – and, I recalled, the manager.

'But the band split up from Rich, so how would they know where he went to?'

'My hope is that they were still close enough to him to know which gig he disappeared from that night. It's a start.

Maybe something happened there. A row – I don't know. A big offer of work – you never know. Anyway, William Gossage may have remained Rich's manager.'

Columba stared at me dismally. 'I don't think, darling, I'll be very good as a private detective. I tried Miss Marple once, and I just could not get inside her head.'

I was hardly surprised, but didn't tell her so. 'You have contacts, and I need them. Stephen—'

'Not his field. I'll have a think about it.'

'Good thing you're not on your honeymoon,' I couldn't resist joking.

She looked blank. 'Stephen?'

'No. Graham Padbury.'

She giggled. 'Graham is no more. I'm very disappointed in him, even as an escort. He seems more interested in a blonde floozie. I have a new gentleman friend.' She gave a little shriek. 'I see it all. Oh, my dear, the answer to your problem!'

'What?' I cried eagerly.

But it was scene's end, and the curtain line came dead on cue.

'My lips are sealed. You shall hear from me.'

Four

Roasts need practice. I had had none, for few single people decide to cook an enormous roast for themselves. I assumed that what I had witnessed at my mother's side would come easily to me and, after all, there were cookery books.

Anxious to impress Quinn's parents with my domesticity, I recklessly picked on a leg of lamb, stuffed it with rice, onion, bacon, celery, and drenched it in cider. It had been marinading for twenty-four hours, and so it was my bad luck that Quinn did not remark on it until ten o'clock on the Sunday morning – two hours before his parents were due to arrive.

'What's this?'

'Lunch, what else could it be?' I popped a frazzled head round the kitchen door, summoned by his shout from the dining room. I had been performing an Indian war dance round the dining table, checking and re-checking the place settings.

The quality of the silence that followed my answer brought me into the kitchen post-haste. Quinn was staring at the lamb, stricken with horror.

'I thought I'd told you my mother is vegetarian. And Father is on a non-fat diet.'

I managed to speak. 'You said keep it simple.'

'That's what I meant by simple. No meat. I'm sure I explained fully though.'

Half of me felt like howling with tears and frustration, the other half thought of the stiff upper lip all wives should learn to exhibit. The first half won by several lengths.

51

The crisis that followed is not relevant to this story, save to show that Quinn and I had a lot to learn about marital communication, both voiced and unvoiced. The trouble was I was by no means sure that Quinn *hadn't* told me, since I had to admit my mind hadn't been fully on what I was doing. I'd been too busy battling to show Quinn that everything was just dandy between us. In many ways it was. In the to- and fro-ing of daily working life deep fears can be laid to rest for a while. In the evenings across the dinner table, I was forcing myself to maintain a normal chatter, even if it meant I was thinking up subjects to talk about beforehand.

The crunch came in bed. To my terror I realised there was an instinctive, if momentary, withdrawal on my part when Quinn turned to me lovingly. It was not yet serious enough to affect our lovemaking, but it suddenly occurred to me that this week I hadn't initiated any myself. Spontaneity might prove the first victim of my problem.

The lamb was the second. I had to fight not to show my edginess.

At five minutes to twelve I was surrounded by hastily prepared dishes. So was Quinn, since he was none too sure, he admitted, that he had not been at fault himself. Amongst the dishes were fish fillets to be poached in orange juice, and an egg curry for my new mother-in-law. Quinn took one look at the latter and remarked, 'Mum eats a little fish.'

I took the hint, and the smell of fish awaiting the poaching pan battled with the smell of lamb emerging from the oven. It was not a good omen for the day, but miraculously all was in place by twelve fifteen, though Quinn's parents had not yet arrived. Nibbles, dips and crudités calmly awaited guests and drinks to join them. The table was set with almost matching cutlery and china, and sparkling glasses, thanks to a wedding present and Quinn's sense of priorities. There was even a posy of late roses and chrysanthemums I'd picked from our garden.

The doorbell rang, and Quinn went to answer it. I was all ready with joyful greetings (genuine, for I'd liked both of them at the wedding), and followed him out into the hall, just as I heard an odd note in Quinn's voice.

'Come in,' was all he said.

Two words that opened the floodgates to hell. The new arrivals weren't his parents. They were mine.

I had an instant fear that I'd had a mental aberration and invited the wrong couple, but I dismissed it. I wasn't that dotty.

'This is a happy chance,' I said brightly. 'Were you just passing?' I was thinking furiously about potatoes and veg. 'You can stay to lunch, if you like.'

'Thanks.' Dad roared with laughter, thinking I'd made a joke. 'We were planning to.'

'You were expecting us, weren't you?' Mum was a little more intuitive.

'Well . . . er . . .' I sent out silent waves for help from Quinn. He voiced it immediately.

'You're not going to believe this,' he told Mum and Dad cheerfully, 'but we weren't. Some silly misunderstanding. Ellie was intending to invite you for next weekend. Anyway, no problem. In fact it's a good idea. My parents are on their way and there's plenty of food – now.' The 'now' betrayed his nervousness.

'You mean Columba didn't tell you?' Mum asked crossly. Dad took the point immediately and prepared to explode.

'Am I missing something?' Quinn asked, quickly taking control as well as hats and coats when he saw the look on Dad's face.

'It *was* today Columba meant, wasn't it, darling?' Mum asked Dad.

'It was,' came the reply. But it wasn't from Dad.

Columba suddenly appeared through the still open door, all beams and smiles. And she was not alone. An unknown man in his thirties followed her, carrying two large wicker hampers, and behind him, of all people, was Jane Griffiths, my assistant.

Lunch for *nine* instead of four? My mind reeled drunkenly. What on earth were all these people doing here? I had a strong desire to run away somewhere so I didn't have to find out. And what about the trifle? I thought distractedly. We'd be lucky if we got a spoonful each.

Mum took charge. 'Shall we all go into Ellie and Quinn's lounge? There might be more room there.' I realised we were all sardined into the small entrance hall, as stationary as stringless marionettes.

We quickly sorted ourselves out. The strange man – obviously Columba's new gentleman friend – apologetically winked at me, which endeared me to him, as he walked past me to dump the wicker boxes in the kitchen. What on earth was in them, I wondered? Cats? Dogs? Irving seemed remarkably interested in them, so I ruled out dogs.

'I realise this is a surprise for you, Ellie and Quinn.' Columba took centre stage in the lounge while Quinn busied himself with drinks. 'But then life *should* be full of surprises. I know how you worry, Ellie, so we've brought lunch with us. Cold, of course. A sort of indoors picnic.' She broke off to sniff. 'What's that terrible smell, darling?'

'Lunch.' My morale hit rock-bottom.

'What a transformation. You never used to cook Sunday lunches.'

'It's for Quinn's parents,' I told her stoutly. 'They'll be here any minute.'

'Splendid.' Columba beamed, ignoring my warning glance. 'I'll enjoy meeting them, won't I, Ellie?'

Sheer panic hit me. Had she already forgotten that Quinn and my parents were to know nothing about the reason for my visit to her? Was she proposing a Gestapo-like public interrogation of Quinn's background?

'I missed meeting them at the wedding,' Columba pointed out to my parents. 'I wasn't there.' She made it sound like a deliberate plan on my part, but it wasn't – honest – though

I had been extremely grateful to Hollywood for hanging on to her.

My panic subsided since no one but me thought her comment at all odd.

Jane was placidly sipping her wine on the sofa. I haven't said much about her so far because she hasn't really entered the story yet. Reader, she is about to do so. Jane is the stable rock of my working existence. She has worked for me ever since I set up Happy Ever After in Tunbridge Wells four years ago. At first we used assorted venues for the receptions, but when Stephen offered me the chance of moving both office and receptions to Charham, I jumped at it, especially since it was within commuting distance from my flat in the Wells.

Then I met Quinn. It was quite by chance. A happy couple decided to have their wedding pix taken at High Rocks and Quinn, visiting the Rocks for illustration background, absent-mindedly walked right into the photograph of bride and groom. Somehow he managed to get himself included in the reception at the nearby Beacon hostelry and in the course of the wonderful fare it produced, he became part of my life. He was living in London at the time, but you'd never have guessed it, because most of his time was spent in Kent with me.

Back to Jane, who still lives in Tunbridge Wells. When Happy Ever After moved to Charham Place, she tried living there, courtesy of Stephen. She found it too large, she said diplomatically. Personally, I wouldn't want to live with that caretaker and his wife either. Nor their Rottweiler. A working relationship is quite enough.

Jane is . . . well, Jane. Thirtyish, dedicated to her work (as all Virgos are), serious-looking and a nicely rounded (Quinn's approving description) size sixteen. She is single, but there is, I gather, a man in her life. He turns up every now and then and mentally yowls for her, but Jane never seems to take much notice. I suppose she must have a romantic soul despite her lack of interest in 'settling down', for one must either be entranced by the romance of weddings or entirely cynical about them to be able to work in our line. She also has a passion for the theatre, which is why she gets on so well with Stephen.

Now back to our lunch party: the stranger – still on his feet, as was Quinn (but not Dad) – coughed politely. Columba – still pacing the room and holding centre stage – remembered her manners. 'Margaret darling, and Ellie, you haven't met John, have you?'

Mum smiled up at the stranger. 'No.'

I grinned inanely at him.

He was about the same age and almost as tall as Quinn, but a lot lankier. His glasses gave him the sober look of a lawyer or accountant until one noticed the quizzical irony in his eyes.

'Ellie is our delightful hostess, John, but it's Margaret you're here to meet,' Columba informed him warmly.

That this was news to Mum and Dad was obvious from the suspicious look that instantly flashed across their faces.

'Margaret, John Curwen,' Columba announced. Then she turned to me. 'Ellie, meet John. He is the answer to our prayer, darling.'

The smile on my face became fixed in stone. The triumph in Columba's voice suggested he was a particularly awkward rabbit to produce from her magician's hat. Furthermore, this might be the new love of her life, but she clearly had some scheme to gallop headlong with this White Knight to *my* rescue in front of everybody.

'It's a pleasure, ma'am,' John said to Mum, establishing without doubt that he stemmed from across the Pond. Then he turned to me: 'Ellie.'

I was still hypnotised, like one of Quinn's Rab-Hit victims, laser-beamed into immobility. The answer to our prayer? Please, Columba, I begged her silently, don't say a word.

'What prayer, Columba?' Quinn asked curiously.

She laughed merrily.

'Another fiancé, Columba? Lining him up?' Dad asked jovially to indicate he'd had enough.

'Nope,' John answered for her. 'Tried it once, sir. Didn't care for it – or rather, she didn't.'

'You married Columba once before?' Quinn enquired politely. I deduced that he didn't care for John.

'Not Columba.' John took it in good part. 'My wife's name was Angie. That was enough wedded life for me.'

'Don't tease me, darling,' Columba said plaintively. 'You know you adore me.'

'As you say, ma'am.' John kissed her hand, and I saw Quinn cringe. Even in my terror, however, I thought I detected a tongue in John's cheek, but I might have been wrong. Columba didn't detect it, anyway. She was reassured.

'Then what prayer?' Quinn patiently pressed again. I waited in trepidation and Mum sat blissfully unaware of her fate.

'I've agreed,' Columba announced with the air of one bestowing an enormous favour, 'that John shall write the Flowerdew family biography.'

It was a moment of Grand Guignol. The assembled company burst into complete uproar, just as the doorbell rang.

I am not even going to attempt a full account of the various melodramas that began at that moment. Quinn's parents innocently walked in to find exactly what type of woman their son had married – a sobbing wreck from a completely crazy family.

I will explain shortly why the mention of a mere biography caused quite such a rumpus. The thought of it still makes me weak at the knees.

I watched helplessly as extra chairs were rushed down from upstairs and another table was rescued from an outhouse, to be speedily set with bits and pieces of crockery and cutlery. Jane and Mum helped me in the kitchen, and in no time it seemed I was sitting down staring at pies, salads, pâtés, fruit and cheese, while a few shivering fish fillets, a small overdone leg of lamb and soggy vegetables sat dejectedly amidst them. No comments were made about the food as the rumpus continued. Everyone jabbed a bit from time to time with spoon or fork, usually coinciding with a vicious point in the argument. Even Quinn lost his cool. Only Jane sat peacefully munching throughout.

I will, however, extract from the nightmare of the next few hours the interchanges that related to my problem. So much was going on, it was hard to recall that this ghastly lunch had started out as the first step in my quest to prove once and for all that the man at the far end of the table was not my half-brother.

Quinn's parents were a quiet couple. I knew very little about either of them, except that his father Ken had heart problems and was a retired schoolteacher. Our courtship, the usual time for information swapping, had been too brief, and in the afterglow of marriage one has other things on one's mind. Now I studied them carefully. They both looked younger than their early seventies. Ken was tall and lean with a soldier's upright bearing. He'd have been too young for the Second World War, but might have collided with the Korean, in '53. Or maybe his National Service days had left a permanent mark. He watched a lot, I noticed, but said little. His wife Bridget did the talking for both, and looked more placid than her husband.

I discovered very early on in talking to them both that neither of them had any interest in theatre, and that they only watched documentaries on TV. They must therefore have been somewhat bewildered by the unexpected entertainment going on at the Lodge and were probably feeling like visitors from Mars reaching a new planet. Perhaps I was wrong though, for I saw a look of amusement on Ken's face at one of the high spots, which was hastily removed when he saw my grin.

Having abandoned lunch to look after itself, I was now able to think of my main motive for inviting Quinn's parents today, and since Quinn was standing at some distance from me and involved heavily in what was going on around him, this was the perfect opportunity – if it arose naturally. I could hardly say, By the way, just where was the orphanage you took Quinn from? I had to work my way round to it.

'How do you find working and wifing?' Bridget Connelly asked cheerfully.

'With Quinn no problem,' I assured her. 'You've trained him well in the kitchen.'

'He was forced into it if he wanted to eat. I work at home, so food gets rather erratic.'

'You're still working?'

'Semi-retired. I'm a book editor. Ken's retired completely, of course, although he still uses his French.'

'So that's why you were in France when you adopted Quinn.' I was relieved it had slipped in so quickly and easily.

'We still go every summer as we used to, for three weeks.'

I plunged. 'Where was the orphanage?'

'In Paris.' I thought she was going to stop, but she continued. 'In Vincennes, on the outskirts. It's long gone now.'

'I wonder' – my voice sounded odd even to my ears, and I quickly dived for another potato – 'why a French orphanage should have given Quinn to you rather than to a French couple. I'm very glad they did,' I added quickly.

A look of slight surprise. 'Put that way, I suppose it does sound odd. The explanation's quite simple. We had friends living in Vincennes at the time, and Marie helped out at the orphanage. She knew we were looking for a child to adopt, and that the staff thought Quinn was English or Irish because of his name, the one fact they had to go on. He'd been there about six months when Marie joined the staff, and the story was he'd been found curled up in a sleeping bag in the chicken-house in the garden.'

'You're joking.'

'No. It was quite logical really. It was winter, and the chicken-house was warm. The noise the chickens would make would draw attention to him quickly enough. Someone cared enough for him to think of that.'

But not enough to leave clues as to how he or she could be traced. I was deeply moved on Quinn's behalf, and cast him several sympathetic looks before I remembered I wasn't supposed to be talking about this subject.

'The police hunted everywhere for anyone who might be his parents, and sent details to the Irish authorities so they could hunt for birth certificates with that name before we were allowed to adopt him. It produced nothing.'

'What about the English authorities?' My mouth felt very dry.

This time Bridget was surprised and showed it. 'I really don't know. I suppose so, although if the child was abandoned in France it's more likely that his parents, whatever their nationality, were living there at the time.' A pause. 'Why do you want to know?' Then she quickly added, 'Sorry, it's the editor in me. Everything has to tie up.' She gave me a sweet smile, but coupled it with an old-fashioned look.

'Oh, it's the same for me,' I said hastily. 'That's why I wanted to know. Thank goodness you went to Vincennes,' I gabbled on. 'I might never have met Quinn otherwise.' I wanted to know if the friend was still alive but dared not ask. Bridget had a point about it being unlikely that a child would be abandoned in a foreign country on a mere visit, and I cautiously scored up a small victory.

'Quinn never remembered much about his early years,' Bridget added. 'When he first came to us he used to chatter but we never knew whether he was talking about the orphanage or his previous life. There was nothing of consequence, anyway. He did have floating memories of some kind of noisy music. They vanish with the years, don't they, and then reappear when one's old.'

Music? My heart thudded right down again.

'There was someone at the home whom he took a fancy to,' Bridget continued. 'A young cook, I gathered from my friend. She may be right, for Quinn came to us already knowing his way round a kitchen. So you see I can't claim credit for that at all.'

It struck me that Bridget Connelly could be given quite a lot of credit for Quinn's balanced outlook on life.

Meanwhile John had been defending his wicket vigorously on the biography pitch, but when Bridget was engaged by my father in conversation – probably to avoid throttling Columba – he turned to talk to me. Columba was quite happy carrying the argument on her own, breaking off intermittently to throw a few family reminiscences at Ken Connelly. Every now and then the dreaded word 'biography' carried clearly over the noise level – not to mention my father's answering growl.

'I gather from Columba you'd like me to do some ferreting on the quiet for you, Ellie,' John said.

'If possible.' Caution was the word here. 'I don't know what she's told you or indeed what your field is. A writer of theatrical history seems a long way from the pop scene.'

'Writing's a sideline, and my theatrical tastes, work-wise, are wide. I'm a freelance showbiz researcher. I take commissions from universities and museums and so forth to buy for their collections – a scout for ephemera.'

'Is that all? I'm sorry, that sounds rather rude,' I belatedly added. I couldn't see much hope here.

'No. I also do research for books, private investigations, tracing artists who've disappeared – anything that comes along.' John grinned at my audible gulp of hope. 'Did Columba tell you about the Flowerdew Museum?'

'No.' What was this all about?

'I'm not surprised, seeing what's happened at the mere mention of a biography.'

61

'Don't get false notions of grandeur. You're not the first in the lioniser's den. There've been at least twenty would-be biographers before you, all torn to pieces at the first hurdle.'

'And that is?'

'The family. Columba is the only one interested in getting it off the gravel, and even her determination can't fight the entire Flowerdew family. And don't tell me there's such a thing as an unauthorised biography, John.'

'I could, but I wouldn't be interested in writing it. A mere career story from press cuttings wouldn't be my kind of thing. Nor,' he added calmly, 'would an *authorised* biography. From what I've seen here today, anything authorised would be blander than hot milk.'

I laughed at his ingenuousness. 'You mean you want family co-operation, but to keep complete control?'

'I do, and I shall get it.'

I almost believed he would. Confidence would take him a long way. Then I realised just what was riding on this, and changed my mind. After all, I too was a Flowerdew. Did I really want its loveable – and less loveable – secrets exposed to the world? Even if Columba had *not* told him about Uncle Ted, he was going to find out sooner or later.

'The museum may be a good entrée,' he continued. 'Get you all used to the sight of my face and the cut of my jib, as you Brits say.'

'Where is the museum going to be? New York or London?'

He grinned. 'Right here.'

This was too much. 'In the Lodge?' I shrieked. Surely even Columba couldn't have persuaded Stephen into this?

'No, I guess she wanted to spare you that. She's arranged for it to be at Charham Place.'

'You mean' – I swallowed hard, for this was just as bad – 'Happy Ever After is being kicked out for a museum? That's my firm. My livelihood.'

He hastened to reassure me. 'No way. It's going to be

62

in the old stables. Stephen is going to convert, heat, and equip them.'

'The poor sap,' I said feelingly, forgetting to whom I was talking.

He looked at me straight-faced. 'Your aunt is a fine woman, Ellie.'

I could hardly retort, You'll discover a few snags. He might not only be Columba's new loverboy, but also a prospective husband. A mere age gap was immaterial to her. 'Of course,' I murmured hastily and, I hope, convincingly. Another sudden thought hit me.

'Are you going to be the museum's custodian, John?'

'No. I'll keep an eye on content, of course. The museum's a good cover for visiting you.' For a moment I thought he was propositioning me, until I remembered my main problem. 'Jane's going to look after the museum,' he added.

I was furious. Didn't I rate at all around here? Columba was going to get a rocket for approaching my assistant without my agreement. I understood now why Jane was here today.

'Is she abandoning me?' I asked bitterly.

'I gather wild horses couldn't drag her away from you.'

I couldn't tell if he was serious or sending me up, so I left the museum for the moment to concentrate on my own fears. 'What did Columba tell you?'

'The whole story about your mother believing that her son by Richard Hart is still alive, and your being worried that Quinn could be Marcus. I see your point,' he said seriously.

'I almost wish you didn't. I'd like someone *other* than Quinn and Mum to laugh their heads off at the very idea.'

'Come now, Ellie.' He was gently telling me to grow up. Fairy-tale happy endings have to be worked for.

'I want to trace what happened to Richard and the main hope is the band.'

'What have you found out so far?'

'Nothing,' I said gloomily. 'I can't ask Mum and I can't

ask Quinn.' I told him what little – good and bad – I had just culled from Bridget.

'Pop music isn't my preferred scene, but I have a few contacts. Should be easy enough to find out what's happened to the Coinmakers.'

'And manager,' I remembered.

'Ah yes, the fascinating William Gossage. I've already studied the photos and done a little preliminary research. I'll get back to you, Ellie. You can rely on that.'

Oddly, I believed him. 'My own theatrical angel,' I murmured in a rare outburst of Flowerdew sweet talk.

'I can't afford the golden harp, let alone to back plays.'

'Oh.' Another dismal thought. 'What are your fees?'

He laughed. 'This is a freebie for Columba.' He might have thought twice about this if he had known where it would lead.

By the gleam in my father's eye, I knew I was for it. He made a beeline for me after lunch, and I wasn't sorry, for I had not missed the fact that Quinn had fallen very silent, and if there was to be a battle I needed to be ready for it. My father was the easier option at present. He took me firmly by the arm for a father-daughter stroll in a very chilly garden.

'I acquit you of *some* blame, my girl.'

'Thank you.'

'Only some, though, because I could see Columba's visit was a total surprise by the look on your face as we arrived. What I want to know is how much you knew about this crazy idea?'

'Of a biography?' I was relieved that he hadn't found out about John's other role. What's more, I could reply truthfully. 'Nothing.'

'The woman is out of her mind and I've told this John fellow that. At the very least, he'd have to rake up the Mighty Rich story again.'

I leapt in quickly. 'No, Pops. There wouldn't be a lot

about Mum in the book since it would be about three or four different generations, not just yours. A brief mention of Rich and a child that died should be enough.' Too late I realised that John knew the truth. He would have to be persuaded to leave Marcus out altogether. Goodness knows, there were enough juicy stories to be had without adding the child's.

'He strikes me as a delver, Ellie. He's a twitchy-nose sort of chap. If we refuse to co-operate – as we shall – he'll delve all the harder.'

'It'll be all right. Most of the crazies are dead.' I met his eye and mine fell.

'You know very well, Ellie, that a biography would either be a whitewash flop or a best-seller. Which do you think he'll go for, given that twitchy nose and that grin?'

'Best-seller,' I admitted. It was all too much and tears miserably began to run down my face.

Dad hugged me. 'Poor girl. It's tough on a happy bride.'

Little did he know the happy bride was living in an unhappy quagmire, with only John Curwen to pull her out. Or push her right in.

I now have to confess I have been guilty of withholding information. It wasn't strictly necessary to provide it at first, for, apart from Aunt Columba, Mum and myself, the Flowerdew family had no relevance to the story of Marcus and Quinn. John's appearance on the scene and Aunt Columba's brilliant museum idea for his cover story would change all that. At first I hoped that a cover story was all it was, and that he had no serious intention of writing a biography, but now I knew that he and Columba were in deadly earnest, both about that and about the museum.

I was economical with the truth when I described our family problems. I implied that Columba is the only mad member of the Flowerdew family. She is not, though she is certainly the most visible.

Sir Claud Flowerdew and his wife Lady Frances (an earl's

daughter who flew the coop) have both long since left this world, and are duly commemorated in St Paul's Covent Garden actors' church. Claud was the first great Flowerdew, though he learned his trade in his parents' travelling portable theatre company, in which he acted everything from stock plays to Shakespeare. Lady Frances joined the family, and their son William, my grandfather, was born in 1897, the first of seven children. He was a hard-working and talented actor, but lacked the spark of genius (or craziness, if you prefer) that his father had possessed. He was secretly happier directing. He died aged eighty-seven in 1984.

His widow Violet is still happily alive, and lives on in the family home in Hampstead, looked after by resident carers. Like her husband, she is tame material for biographers. She is not tame in other respects, though. My grandmother is where most of the would-be biographers founder. They think they're in for an easy ride, and find out – too late to readjust their plan of campaign – that she is not.

Columba on the other hand is a throwback to Claud. No doubt about it. Claud and Lady Frances's other six children dispersed themselves around the theatrical world. I will spare you details of their vastly chequered careers (both on stage and off), save for Great-Aunt Cecilia, the youngest.

She too is still alive, at a sprightly ninety-one, and lives in an amiable crazy mist interspersed with intervals of sheer lunacy. This is not due to her age. She has always been completely scatty, my grandmother informed me. She had five husbands and outlived them all. Only two retreated in divorce; the others remained devoted to her until their respective deaths. The first was a big game hunter; the last was the love of her youth, a character actor called Jacob Crichton. Cecilia also played character parts, specialising in dotty old ladies with whom she had no trouble at all identifying. She still appears very occasionally doing a sort of John Gielgud in cameo film roles. So what makes her dotty? Wait, dear reader. You will be meeting her.

There is only one other fact you need to know about Great-Aunt Cecilia and my grandmother at this point: they loathe each other. The reason for the feud is lost in the mists of time – they've probably forgotten it themselves. Rumour has it that Cecilia once made a disparaging remark about William's acting ability, with which he fully concurred. My grandmother did not – to her he was Irving, Beerbohm Tree and Gielgud all in one. Cecilia and Violet never see each other, and so the volcano is dormant, awaiting its time. With the biography, it may well have come.

The real horror of the Flowerdew family, however, is Uncle Ted. Columba and Mum weren't William's only children. Edmund Flowerdew was the eldest. He did exceptionally well in the Flowerdew tradition on the stage in the late fifties and sixties. He married a delightfully madcap lady called Flossie who, believe it or not, had a pedigree almost as good as Lady Frances, and settled down to marital bliss and stardom, producing many triumphs on stage and one child off it – my cousin Imogen. All was set fair until suddenly he disappeared in the middle of a provincial run of *As You Like It* in 1972. Completely disappeared – just like the Mighty Rich. Or not like him, for some years later Columba discovered he'd just been released from prison, where he'd been in on a charge of bigamy under the name of Charles Merridew.

The two ladies in the case had apparently filled a role that Flossie failed in – quiet domesticity. Joan Trent was a former haberdasher's assistant, lived with Charles in the north of England and provided him with three daughters; Patsy Harding was an excellent cook, lived with Charles in a neighbouring town, and provided him with a daughter and a son. These households co-existed for several happy years until 'Charles Merridew' made the mistake in 1978 of registering two of his offspring virtually simultaneously and was recognised by the registrar, who, unluckily for Uncle Ted, had just moved from Joan's town to Patsy's.

Even then the Flowerdews might never have known of

'Charles Merridew', since television in those days did not have today's power in spreading theatrical faces instantly around the globe. Joan and Patsy, only just recovering from the shock of discovering about each other, were informed of Flossie's existence by a gleeful Columba, and Flossie became acquainted with her husband's iniquities. Columba then presided over a family summit, where she suggested for the good of all that none of the children should be told, and that all enquiries on Edmund Flowerdew should meet with the news that he had been killed in a crash while on tour in Australia.

Not for the first time – or, alas, the last – Columba's plan came somewhat unstuck. Flossie immediately set off after her missing husband, and so did Joan and Patsy. Edmund took to the road to escape them all, and so far as we can gather is still working his way round the world, performing under false names in small companies. This King Lear, Macbeth, fraudster, alcoholic, tramp, bigamist, darling of the race tracks, is the black sheep of the Flowerdew family, who occasionally bobs up like a yo-yo to ask if there are any pickings to be had. No one ever *sees* him, and he never stays long at any one address, since Flossie, and presumably Joan and Patsy, are still after him.

Occasionally, Charles Merridew is picked up and dumped in a hostel or cell. It is hardly surprising. He marches along the road – according to the police – spouting chunks of Prospero or Lear, or Noel Coward or Toad of Toad Hall. People back nervously away, report him, and he has to fight for his freedom all over again. He always sends for help from Columba, who provides it, but he never stays to thank her personally. When he had a nice win on the lottery last year, however, he charmingly sent such nice presents to Columba and Margaret that they were completely disarmed.

No one has actually seen Uncle Ted for nearly thirty years now. I was entrusted with the truth on my twentieth birthday, but poor Imogen is still under the impression that dear Daddy is dead. Imogen is now forty-one.

I could go on, but it should now be clear why a biography of the Flowerdews would not only be a best-seller, but wreck quite a few Flowerdew lives as well.

Did Quinn know any of this, you may ask?

He did not. Columba was enough to be going on with. I had been waiting for a chance to break the happy news, and it hadn't come. I realised I would shortly have some explaining to do, in view of today's uproar. It was small comfort to remember he might well prove to have Flowerdew blood himself.

Five

It began over the washing-up. Don't most marital rows
do that? It's the fault of technology. Once upon a time
washing-up was a relatively peaceable sort of affair, passed
in an afterglow from the meal. It had its preordained rules:
a slow, gentle beginning with the glasses, then the cutlery,
followed by delicate china, then not so delicate. By the time
one had worked one's way through to the nasties – the pots
and pans and insufficiently greased flan cases – a working
relationship had been established in a mutual desire to get
this chore over with.

Not now, not since dishwashers took over. The ritual now
consists of short sharp jerks as dishes are categorised into
'will it' or 'won't it' be dishwasherproof, then rinsed, then
packed away into the machine. Then it's on to those horrible
items so mucky that the dishwasher disdains them. This
was the stage we were at, after the last of our guests had
departed – exhausted from battle – to leave the newly-
weds alone.

I couldn't look at Quinn. I busied myself with trying to get
the roasting tin clean and thinking, Any moment now he'll
be asking me more about the mad Flowerdews of whom he
must have heard such entrancing snippets this afternoon, and
why I never told him about Uncle Ted.

He didn't. He said nothing. He said nothing for so long
that I couldn't stand the suspense and asked inanely, 'What
are you thinking about?'

The answer came promptly enough. 'You.'

'Why?' My voice sounded like a declaration of war, though I didn't mean it to.

'And families,' he added.

'Mine?'

He shrugged and paused while he wiped a saucepan so dry it almost thanked him. 'And mine,' he replied at last.

'Look, I'm sorry.' My nerves were so on edge, I yelled at him. 'I'll apologise to your parents. Okay? I'll wear sackcloth and ashes and go on bended knee before them. All right with you?'

'No. They'll think you're round the twist.'

That did it. 'Like all the Flowerdews, I suppose. Wife belatedly reveals insanity in her family. Have you inspected our attic, by the way? Maybe I've got my first husband locked up there like the first Mrs Rochester.'

He laughed. Normally I wouldn't have minded, but today I did. This was far too serious a moment for that.

'Don't think I'm joking,' I shouted.

'I'll go and inspect. He might give me a few tips on how to deal with you.'

'So you think I need dealing with. Well, thank you. The whole thing's my fault. That's what you assume, is it?'

'Hey, quieten down, lady.'

I should have seen the red signals, for he was dangerously quiet himself. I didn't. Instead I rushed on through every barrier reading 'Don't go there':

'All the Flowerdews are mad, excepting my mother. Can I help it? Is your family entirely without flaw?'

Quinn's eyes flickered. Too late, I realised how tactless this was. Moreover, his family might be mine, and if by the Grace of God it wasn't, he could be descended from Jack the Ripper for all he knew.

'Seeing you in a Flowerdew context gave me pause for thought, that's all.' The reply was mild enough.

'You're regretting marrying me?' I snarled.

'No.'

He was doing his best against great odds, but his 'no' wasn't convincing enough for me. I wanted him to trumpet it, to clasp me in his arms, to stare deeply into my eyes, assure me I had filled an aching void in his life. I'd even settle for a kiss. I just wanted him to convince me. And he didn't. Perhaps he still thought reason would help.

'I think maybe you've retreated into family too much these last few weeks. And you're showing all the signs of getting in even deeper since you've seen Columba.'

I went cold. I hadn't even told him about my visit to her. Yet somehow he knew. Or he'd guessed. And that meant he'd guessed what I was doing.

'And perhaps it's not wise,' he continued, 'to be deep in the family you came from just when we should be starting our own.'

'Having a baby?' I had to force the words out. Why, oh why, did he have to raise this now of all times?

'Perhaps. If you'd like to. Or leave that while we try to establish ourselves as heads of a new dynasty. You and me.'

'*Try* to?' I kept my voice calm by superhuman means.

'Having a baby could help that. Besides,' – he gave the rather sad, twisted smile that usually (not today) turned my heart over – 'I'd like it.'

Oh yes, Quinn knew what I was up to. He could read my secret mind. He knew that I was still following up the mystery of his parentage and that Columba was helping me. His obvious instant dislike of John was ample proof of that. He, in his simple male way, thought having a baby would solve everything. Take my mind off it. Or did he secretly fear the same as I did? If so, the difference between us was that he wanted to have a baby to settle the question. I wanted to run like hell.

'How can we?' I replied, though I hardly knew whether I spoke to him or myself. The words just came. 'It might be incest.'

There are moments that turn one's life irrevocably onto a different track, like points on a railway line. And someone – me – had just pulled the lever that switched ours.

I watched, appalled, as the face of the man I had married changed into that of a stranger. I was quite detached, frozen into the calm of terror. A red flush hit him, and when it had died away, I no longer knew the man I had married, whom I loved more than anything else in this world, and with whom I had been going to live happily ever after. No fairy godmother was going to appear to wave her wand this time. I'd had my chance and blown it.

The last gasp of love's latest breath – never had Drayton's sonnet seemed more relevant or more hopeless in my case. *Now if thou would'st*, it ended, *When all have given him over, From death to life, thou might'st him yet recover.* Only in real life – in mine at least – it never happened like that. Farewells were permanent, there were no eleventh-hour reprieves. One look at Quinn's face and I knew I'd gone a bridge too far.

'You're still stuck on this crazy idea that I'm your half-brother, aren't you?' Quinn sounded incredulous – or was it an act? No, this was no play-acting. I'd made a mistake. He hadn't guessed about my obsession, nor about my visit to Columba.

'I can't believe it, Ellie,' he went on. 'I thought something was wrong, but not as bad as this. I ought to have realised. Even when my mother said you'd been asking about the orphanage this afternoon, I thought nothing of it. Idle conversation, I thought. My God, you fooled me. So now you can tell me just what you're up to.'

'I'm following up every possibility, just to make sure for our own peace of mind. Don't you see?' I pleaded. 'I've got to know.'

'But there's no bloody reason for there to *be* anything to know,' he roared at me. 'Can't you see that?'

'No, I bloody well can't.' I decided to stand up for myself. 'There's the timing, there's your name—'

He groaned. 'Go to Ireland, Ellie, and try telling people there you think I'm your brother because I'm called Quinn. They'd laugh in your face. If I were called Robert Smith, you wouldn't think that was grounds for suspicion. Use your common sense – if you have any, which I'm beginning to doubt.'

'I knew you'd think I'm crazy because of the Flowerdews,' I shouted back. 'That's the root of it. It's nothing to do with what I'm doing.'

'Wrong again. I think the Flowerdews are fun.'

'Good, because you may have their blood in you.'

How could I have said it? I had no idea and didn't care. I just burst into tears. He did come to me then, but the arms around me, I convinced myself, were there for mere comfort, not because he loved me.

'Give up this pointless chase, Ellie,' he whispered. 'The answer isn't there to find, because there's no problem.'

'It's in my mind, Quinn. I can't get rid of it.'

He released me. 'All right, Ellie.' All the anger had gone now; he just sounded tired. 'Go ahead. Go on hunting your Snark. I can't stop you.'

'Perhaps' – I hauled what was left of me together – 'it will softly and suddenly vanish away.'

'I can't see,' he said sadly, 'that that would help. We'd know it was there – in your mind.'

'I can try.'

'It's dangerous ground.'

'Then I'll tread lightly.' I felt sick in my stomach.

'How are you going about it? I presume you're not dragging your mother into it?'

'No. John—'

'Ah. Mr Charm and Balm,' Quinn sneered. It wasn't his usual style, and I stared at him in amazement.

'I realise you didn't take to him, but I can't see why.'

'I didn't like the way he handled the biography issue.'

'But he didn't do anything. He let the row swirl around him.'

'Quite. Point made.'

'I don't see,' I said angrily, 'that being a bit of psychologist-cum-diplomatist is such a bad thing for a potential biographer. Mother liked him, even though she's against the book.'

'Good,' Quinn said smugly. 'I don't, though.'

'And he's on Columba's list.'

'That's a recommendation?'

'Oh!' Here we go again. This time it was my turn to struggle for composure. 'You said you liked Columba – in a way.'

'I do, and that way includes your as-yet-unmet grandmother, your dotty Aunt Cecilia, and the late Uncle Ted.'

My heart sank. He hadn't heard the full story. Slowly, almost pompously, I told him about 'Charles Merridew'.

He roared with laughter – until he saw my face. 'Come on, Ellie. Try to see the funny side.'

I tried. Then I tried harder and eventually a faint smile emerged even though my stomach didn't agree. 'What do you think will happen to this biography? Do you think it will still slip through in the excitement of the museum?'

Quinn outlined a few scenarios, and then I offered my own olive branch. 'Perhaps you could do a cartoon strip on Uncle Ted, as a kind of Flying Dutchman wandering the world trying to escape from his three women.'

He laughed. He genuinely did. And so did I. Only when we went to bed exhausted and held each other tight did it occur to me how topsy-turvy the situation was. Here we were finding a meeting place in the Flowerdews – the very thing I had feared might divide us for ever. In a way it made matters worse. The darkness of doubt lay not in the Flowerdews but in me, and what lay between myself and Quinn. That hadn't gone away. It was still there. I was committed now for both of us, for our marriage – if it could even survive this first terrible test. I had to find out the truth about his parentage.

His arms were around me, but he made no move to love me, and I was too scared to make the move myself.

*   *   *

'Message for you,' Jane sang out as I arrived in the office a week or two later. 'John Curwen's coming down next Tuesday.'

This was good news. 'Great.'

'With your aunt.'

Not so great. Life had settled down into an uneasy truce between Quinn and myself since the Flowerdew lunch, as I had mentally named it. We kept away from the subject in conversation. He talked about his work, I talked about mine. No mention was made of half-brothers, and there was only the occasional polite enquiry about the museum, even though this was beginning to affect our lives. Work on it had already begun. Each morning a couple of heavily loaded builders' lorries or vans trundled past our home up to the stables.

Not that I had forgotten about my hunt. John was concentrating on tracing the band, and I was doing what I could in any direction I could think of. My mother and her family – save for Columba – were a closed door; so apparently was the orphanage where Quinn was found. The band and John's other contacts were therefore the only open source.

I read a guide on how to trace long-lost family and friends, and considered how its suggestions might help. Family for instance: Richard must have had family of his own, but Mum never mentioned it, and now I could not ask her. Another line of enquiry might be old photographs and press cuttings: I dismissed the first. Any clue they contained about Richard's friends would have been followed up by my mother, and the band would have known the musical circles he moved in. Unless one or all of them were deliberately lying to my mother about their knowledge of his whereabouts, photographs and press cuttings were not going to help.

National insurance records, bank records, death certificates and so forth would all have been covered long ago, while the divorce process was going through. I had a faint hope that a later death certificate might have escaped Mum's notice and considered writing to check. There was only one snag: if he had died under his real name, someone would have caught up with it by now, and if he had died under an assumed name, I had no chance whatsoever of tracking it down.

My bright hopes boiled down simply to reading as much about the pop culture of the late sixties as possible, to glean every mention of the Mighty Rich. It was from here that my one remaining hope sprang. I scoured the Internet for information on the Mighty Rich, but what was produced was very sparse. What I did find myself staring at was a number of fan clubs for pop stars of that era. Some of them were for idols no longer alive, but Rich wasn't one of them. Still, he might have had a fan club at the time, and fans were like Rottweilers: they wouldn't let their prey go easily.

I spent a couple of tedious days at Colindale going through old newspapers and magazines, and at last my patience was rewarded by finding an interview with a beehived, doe-eyed lady who claimed to run the Mighty Rich fan club. Her name was Angela Parsons, she was married to a soldier, and she ran the club from her home in Brentwood. It was manna to feed my starvation, and I couldn't wait to see John to tell him. Needless to say, I rang every Parsons in the Brentwood telephone directory with no success.

For this reason if for no other Jane's words about John were music to my ears.

'And,' she added, 'Stephen's flying in on Monday.'

'Jealous of John?' I remarked absently, then pulled myself together as I saw her staring at me oddly. I forgot Columba was still an idol to her.

'No, to see how the building work is going and to discuss finances.'

'For what? I thought the building estimates were agreed.'

'The museum has to be filled with something.'

'But won't the stuff be donated by the family?'

Jane looked at me even more oddly. It was clear that in

her books I didn't deserve to have Flowerdew blood. 'I seem to remember something about a biography.'

I groaned. I'd been so preoccupied with my Missing Persons mission that I had all but forgotten the bone of contention. It was time I caught up with events, and I decided to pay a call on Columba tomorrow, which was a Friday. I had a client in Victoria, so there was a pretext. It was needed not for Jane or Quinn, but for my conscience.

When I arrived I found John there, ready to take us both to lunch. Columba put on her huge dark glasses with the dramatic horns on them to escape notice from fans.

'How's the biography going?' I asked them both.

'As you'd expect,' John replied cheerfully. 'Columba and I are for it. Your mother and grandmother are against it. Imogen is all for it, though I guess she doesn't realise quite what it would lead to.'

'You've told him,' I accused Columba crossly. It was too bad to tell John about Charles Merridew before he got the go-ahead from the whole family.

'Of course, Ellie darling. Why not?'

'Hey, you can't blame her,' John said quickly. 'I asked where his grave was. I go to Australia once in a while. When Columba told me the truth, I wanted to know where he went after his prison sentence.'

'How can you find that out if his own family doesn't even know?'

'Not that hard. I can pick up the trail somehow.'

'Then you won't need to speak to any of the family. You can go ahead,' I said bitterly.

'Just what I told him, Ellie.' Columba seemed highly pleased. 'The silly goose refuses to do that on principle.'

'I'd like the family blessing,' John said meekly.

'To avoid stink when it's published,' I retorted.

'Stink, Ellie, would sell books. I'm sure you believe I couldn't resist that.'

I caved in. 'I'm sorry.' I really was. 'I suppose I'm

getting too caught up in it, worried this Rich story will come out.'

'Trust me,' murmured John. 'I'm a journalist.'

I grinned at the joke and all was forgiven. If only things were so easy with Quinn.

'What about Great-Aunt Cecilia?' I asked curiously. 'Does she know about the biography?'

'Cecilia is, I think, for it. If only to annoy your grand-mother.'

'Why do you say you *think*?'

'Because Flossie's against it, on account of Imogen's lily white innocence – and Imogen lives with Cecilia. I'll know for sure what your great-aunt's view is when I meet her.'

'She's agreed to see you? Violet will slay her,' I said incredulously. 'Or does she think you're coming to inspect the drains? She's completely dotty.'

'No, she thinks I'm coming to talk about the Mighty Rich.'

Floored again, and this time I was out for the count. 'What on earth would Great-Aunt Cecilia know about him?'

'I gather she was close to him.'

'Was she?' I was obscurely riled that he should know this when I, a member of her own family, did not.

'You can come if you like,' he offered pacifyingly. 'Even though Rich is not the only reason I'm going to see her. He's the back door.'

'I'll think about it,' I declared offhandedly, though I'd no need to do so. I wouldn't miss this meeting for worlds.

On Tuesday morning I had a sudden panic. Nothing had been said about where John and Columba were to stay. Were they by any terrible chance planning to grace the Lodge with their company? I put the question to Jane as casually as I could, and was told to my relief that Stephen was putting them up in Charham Place. I had a sudden irreverent curiosity as to how the sleeping arrangements might work out. John seemed to be seeing an awful lot of Columba, and my theory that he was high up in her love-life league did not seem far-fetched – particularly in view of their parting exchange when he had left us after lunch last Friday.

'Dearest, I must fly.' A peck on Columba's cheek.

'Tonight on gossamer wing?' she giggled.

He glanced at me, and kissed her hand. 'Where are you off to now, Columba? The moon?'

I could make nothing of it, except a vague memory of a Cole Porter song. On the train going home, it came to me. Gossamer wing was or had been American slang for a condom. It took me back a bit, but they were both adults, so there it was.

In the event, it turned out that Columba was sleeping in the Tower Room – like some inviolate Sleeping Beauty – and John on the far side of the house. The Tower Room was one of the bridal suites so I knew all about it – including the fact that Stephen's rooms were much nearer than John's.

John read my face correctly as we plonked Columba's luggage in her room, and set off on the long march to his. 'I'm saving myself for my wedding night,' he hissed at me, so that Jane could not hear.

I giggled, and supposed that if I were Columba I might well fancy a mid-thirties bridegroom with John's urbanity, and if I were an ambitious theatre buff I might well fancy marrying into the Flowerdew family.

'If you're after a Flowerdew, there's always Imogen,' I reminded him.

'Ah.'

Imogen, like John, had tried marriage once and didn't like it. She'd moved out after six months and taken up a career in bookselling, as though whatever-his-name-was had never been. Now, at forty-one, she leads a bracing life of healthy country walks, bookselling, and helping with the care of her great-aunt, in whose house she now lives and which is conveniently near to Imogen's work. She shows no signs of discontent – or of wanting to tread any theatre boards.

Since I had seen John so recently, I hardly expected him to have any more news for me, but on the Wednesday he suggested that we leave Stephen, Columba and Jane – who were busily at work discussing the contents of the museum costume room – and take a walk in the grounds. I grabbed my coat against the early November chill, and we strolled down to the lake.

'This is some place to work,' he remarked admiringly, as a duck waddled onto the bank to point out that winter was nearly here and so I'd better get some practice in feeding him.

'It is. And I'd like to keep it. So don't extend the museum for a while.'

'Jane will see to that. She needs this job, because she won't be parted from that museum once it's open.'

I wondered if the word 'flop' ever entered this American's vocabulary, and decided it didn't. Perhaps that wasn't so bad a way to live, provided you could then deflect one at a moment's notice if it did chance your way.

'You couldn't have a better custodian, John.'

He nodded. 'Guess you're right, Ellie. I'll bear that in mind. Now, about your problem.'

'Have you discovered anything new?'

'Yup. The royalties. I asked around, as they say. The recordings Richard made with the Coinmakers get split between the four of them. Forty per cent to him, twenty to the other three, minus ten to the Great Manager Gossage. After Rich went solo he received one hundred per cent of course, of which fifteen per cent went to Gossage. After Rich disappeared – and that was only seven months after going solo – everything was held back until the divorce. Then your mother received half, and the remainder was held against Richard's return. When the presumption of death case—'

'The *what*?'

'I thought you might not have heard about that,' John said smugly. 'Didn't your mother tell you about it?'

I wasn't going to betray Mum. 'She may have said something.'

'Ah. An application was made by Richard's father in early 1977, and granted by the High Court.'

I scrabbled in my memory. 'But don't you have to bring evidence of probable death?'

'Apparently there was. Richard died during an LSD trip in Nepal in 1972.'

'Who says?' I was grappling with all the frightening implications of this thunderbolt.

'The Great Gossage did, in 1977.'

'But my mother – she thinks he's alive, yet she must know about this.'

John's compassionate look made me even more defensive. 'Can you talk to her about it?' he asked.

'No.'

He sighed. 'There's an odd thing I thought she might explain. After the High Court case, Rich's share of the royalties was released to his father, but Gossage's percentage went up to thirty per cent. I thought she might know why. His father can't remember – so he claims.'

'You've *seen* him? You've spoken to him?' Everything was moving too fast and the reins of control were slipping from my hand.

'Sure.'

'But how did you find him?'

'Through your Great-Aunt Cecilia. She told me on the telephone that she'd kept in touch with him – and Richard's brother too.'

'What on earth for?' I was irrationally disappointed at this simple explanation. Magic tricks are never the same once they've been explained.

'I told you she was close to Richard.'

'Any news about the band?' I decided to refrain from

further questions about Richard's family till I'd seen Cecilia
myself – and spoken to Mum.

'Give me a chance. Only one of them so far. Michael
Patterson is still on the circuits, in a group called The Goldies
– all of a similar age to Michael, all names of a sort built up in
the sixties and seventies. It plays the clubs, makes occasional
recordings. It does reasonably well, apparently.'

'When are you going to see him – or have you been
already?' I asked suspiciously.

'When he gets back from New Zealand, Ellie. He's on
tour. Back for the Christmas season.' John grinned. 'I'll
be on the trail of the other two just as soon as he hits our
shores again.'

'Three,' I pointed out. 'There's William Gossage.'

'There I do have news.'

'What?' I asked eagerly.

'He's disappeared.'

'I kept clear of her nap times,' John said as we arrived at
Great-Aunt Cecilia's door at five o'clock later that week.
She still lives at Stedham House, which Claud Flowerdew
bought in 1910 as another country retreat. (Hampstead, where
Violet lives, was still countryside then.) It wasn't much of a
retreat. The place positively bulged with naughty Edwardian
house parties, from what I can gather. Cecilia lived there
after her parents' death, and simply imported one husband
after another.

'She doesn't have them,' I said. 'She isn't like most
ninety-one-year-olds.'

'Then she won't be fazed by my tape.'

'She probably won't know what it is. She's not a great
one for modern inventions.'

'None of them?'

'She has a TV and can even make the hi-fi work if she's
keen enough. Oh, and a video. She plays old Flowerdew
films, including the silent ones.'

'*Silent?*'

I mistook his eagerness for ignorance. 'Oh yes. Claud did a series for Hollywood around the time of the First World War, just as Beerbohm Tree did.'

'I knew about them. I just didn't know there were any in existence. I thought they'd self-destructed years ago, as so many others have.'

'Play your cards right, and she'll show them to you – for days on end. Claud as Hamlet, Claud as Lear, Claud as Sir Toby Belch. William struggling with Romeo.'

'Now that I did not know about.' The hunter was after his prey.

He found lots more of it as soon as he entered the house, which was stuffed with Flowerdew memorabilia. The walls groaned under prints and pictures, bookcases were overflowing with books about them, and everywhere stage props were stuffed in no particular order. Only I knew, of course, that that battered walking stick had seen Sir Claud across many a stage in his later years, and that the wooden chair facing us had in times past been the throne of kings. John, however, cottoned on remarkably quickly, and was almost panting with enthusiasm.

'Down, boy, down,' I said soothingly as we marched over to the drawing room on the carer's heels. Imogen was still at work.

'Here we are, madam,' the carer announced us.

Madam? Oh yes, my great-aunt had everyone trained.

'Thank you, Agnes.'

Great-Aunt Cecilia – or Aunt Cis as she is known today in her family – is a tiny doll-like creature now. You have to search for her. We had to search extra hard that day, for she was hidden behind a papier mâché replica of a Greek temple. She emerged, and posed for us in a variety of Indian skirts and shawls. Another day she might fancy playing Miss Havisham and appear in a white wedding dress. Even, heaven forbid, Salome. My personal favourite is Giselle. She is a great dancer. She can't do pliés any more, but her limbs are supple enough for her to make a good stab at most forms of dancing. Unfortunately she is also a great faller and to everyone's alarm has broken arms, legs and a hip in her attempts to rival Fonteyn, Rita Hayworth or Ginger Rogers – whoever happens to be the heroine of the day. It never stops her. Nothing can (I hope).

'Darling Ellie.' She floated gracefully towards us and her chair. 'I am Hermione, of course. I am returned to you, a stone statue come to life. Who is this delightful young man?'

'John Curwen, ma'am. We talked on the phone.'

'Ah yes, Columba's protégé. We used a different word in my young days.'

'Boyfriend, sweetheart, swain?' John asked blandly, for my benefit. I'd get my own back.

'Oh no.' Aunt Cis puzzled over this, and then smiled. '*Amitié amoureuse*. You, young man, are an amorous friend.'

'I'm wearing a different hat today, ma'am.'

'Of course you are. You've come about dear Richard, haven't you? How I recall his *Lady in a Mist* – or was it *Love in a Mist*? No matter, it went something like this.' She struggled to her feet again (because of the Indian draperies rather than age), posed once more by the temple doorway, and broke into a reasonably lively rock and roll dance. John promptly partnered her and my role was to sing – which I did. I was well used to this routine. 'What jigs he and I used to have,' she said as we all sank down again at last.

For some reason this brought Richard alive for me in a way nothing else had yet done. A picture of a young pop star dancing with a sixty-year-old lady. I saw his present, surrounded by nostalgia for the past. And a sweetness and thoughtfulness that none of his pictures or what I had heard of his life had yet suggested.

Six

I am very fond of Great-Aunt Cecilia – although perhaps fond is the wrong word. There are too many years between us for that. I love her, I like her, but fondness implies a bond, and that is missing. There could be one – if only Cecilia wasn't Cecilia.

Old ladies of ninety-one are usually accepting of their years, content to settle down, however unfairly, into the image society has of such an age group. Cecilia insists on fighting the world on her own terms, whether she decides to be a teenager for the day, or a wise old sage who has seen it all, done it all. The only role she rarely plays is that which society expects of her.

Please don't mistake me. I'm not knocking the fact that she's her own woman; I think it's terrific, and I hope I'm in such form in sixty-odd years. Its result, however, is that it's very difficult, as with many actors, to fasten onto a point of contact unless one is an actor oneself.

Strangely, I've never had this problem with Columba, partly because Columba treats me as a participating audience, but Cecilia does not. To her, I am a Flowerdew gone wrong, and so is my mother. *Why* don't we want to be on the stage, is her line of thinking? *All* Flowerdews belong there. Imogen seems to have won herself a special exemption, for she gets on with Cecilia like a Boswell with a Johnson. I found it all the more interesting that Aunt Cis and Richard were close. Gender, perhaps. Cecilia always had an eye for men.

Her carer brought in an uninspiring tea. I love the word

'carer'. It conjures up a motherly picture of older times when one person was prepared to devote themselves body and soul to the cared-for with the commercial aspect gently glossed over. Nowadays, it's usually just another job, and Aunt Cis's team changed with rapidity. Sometimes they were dedicated, sometimes they were not. This one was one of the latter. She wore a martyred look as though tea-making were beneath her, though she perked up when Cecilia thanked her as warmly as if the tired Madeira cake were oven-fresh scones and cream.

'Now what did you wish to know about my dear Richard?' Aunt Cis poured Earl Grey tea like a trouper. Her favourite teapot is enormous, and she drinks the tea so weak that only one teaspoon of tea is ever permitted to hide in the bottom of the pot. One leaf over the limit, and back it goes to the kitchen. She has a special smile for such days, and there's never any protest from the carers. It's always a pleasure.

'Mum believes Richard is still alive somewhere.' I held back on Marcus.

'She would, of course.'

'Because she still secretly loves him?' I was amused. 'I don't think so.'

'Before I answer Ellie's question, young man,' – she turned piercing blue eyes on John – 'might I enquire what your concern is in this matter? You claimed to be a prospective biographer of my family. Do dear Ellie's questions about Richard pertain to that?'

No flies on Aunt Cecilia's currant cake. Nor on John's either it appeared.

'I'm also helping your niece Columba and Ellie to find out what happened to Richard.' (I noted John wasn't referring to his 'presumed death' either.)

'And why might that be?'

'To make the story complete – and also the museum. You have heard about that?'

'My dear young man, I *live* in a Flowerdew museum.'

'And very fine it is too, ma'am. Nothing could match this. But it's time the public at large recognised what the Flowerdews have contributed to theatrical history.'

'You make your museum sound a charitable work, Mr Curwen.'

'It is, ma'am. Unfortunately I can't offer my services free for the biography, however. I need a publishing commission. No problem about that, but I have to be sure that I have a story to tell.'

Cecilia handed him the sugar tongs. Tarnished, but their elegance shone through, as did hers. 'And you expect me to co-operate in your digging in the dirt for Flowerdew nuggets?'

'Expect, ma'am? I wouldn't do that. And however dirty the soil is, my nuggets will be golden.'

'With halos?' she enquired politely.

'Golden with truth, ma'am, but that doesn't include irrelevant truth dragged in for sensation.'

'And who decides irrelevancy?'

'I do.'

'Is Violet co-operating?'

John didn't hesitate for a moment. 'She is not, ma'am.'

Cecilia cackled with glee. 'Typical. Very well, John, you have my support. When do we begin?'

'After you've told us about Richard,' I intervened. I saw my precious quest sidetracked into another Flowerdew backslapping session.

'Dear Ellie.' Aunt Cis shot a conspiratorial glance at John. 'John, you must return tomorrow.'

'I'd like that, ma'am. Shall I bring Columba?'

'Much better just the two of us to begin with. So much more intimate.'

For a moment, I saw the raver Aunt Cis must undoubtedly have been, no beauty but with an appeal that could lasso men at a hundred paces and entwine them in her toils. John was almost purring his satisfaction and I wondered cynically what role she would play tomorrow. Hermione could all too easily switch to Cleopatra, or, looking on the bright side, Rosalind.

'I'm waiting, Ellie,' she announced.

'What for?'

'The truth. I am a great believer in it.'

'Even when there's not much to tell?' I can play roles too. This was a virtuous one.

'Try.'

Why had I ever hoped I'd get away with controlling this conversation so that we talked solely of Richard and not of Marcus? It had seemed a simple task before I came. Now I saw it was impossible, and yet for my mother's sake, I could not tell her the truth.

'Ellie, dear. Perhaps I should help you.' Aunt Cis has been reading faces for a long time. 'It's to do with Marcus, isn't it?'

Relief struggled with caution. 'What about Marcus?' I asked.

'I always thought that so private a funeral was odd. One of the few things on which my sister-in-law Violet and I agree. The alternative is that Richard abducted the child. Though why, in that case, did Margaret not seek help?'

'She did. The police could find no trace.'

Aunt Cis frowned. 'I am an elderly woman, Ellie, but quite capable of clear thought. By help, I also meant the family. Why did she not breathe a word?'

I surrendered. 'I don't know, but you're right.'

'I knew I was right to choose Hermione today,' Cis told us reflectively. 'I am gifted, you know – I do have second sight. I was a seventh child, of course. I was communing with Hermione wondering how she felt when she met Perdita, the baby she thought had died at birth, for the first time as a grown-up woman. Marcus is a Perdita, isn't he? I suppose, correctly, a Perdit*us*.'

A picture of Quinn, laughing at me in our new home,

overwhelmed me so I could hardly speak. I choked and struggled to regain my composure. Not that Aunt Cis would notice. She was still on some stage of her own. 'Didn't you ask my mother about it?'

'No. The funeral, we were told, was *very* private, and yet the Flowerdews have never been private people.'

'Some have.'

'Not deep down, dear. Do you know, I do believe that's why Violet and I never saw eye to eye. She was jealous of my talent being superior to William's.'

'Of course,' I murmured, but then I could not resist. 'What about Uncle Ted – and Imogen?'

'That is quite different,' she rapped back, as I fully deserved. 'Dear Imogen, I am convinced, carries the flame within her; she is at the shrine, waiting for the Flowerdew spirit to pass into her.' Even Aunt Cis seemed to think this was over the top, since she added, 'Not that I can see Imogen in a religious light. I speak metaphorically, of course, like Canon Chasuble. Such a dear man, Oscar. I do wish I'd met him. When I played first Gwendolen, and then Lady Bracknell, I felt a keen rapport with their author. *The Importance of Being Earnest*, babies abandoned in handbags. My dear, we are positively *dwelling* on the theme today.'

A spasm of fear clutched at me. Please, please, don't make the other connection: the long-lost brother.

Aunt Cis smiled at me. 'The Importance of Being . . . Marcus.'

Was she rambling or was she fishing? John saved me.

'I'll write you a Flowerdew play to match if Ellie manages to track down Marcus.' He was grinning, but Cecilia took it seriously.

'If Columba plays Margaret, as I've no doubt she will, I demand first refusal on Lady Bracknell.'

'There is no Lady Bracknell in the Flowerdew story.'

'There is *always* room for a Lady Bracknell.' Conversation concluded. On that topic, anyway.

'The Mighty Rich,' I gently reminded her.

'I knew him as Richard.' Said with a tone of reproof, I felt I had been guilty of a crass beginning, as my great-aunt had no doubt intended me to feel. 'Such a sweet boy, so talented. He could almost have been a Flowerdew himself.'

'Did he act?'

'In his stage performances, yes, but I meant in his sheer artistic talent. He was an artist in his own right. A poet, too. Much is made of the Beatles, but my darling Richard could outshine them with his lyrics. For every *Penny Lane* he could write a "Tuppence Highway", for every *Strawberry Fields Forever*, a "Framboise Délices Today", for every *Hey Jude*, a . . .'

I longed to suggest 'Hallo Dolly' when she paused, but held back this irreverence as John contributed gravely: 'An Elegy to Holofernes.'

'Exactly.' Aunt Cis approved this Biblical triumph. 'Judith is a role I've always longed to play. A combination of Salome and of Charlotte Corday. Richard's greatest solo after he left the Coinmakers, *Seven Wives*, never received the attention it deserved. It would have been the cornerstone of another *Sergeant Pepper* album, given time. I am proud it was inspired in this very room, as we trailed clouds of glory . . .'

John was quicker than I was. 'Are you saying you smoked pot together, Mrs Bennington?'

'Flowerdew, if you please. It would be unfair to my five husbands to choose one of their names for posterity, so I retain my own. And yes, we did smoke pot.'

I gaped at her, hardly believing what I was hearing.

'I revelled in it,' confirmed Cecilia complacently. 'Not if I was due on stage, of course. It would hardly have helped my interpretation of Cleopatra – or perhaps it would have done.'

My mind still boggled. Aunt Cis would have been nearly sixty when Richard went solo.

'Did my mother take it?' I asked weakly.

'I believe she experimented with it in the early days, but she stopped when she became pregnant. Always so *sensible*, Margaret. After all, the sixties were an age when one was forced to experiment if one wished to participate.'

This kind of labelling always makes me suspicious that it comes from hindsight rather than memory, but who was I to speak? The sixties were over when I appeared in the world. I struck a small blow for reason. 'Did you participate, John?'

'I was a kid. My parents did. They went to Monterey and Woodstock. Wore the flower-child uniform, raved over the songs.'

I shut up. After all, it was Richard I wanted to talk about, not olden times.

'Did you see Richard after he split up with the Coinmakers?'

'Naturally. Without the band, he needed more than ever to talk to someone and he came to me.'

'What about his manager?'

'Ah, Mr Gossage. A most strange gentleman. He and I did not get on well.'

No hope there, then. She would hardly have kept in touch with him. 'Could you tell me when Richard disappeared?'

'The last time I saw him was in July 1969. He came to see me with Marcus and told me about the gig he was going to in Richmond. He often took Marcus with him if the venue allowed it, but Richmond was a long way from Sussex for a child. I wasn't surprised therefore when Margaret told me later Marcus had stayed with her. I heard nothing after that visit, and assumed Richard had returned. It wasn't until the following spring that I heard Marcus had died and that Richard had left her. We weren't in constant contact, for I *was* busy travelling in those days. I *was* surprised when I found out that Violet hadn't been told about the funeral either, and that's when I began to wonder what had happened, and whether Richard had simply run off with the child. However, as I said earlier, that seemed equally unlikely.'

'Weren't you surprised that Richard didn't contact you?'
I decided to delve deeper.

Her eyes flickered. 'Richard was a free spirit. He often
went to a gig, heard about another, and went straight on
to another; they were hardly planned with the regulation
of theatre performances. They were spontaneous; the pop
world was still young, flowering into its maturity. He rode
with the winds of change.'

That boiled down to precisely nothing in my view.

'Was he an irresponsible man?'

'Margaret always said so. But I do not believe it. He
went where his art took him. To be an artist carries a great
responsibility, as I know full well.'

Rubbish, I thought. 'What do you think happened to him
then? That he was tired of my mother and decided to set up
home elsewhere? Do you believe like many people that he's
dead? After all, according to her he took no money with him.
It sounds irresponsible enough to me.'

'He is an artist,' she repeated patiently.

A con artist, if you ask me, I thought, fiercely protective
of my mother.

Aunt Cis seemed to read my mind, and felt some further
explanation was called for. '*Sergeant Pepper* brought in a
new age. After that, pop music became deeply introspective.
Artists examined the world we live in. Vietnam too made a
deep impression.'

'Are you saying Richard was politically active?' John
asked.

'Richard didn't know a Tory from a Red. He searched
inside himself for the truth.'

'With the help of LSD,' I pointed out.

'Rarely,' Cecilia supplied, not at all put out. 'Mostly we
smoked pot. Like sex, we considered it delightful in itself,
and unlikely to lead to bad habits.'

'Back to Richard, Cecilia,' I said gently. I hardly agreed
with her in an age of paedophiles and pornographers, but sex

was a subject on which she could talk till the cows came home – or in this case, Imogen, who would shortly be home from work.

'The twenties were an unreal time too, like the sixties. The difference,' Aunt Cis reflected, 'is that the sixties were shared by the youth of all classes, whereas you needed money to enjoy the twenties. I admit it helped in the sixties too. Getting to Nepal can't have been cheap.'

'Nepal?' I picked up. So she did know about his presumed death. Then why . . . ?

Aunt Cis stretched out suddenly for the cooling teapot. 'Everyone went there . . . or India,' she said after a moment. 'Gurus, you know.'

What I *knew* was that she was covering something up. I got it in one leap. 'You've met Richard since he disappeared,' I accused her.

There were genuine tears in her eyes – unless they were genuinely part of some new role.

'Not met, Ellie. Oh, not met. I did have one postcard. Such a pretty one, from Nepal. It came a few years after he left, merely to tell me he was all right.'

'And you never told my mother?' I asked incredulously.

'He asked me not to.'

'Even though she was looking for evidence of his whereabouts for the divorce case? And' – I plunged – 'you must have heard about his family's successful application to have Richard presumed dead. Didn't you even tell the court about the postcard?'

'No.' Cecilia smiled smugly. 'I believe in keeping my word, and after all, my silence enabled her to achieve her divorce more quickly. You should be grateful.'

Grateful? I'd think about that later. Meanwhile the million-pound question. What of Marcus? If Marcus was with Richard in Nepal, there was a good chance my quest was over – he wasn't Quinn. If Richard was on his own, most certainly it wasn't. I could hardly bear to put the question, but I had to, and did.

'He didn't mention him, to the best of my recollection. I do have the postcard somewhere. I was so fond of him. I'll look it out for you.'

'*Now*, please.' A yelp seemed to come out. Where did this leave me? None the wiser, save that Richard had been in Nepal – along with thousands of other young Western seekers after the truth of life – a few years after he left my mother, and that this tied in with the presumption of his death.

Aunt Cis looked pleased that she had obviously scored a point and rang the bell. This time an anxious Imogen galloped to the rescue. That sounds condescending, but I like Imogen. She's tall, sturdy, and fifteen years older than me, which means she was in my eyes a glamorous young woman when I was a child. For a while she was a role model and, more to the point, she protected me in family arguments as the Flowerdews metaphorically poked and prodded me as they inquired into why I showed no signs of thespian talents. I realise now that Imogen was thereby protecting herself as well, but nevertheless I remain in her debt.

'We are discussing Richard Hart, Imogen, your aunt Margaret's first husband. the Mighty Rich, he was called professionally, although you won't remember him.'

'I do.' Imogen is never one for nuances, and there had been a definite warning in Aunt Cis's voice. 'I remember being popular at school because the Mighty Rich was my uncle.'

'What happened when he disappeared from the pop scene?' I asked, on tenterhooks for the postcard.

'Everyone thought I knew where he was,' Imogen replied. 'They believed at first he was incommunicado, preparing some great album to change the world. By the time I left school, one or two believed he was still alive, like Elvis, but mostly they'd forgotten all about him. Such is fame. Had enough tea, Aunt Cis?'

'Yes, dear.' Aunt Cis smiled trustfully up into Imogen's

eyes, playing the role of grateful elderly relative. I wondered if she still smoked pot and if so, what would happen if Imogen found out.

'Did you know Richard yourself?' I asked.

'Of course. I was a chubby five-year-old bridesmaid at their wedding. He wasn't much of a name then, I gather, and anyway, I hadn't even heard of the Beatles then. I met him from time to time, at family events, but I was only twelve when he vanished.'

That seemed to end that, and Cissy despatched her in search of the precious postcard.

'About Richard's family,' I began brightly. 'How did his father and brother react to his disappearance?'

John remained silent, to my relief, though I was surprised.

'My dear Ellie. You know very well. They reacted with a court case so that they could apply for his estate.'

'You don't like them.'

Dear Aunt Cis glanced at John, rearranged her draperies, and disappeared into *The Winter's Tale* again. 'Poor Leontes. At least he welcomed my return.'

At that moment Imogen came back in waving her trophy. Aunt Cis handed it to John, who was sitting nearest to her, and though he passed it to me immediately, I knew he'd managed to skim through the essentials.

I missed *the* essential, so eager was I to see what Richard had written. It was short: 'Darling Aunt Cis, dance on. Its lord still does. Don't tell the tribe. Dream the last waltz with me.' It was signed 'R'.

So what was the essential? John told me. 'The postmark, Ellie.'

For a moment I didn't get it, then I realised. It read July 1973, and his presumed death was 1972.

Aunt Cis looked guileless, but I'm certain its significance had not passed her by – neither in 1973 nor today.

Trust Imogen to prevent my following this up.

'What about this biography that's going to ruin Sir Claud's

reputation?' she demanded of John before I could speak. 'Aren't you the man writing it? My mother says you've persuaded Aunt Cis to help you.'

Trust Flossie. Chatter flows out of Flossie's mouth like Niagara.

'Yes.' John grinned at her. 'That's me. The Monster.'

Imogen has no humour in her. 'You don't look like a monster.'

'Thank you. Does that mean you're in favour of the biography?'

He was intentionally treading the path to disaster. John was fully aware of Imogen's ignorance of Uncle Ted's little peccadilloes. Oh, where was Quinn to ward off the dragons?

'Certainly,' Imogen declared. 'It's a splendid idea. I'll help. I don't believe in family secrets.'

Quinn looked up as the remains of me staggered in after this fresh pit opened up before me.

'I've put a casserole on for supper.'

An overture. 'That sounds good.'

'How about a drink?'

A definite olive branch. 'Thanks. White wine please.'

'How did you get on?'

No overture, no olive branch. This was a planned campaign. 'Where?' I asked stonily.

'I walked up to the house to take a message to Jane, and Stephen said you'd gone to see your great-aunt with that Curwen fellow.'

'I did. John wanted to talk about the biography and needed me there to—'

'And you wanted to talk about the Mighty Rich.' Quinn cut off my over-wordy defence.

'So?' I took the glass hoping I didn't sound as aggressive as I thought. Apparently I did, however.

'Look,' Quinn said peaceably, 'just tell me what's happening, that's all. Columba handed over to me a whole pile of video recordings and press cuttings of Rich and the Coinmakers. The Great Cur collected them for you.'

'I presume by the Great Cur you mean John.'

'You don't seem too excited.'

'I'm not.' I couldn't tell him I'd spent a couple of useless days wading through press cuttings, and this new stuff could only have peripheral interest. Quinn was waiting for an explanation so I had to give one. 'I'm trying to find out what happened to Richard *after* he disappeared, not what happened to him before.'

'Hum.' Quinn thought for a moment, then said, 'Okay, so what have you found out from your great-aunt?'

'Not a lot,' I stalled half-truthfully.

'Why did you go to see her?'

'She knew him.'

'And what did she say about him?'

'Nothing helpful.'

Quinn sighed. 'Ellie—'

'Look,' I interrupted, 'I'm frightened to talk about it. All right?'

'*Frightened*? Of what? Not of me, surely?'

'No. Of what it might do to us. The "us" factor might disappear.'

Quinn stared at me with a hopeless look in his eyes, but I was powerless to fling myself into his arms and let the pent-up terror inside me pour out. Instead I listened dumbly to his reply.

'It *is* disappearing, Ellie.'

I had to say something to bridge the gap or it would yawn too wide to cross. I was forced to offer the only plum I had.

'She had a postcard from Richard in 1973, a year after he was presumed dead. It was from Nepal. Nothing since.'

'So what did it say?'

I could hardly bear to watch the eagerness die out of his face as I replied, 'He didn't mention Marcus.'

'Supper's almost ready,' he said at last. 'Set the table, will you?'

The routine of marriage can provide a defensive rampart in a battle, and I accepted its shelter gratefully. No more was said of the Mighty Rich, nor even of the Flowerdew biography. Supper was followed by an hour's television, during which we sat side by side with a great distance between us. A hand on his thigh, or his on mine, would have crossed it, but instead it grew wider and wider while I struggled for something to say.

It must have weighed on Quinn as it did on me, for that night we made love with a passionate intensity that was all the more beautiful for the knowledge that it solved nothing. There was no red sunset to foretell a bright tomorrow.

Seven

It was with feelings of some trepidation that I set out with John to drive to Sumner Court near Guildford. A somewhat offhand Michael Patterson had suggested we could 'grab' him while he was setting up for a Goldies' gig at this country hotel-cum-conference centre.

Its range covered weddings, anniversaries, and similar events, and fêtes in the grounds. At the end of November fêtes weren't on the menu, but office parties were. I'd been here previously, before Stephen took Happy Ever After under his wing. I'd even used it as a venue on occasion. The gardens, so luxuriant in summertime, now looked desolate and bedraggled, which managed to remind me of my marriage, and I had to fight to keep my British chin up. It wasn't fair on John to burden him with my marital problems, but I think he guessed that my quest for my half-brother was taking its toll.

Sumner Court was aglow with glitter, holly and mistletoe, as though presenting its credentials as part of the perfect bliss of Christmas. To me, however, the Christmas to which I had so eagerly looked forward in July – since it would be my first with Quinn – was beginning to assume the proportions of a nightmare, and I was glad to be able to enjoy a day away from home territory in John's relaxing company. Americans appear at least to carry their internal baggage more lightly than my fellow Brits, and John never seemed to have a care in the world. Perhaps he didn't. He never mentioned women – other than Columba – yet he didn't strike me as being gay. Was he a mother's boy or sworn to celibacy after his former marriage? Did that explain his attachment to my aunt? *Was* there a sexual attachment? I quickly dragged my thoughts away, believing that it's usually better to work on the principle of 'what you see is what you get' in a friendship.

We tracked Michael Patterson down with no difficulty thanks to the sound of distorted vocals through amplifiers and weird noises from effect units, interspersed with the odd curse and shout. The former ballroom, which I'd last seen at a sedate wedding of a couple in their sixties, resembled an auto-jumble. Strewn out across the stage and a large part of the floor were leads, batteries, wire cutters, fuses and soldering irons. In and around them several men in their forties to sixties were busying themselves like the gardeners waiting for the Red Queen in *Alice*. I longed to shout 'Off with their heads!' but in the interests of fraternisation refrained from doing so. The thought cheered me up, anyway.

'Mr Patterson,' John bawled over the caterwauling sound effects. There were quite a lot of silver threads among these golden oldies, and one finally disentangled himself from his electrical problems, cursing, 'You'd think they'd have bloody warned us the stage was a twenty-one footer.'

I quickly agreed, since it seemed simpler.

The years had not dealt kindly with Michael Patterson, and the lines left by what I suspected were years of bewailing his lot in life contrasted oddly with the lank, long, once golden hair.

'Com'n'ava beer,' he invited us, summing us up apparently to his satisfaction. By which I mean we fulfilled his worst suspicions. In the bar, we eventually prised someone out of deep meditation to serve us with a beer and sandwich.

'What do yer want to talk about Rich for, anyway? Another bloody article?'

'No.' I had nothing to lose by telling him the truth. 'John's setting up a museum devoted to Rich's wife's family, and secondly, since she is my mother, I want to know if the rumours that he's still alive are true.'

He surveyed me, drained his glass, and said with ill-concealed glee, 'You won't want to hear my views on him, then?'

'You've heard nothing of him?' John's rather formal dressing had impressed Mike as little as I did. I'd suggested to John when he fixed this deal that we went casual for the day. He had refused. 'If he can dress how he likes to show his identity, then I can too.' Point taken.

'No, and that suits me.'

'But do you think he could still be alive? The High Court presumed him dead in 1977 after hearing he died of drugs in '72.'

'That self-serving bastard wouldn't kill himself.'

'Accident?'

'Nah. Too fond of himself to overdose.'

'So you think he chose to disappear?' I asked.

Mike shrugged. 'Look at the way he just walked out on the Coinmakers. The bastard just upped and left us. Said he wanted to go solo, but it finished us.'

'And that's why you don't like him?'

He shot me a glance. 'Never did. Always one for his own way was our Rich. We were meant to be a band of four, but you'd never think so. It went okay till he got this bug about writing his own stuff like he was a John Lennon or something. It was drivel – or we thought it was,' he amended. 'He did okay with it later. But it was written for him, not the band. We were only back-up, and didn't he make us know it? Even me, and he'd been the one to insist we had two vocalists, not one. When he wrote his own stuff, he dropped out as a vocalist. Said the Beatles had done that. We were going down a new path – *his* bloody music. The way we saw it we'd done all right with buying stuff in from the professionals. Will Gossage had a good eye for a song. *Demolition Squad* reached number two, and *Last Night, Next Night* would have hit number one if it hadn't been for *Sergeant Pepper* coming out that week. We were on our way – our own fan club, about to release a second album – and then Rich upped and walked out on us.'

'And your manager went with him?' John asked.

'Our *manager*?' He mimicked John's accent. 'Good old Will Gossage? Rich thought the sun shone out of his arse, but we didn't reckon him. We weren't where we should have been.'

'What's happened to him then? Do you know?'

Mike sniggered. 'My guess is he and Rich ran off together, and they're an item on a desert island, strumming and crooning away to their hearts' content.'

Now that was an unpleasant thought, and one that hadn't occurred to me before. It could explain the lie about Richard's death – if it was a lie. 'He took his son with him . . . Marcus,' I reminded him, remembering too late that Marcus was supposed to be dead. Fortunately Mike wasn't interested.

'Did he? Wouldn't surprise me. The stuffy Flowerdews were one thing, that kid was another. Rich thought the world of him, but said he took too much after his mother – serious like. He was going to turn him into a poet, he said.'

I wondered if I dare mention royalties, but as I hesitated, John did it for me.

'Half his royalties go to his family, after a hefty percentage to Gossage. Do you think he's made a career under a different name and the family's covering up for him?'

'Nah. A voice like that? I'd have heard about it. There are a couple of lookalikes of Mighty Rich doing the rounds, so believe me, I'd have heard the rumours.'

Mike condescended to address me again when John went to get more drinks. 'So you're one of the Flowerdews, are you? The only one Rich had any time for was his old lady, as he called her – not his wife though.'

'Cecilia.'

103

'He and his wife were heading for the rocks,' Mike informed me complacently. 'And for what? Rich was his own man and she wanted to shackle him, make him conform.'

I bypassed this and doggedly got back on the trail. 'Cecilia heard he was in Nepal.'

'Could have been. Picked up a stolen passport there and he was away. May still be there with dear old Will.'

'Did they disappear at the same time?' I ignored his obvious intention to go for the jugular.

'Gossage went later. Bloody poseur, he was. Dropped us Coinmakers like a sack of potatoes when Richard went solo, and went to manage him. Then after Rich disappeared he strolled back, cool as brass, and said he'd run us again. We told him to piss off. We got our pride. A fat lot of good it did us, and I reckon we made a mistake there. Couldn't stand the bloke, but he knew the trade. He could sense change coming, and rode the surf. That's what he told us, and he was right. It was late '69 when he came back, and two weeks after we'd turned him down, Altamont Speedway happened. Heard of it? It was meant to be another Monterey or Woodstock, but the Hell's Angels took over – stabbings, violence. Peace and love were out, so were hippies. The Beatles split up, the Rolling Stones were in. Everything began to change. The Coinmakers were caught; we were too way out to be Beatles, and not way out enough to rival the Stones. We messed around for a year, and then we split up, getting jobs when we could.'

'What's happened to the other band members? The drummer, Colin Atley, and the bass Bryan Whatley? Are you still in touch with them?'

He took a gulp of beer. 'Ah well, they shall not grow old and all that.'

'Dead?' I asked, taken aback.

'Bry's running a pub somewhere – Dorset, I think.'

'And Colin?'

'Clashing his cymbals in bloody heaven,' Mike replied

savagely. 'Killed himself, didn't he? *That's* why I hate the name of the Mighty Rich. I liked Col.'

'But what did Rich have to do with his death?'

'If Rich hadn't gone, we'd all four have been together. Col always felt an outsider; there was us three guitars – and him, drumming away on his own. He couldn't hack it after Rich went. He took it harder than we did. Died in '76. He was a bloody good drummer – but moody, you know,' Mike said as though he himself were the most cheerful guy around.

'Was he on drugs? Was it an accident like the death of Brian Jones?'

'He was high, but Col meant to do it. His girlfriend chucked him – he blamed that on Rich too – he couldn't work, so he killed himself. And that, folks,' he said glowering at us, 'is the happy story of the Coinmakers.'

'You've done well for yourself,' John observed.

He received a glare for his pains. 'Yeah. I miss the old gigs of the sixties, but I wouldn't swap today for yesterday. Look at it this way. I still get a buzz from the old guitar throbbing away, and the pay's okay. I'm not even on pot – I'm a family man now.' He stared gloomily into his beer, and answered the query that obviously came to mind. 'So if you wonder why I hate Rich Hart so much, it's this. We could've done more, and he put the kibosh on it. We trusted him. He built us up, and then he kicked us in the balls. You don't forget a thing like that.'

Bryan Whatley wasn't too hard to track down, once given the clue. John wanted to leave him till after Christmas, but I was all for visiting him before. I'd been depressed by the lack of information we got from Mike Patterson. Atmosphere and background were all very well, but they achieved nothing. I wanted – oh, *how* I wanted – just a little something more tangible before I faced the ordeal of Christmas. John was happier than I was, since Mike had offered to send him a few photographs of the Coinmakers in the early sixties, when they were still making their way up the charts.

We would hardly be welcome at a pub in the midst of the Christmas season, but Bryan Whatley had agreed we could come, and I set my hopes on him. Perhaps I had some vague dream that Richard might be masquerading as a barman in this quiet hangout.

Bryan Whatley's pub turned out to be in a village near Sherborne, and if we were expecting its owner to be a Mike Patterson lookalike, we were in for a surprise. He was just closing for the afternoon when we arrived – no all-day opening here – and he was as unlike Mike as he could possibly be. He reminded me of the old Laughing Sailor of the slot machines you still occasionally see; he was still the big, broad man of the seventies' photo, and had a laugh to match. He bore little resemblance to the photographs of the sixties, however. In those he was the young pop star idol, slim, dreamy, good-looking; now he was doing a good impression of Mine Host.

He took us into his private parlour where his equally jolly wife Peggy awaited us.

'How is old Mike? Getting old, like all of us?' he asked. Guffaw.

It was hard not to grin back, as though we were all in one vast conspiracy. There seemed a genuine warmth about Bryan though – and so I told him, albeit somewhat cagily.

'Still in the trade then,' Bryan remarked. 'Good for him. Still the same old stuff?' It was hard to tell if he was envious or curious.

'Basically yes,' I replied. 'Golden oldies of the Coinmakers, together with other sixties hits, he says.'

'Do you miss the scene yourself?' John asked.

Peggy chuckled. 'Not bloody likely.'

'No.' Guffaw from Bryan. 'You heard the missus. The folks who come in here hardly remember the Coinmakers or Rich. I've moved on.'

I believed him. All the photographs I'd seen on the bar walls as we came through, and the few in this room, were of Bryan and Peggy, Bryan catching a large fish, Bryan on the golf course. I saw none of the Coinmakers.

'You've got to put the past behind you, or you go into the future bum backwards,' was Bryan's final verdict. 'Now tell us what you're here for. Museum you said, and information for a biography.'

Once again I trotted out my stepdaughter line, ending up: 'Basically I want to know whether Richard is still alive, if you ever heard from him after he disappeared or have any idea where he might have gone.'

Bryan stopped grinning. 'Mike told you about Rich going solo?'

'Yes. He obviously felt very bitter about it.'

'Didn't surprise me. Always going off on his own was Rich. Blooming marvel he ever made it to a gig at all, he was that absent-minded. Thinking his own thoughts, he was, so he just went in the direction he wanted. Always after something new he was. One day he was going to climb Everest, the next he was going to be another Michelangelo or the next Gary Rhodes, or the next Poet Laureate. Never satisfied.'

'Even with his wife?' John murmured.

'Ah, now, there's a question. You being her daughter, miss, I oughtn't to speak of it, but I daresay Mike didn't hold back, so nor will I. When you're out there in front of thousands of little darlings screaming their heads off, it's all too easy to forget the little darling back home. No use you looking like that, Peggy my love,' he guffawed at his wife. 'It's water under the bridge – and anyway you were one of them. Gave all that up for you I did.'

'And never regretted it,' Peggy supplied.

I got the impression this was a well-worn bar routine, but that didn't mean it wasn't true.

'Rich was one on his own, picking and strumming his way through life like there was no tomorrow,' Bryan continued.

'He never played the field though. Too interested in himself if you ask me. I don't say that he never had a fling – we were all on pot at least, not to mention drink. Did we think of tomorrow? We thought of it all right. But tomorrow was ours, to do what we liked with; we had freedom, we had choice, and the youth of the world knew it. To my mind, Rich was happy enough with Margaret. She came along to the gigs occasionally, but after she had the kid we saw less of her. Rich adored that kid. He even brought him along to gigs with him. He popped him on the stage and he'd sit there good as gold while the noise racketed all around him. He was educating him, Rich said. Poor little sod.'

'Why do you think Rich left?'

'I reckon he just took himself off on a whim. He wasn't the sort to plan a disappearance. Why should he? He was riding high in the charts.'

'But why take no money?' John said.

Bryan gave us an old-fashioned look. 'There was the kid, wasn't there?'

'But he—' I struggled to remember my script. 'Marcus died.'

'*After* Rich left, so that wasn't the reason he went.' No flies on Mine Host. Not even one. 'Look, Ellie – you being Margaret's daughter, I reckon I can call you that – let's come clean. I'll tell you what I think, and you can tell me if I'm right. Margaret came to see all three of us after Rich disappeared. First visit was in September, desperate to know where Rich was, and the last a few years later, to find out if we'd heard from him. She wanted to marry again. Mike could never wait to get rid of her, but Colin and me, well, we did what we could to help – gave her intros, etcetera. From what she told us, he disappeared not long after we last saw him at this gig in Richmond. That was after we'd split from him, but we agreed we'd make this joint appearance. He had the kid with him, and pushed off home as soon as he could. That's all we could tell her. Not long after her first visit she came again to tell us the kid had died and had we heard anything at all from Rich. If Rich did contact us, she said, we were to tell him about the kid. I always reckoned that Rich had taken the kid with him, and *that's* why she was so obsessed with finding Rich.'

'I didn't agree. Why would she lie about his death?' Peggy said. 'She'd have been screaming the odds about abduction. Sorry, dear, but don't you agree?'

I thought of Mum, alone and desolate. I thought of the Flowerdews and the almighty scenes there would have been. Everyone would have been determined to drive Mum out of her mind by 'helping'. I thought of all the efforts she'd put into finding the child, and failing. I thought of Mum not being able face it any more, and giving that one simple lie to someone – her mother probably – so that they would leave her alone.

'There may have been family reasons,' I said quietly.

'Thought so,' said Bryan. 'Cards on the table. Rich took him, didn't he?'

'Yes.'

'Then that explains it. Marriage breaking down, Rich didn't want to lose the kid . . .'

It didn't explain it, because the marriage wasn't breaking down, but I let it pass.

John took over. 'What about William Gossage? Mike suggested he and Rich might have been an item.'

Bryan roared with laughter, to my relief. 'They were an item, all right. Dedicated to *sound*, not sex. He was our George Martin, not just our Brian Epstein. In other words, like the Beatles, our musical "ear" and our manager, only we had them in one man.'

'So they *could* still be together?'

'Not if Rich isn't singing any more. Gossage put sound before people. Rich wasn't like that.'

'Then what happened to William Gossage?' John asked. 'No one's heard of him since '77, when he claimed Rich was killed in Nepal five years earlier. Falsely claimed, we believe. So why did he disappear?'

'Don't ask me. He was an odd one. Tall fellow. Looked a bit like Tom Baker as Dr Who. Only with him the trademark wasn't only a scarf, but a carnation in the buttonhole. Fancied himself as a natty dresser, Homburg and all.'

'Did he go in a clap of thunder, or just slowly disappear from the pop scene?' I asked.

'The latter. We told him – or rather Mike did – to get lost when he came crawling back to us. That's Mike's way of putting it. I saw it as more of a "I've come to bail you out, chaps." Never heard a whisper from him since.'

'What about Colin Atley?' John asked.

Bryan glanced at Peggy, who answered for him.

'Colin couldn't hack it solo. All that success and girls throwing themselves at him, and then it vanished. His marriage broke up; he couldn't make the effort to go on playing, but couldn't turn his back on it, like Bry.'

'Mike blames Rich for Colin's death.'

'Mike would blame the Archangel Gabriel for not filling his beer mug,' Bryan said soberly. 'Things happen in life. You have to deal with them yourself.' Then he guffawed. 'Mind you, a good wife helps, eh, Peggy?'

'Did you know Rich?' I asked her.

'Oh, *yes*. What a performer.'

'Did you meet him?'

She looked surprised. 'Well, of course. Bryan and I married in '68, and Rich and Margaret were our best friends.'

'So you *liked* Rich?' I said incredulously to Bryan.

A shorter guffaw this time. 'Easy to tell you've been talking to Mike. Sure I liked Rich, for all his blasted dreams and selfishness. I liked him better than anyone I've met before or since, save for Peggy here. He was a gentle sort of guy; you couldn't help but like him. Charmer to women, and a good friend – when he was thinking of you, not himself. He didn't like anyone to be in pain, hurt, you know? He wanted to wave a wand, or sing a song, to soothe it away. I tell you, I still miss him.'

The time after Christmas is a busy one for Happy Ever After, since lots of questions get popped under the mistletoe, but the days before Christmas tend to be correspondingly slow. A good thing, for I was able to catch up with such Christmas preparations as I had to do. I was determined that I would play my part to make it a good one, to make up to Quinn for the gap between us. I was buying time, and Christmas had therefore assumed the proportions of a terrifying watershed in my marriage.

Somehow I hadn't managed to tell Quinn what had been going on, not because I didn't wish to do so, but because there was nothing concrete to reassure him. Interesting though it was to hear Mike and Bryan's opinions, I was no further forward in the big question of where Rich was now. I suppose I had expected that one of them would say, 'He's in Tahiti or California,' or 'I had a postcard complete with address the other day.'

John thought I was expecting too much, and that we had to build up the picture little by little. I didn't agree. We hadn't added any pieces at all to that jigsaw puzzle. Save for Aunt Cecilia's nugget that proved he hadn't died in 1972 in Nepal, we were precisely where we started. There was no help for it, I realised – if I was going to get through Christmas, I had to put my head in the lion's mouth.

The lion was not my mother, since she didn't have a clue where he was either, but Richard's father. The only outstanding business with my mother was why she hadn't told me about William Gossage's claim.

John insisted on coming with me to see Thomas Hart, although I had mutinied and said I'd do it on my own. If he were such a dragon as he sounded, a woman would do better at taming him than a man. John said he hadn't seemed too tough over the phone, and that he would come anyway. I only hoped Quinn didn't hear of this rash of companionable visits. With his growing dislike for John, he would be highly suspicious as to his motives.

Thomas Hart was reluctant to see us, even though we diplomatically stated the reason for the visit to be the Flowerdew museum. He was a retired civil servant living on his own in a terraced house in North London, where they'd moved to from Ireland when Richard was five. A carer let us in. Looking at Richard's father, it didn't seem that much caring was necessary – although in his mid-eighties, he seemed perfectly capable of caring for himself.

The dining table was set for a solitary dinner, but there was an extra visitor at the moment, introduced as his son Philip, Richard's brother. The father's face and manner were a mix of Old Testament severity and Greek God hero, and his ramrod-tall figure spoke of military bearing. The brother had none of these admirable qualities. The words 'sly' and 'mean' came to mind as I shook hands with this grey, middle-aged, sharp-featured weasel. Okay, I exaggerate, but events were to prove me on the right track.

'You wished to see us about my late son, Richard.' The Harts, father and son, sat down in leather armchairs and waited.

John launched into the story of the museum. They heard him out in silence, never taking their gaze from him, and the silence lasted for a time after John finished speaking.

'There are many photographs and memorabilia of my late son.'

'Not childhood ones, sir. Very few of those.'

'They have been destroyed,' Philip informed us smugly.

I wondered what Richard's Irish mother had thought of that, and as if on cue, Father Hart continued, 'My late wife kept them. I destroyed them after her death.'

'Why?' asked John boldly and, oddly enough, received a reply. Maybe it was the American accent, which I've noticed can work wonders.

'I saw no need of them. My son was dead.'

'Are you sure of that?' I asked.

A *very* heavy atmosphere now. 'And now I see the real reason you came here,' he replied. 'Another of these foolish fantasies.'

'Perhaps you are not aware,' the Weasel added, 'that my unfortunate brother was legally pronounced dead by the High Court many years ago.'

'Sure,' I said steadily. 'But Richard is, or was, married to my mother. I have the right to find out for myself if rumours that he's still alive are true.'

That did it. '*Right?*' the Old Testament hurled at me. 'No one has that right except for me, as your mother has married again. I am not myself interested in pursuing such illusions.'

I was in so far I could do no more harm now. 'It's a question of your grandchild.' Even as I said it, I wondered why the royalties had gone to Rich's father, with no mention of Marcus. Another mountainous query – and Mum's face – arose before me.

'He too is dead.'

Too late I realised that my mother might not have told even Richard's parents the truth about their grandchild, though that still didn't explain the royalties. This was territory too dangerous to enter, so I gabbled some story about wanting to find out what I could about Marcus. 'You have no photographs of him, you say. What do you remember of him?' I asked. I must have sounded half-witted, but it seemed to pass muster.

'He was an earnest child. Brown hair. He took after my son.'

'Richard's hair was blonde.'

'My son Philip here. A financial adviser.' Thomas Hart's face came to life as he looked at the Weasel, and I saw in a moment that Richard the musician had been of naught beside the glory of the son who had trod in Father's secure footsteps.

113

'You must be very proud of Richard,' I said demurely. 'Even if he is dead – and that is by no means certain – he has left a legend behind him.'

'To make one's way in the world one needs more than songs. I should make it clear that Richard left this house when he was eighteen, having refused all advice on his career. He never returned.'

'But his mother—'

'Took my view.'

'Yet you laid claim to his royalties in the High Court.' I did my best to remove the sting from this but did not succeed, for the Weasel sprang out with all claws bared.

'And why not? My brother was dead. The child was dead. Your mother remarried. I hardly think you are qualified to judge the situation. I am.'

John swept up the shattered remains of the encounter as I reeled from this new information, and we retreated reasonably gracefully.

'The vicious old patriarch,' I said, relieving pent-up fury after we left.

'He's not that bad.'

'The weasel brother is. Anyway, Father threw Richard out when he was only eighteen.'

'As Richard no doubt intended. It was all the rage then to be chucked out of home. A status symbol. Anyway, there are two sides to any argument. I quite liked the old codger, though I agree with you about the brother.'

'That's because you're American,' I said gloomily. 'Father Hart is your idea of the typical Englishman.'

He laughed aloud. 'While you were striding down the steps, he whispered to me that he still has Richard's first guitar somewhere. He'll hunt it out for the museum. Sure sounded good to me.'

'Wonderful,' I said hollowly. 'But it doesn't tell us where Richard is.'

'Or was,' John gently reminded me.

*   *   *

Quinn and I had amicably settled our Christmas. Romantic ideas of Christmas stockings, trees, dinner and Midnight Mass *à deux* were tacitly laid aside in favour of numbers. We would spend Christmas Day with my family and Boxing Day with Quinn's. We would even stay overnight in Sussex, so that we had no need to make polite conversation at home or cater for meals we no longer lovingly shared. My fault – but what help was it to acknowledge that?

When I say family, I mean extended family. Someone decided – probably Columba – that it would be nice to have a Flowerdew Christmas, in view of the museum to be opened in the spring. Cecilia and Imogen, Violet, Flossie, Columba herself, myself and Quinn, Mum and Dad, and an extension was granted to Stephen.

Not to John, however. In my innocence I assumed this was to avoid hurting Stephen's feelings. I should have known better. Fortunately John mentioned vaguely that he had other plans.

'How nice,' Columba beamed as she swept through the front door of Kingsgate House with Stephen in tow. 'A real family Christmas. Now we can all discuss this biography peacefully.'

'Over my dead body,' Dad growled, and even Columba blenched. Then she made a comeback.

'Perhaps later on,' she conceded graciously.

The entire Christmas luncheon, the giving of presents and downing of good food and wine, passed like a dream, and I at least was lulled into the happy thought that the Flowerdews weren't so unbearable after all. Even the feud seemed to have declared a truce for the day. Cecilia was chatting animatedly to Flossie, Grandma Violet was deep in conversation with Mum, and I even half-expected Uncle Ted to wander in to complete this family circle. Quinn seemed to be enjoying himself, so far as I could gather, talking to Stephen and

115

Columba, and I blissfully relaxed into the usual coma of Christmas afternoon.

Mistake. At six o'clock, when drinks again made their appearance for those lucky enough not to have to drive home, Columba was still as bright as a button. She welcomed Violet and Cecilia down from their naps (in separate rooms) with, 'Good, here you are. Now this lovely museum Stephen has given us – do let's have a launch for it,' and plunged headfirst into discussing the invitation list with every star of stage and screen on it. If they all came, we'd have to have the entire lawn covered in marquees.

'If we're ready by late May,' Stephen said dubiously. 'We're still short of exhibits.'

Discussion resumed about who would donate what, turning into a sort of auction in the bidding for prime approval from Stephen. Mum even volunteered the garments she'd worn in the early sixties as Peaseblossom in *A Midsummer Night's Dream*. I thought Columba was going to refuse them, but fortunately diplomacy won. Having accepted the gift gracefully, in her mind at least, smoothed the path into what Columba really wanted of my mother.

'Does that mean you're becoming a Flowerdew fan at last, Margaret? Thank heavens, that means we can get the biography under way.'

What was rapidly under way was another full-scale pitched battle, with enough of us present to form two formidable teams: those for the biography and those against. Stephen's vote was reluctantly counted, since he was donating the museum. Quinn decided to be umpire, with a side wink at my father.

'Suppose you all make your pitch, and I'll count votes as we go along. Columba, you begin, as this is your project anyway.'

'Certainly. We as Flowerdews have a heritage to protect and nurture. We owe something precious to the public. They need the opportunity to revere it, and the historians in the future need to have a research resource.'

'That's enough of Columba's pitch,' Dad said testily, and she shut up, smiling sweetly.

Everyone had his or her say, down to Flossie's simple: 'I don't think it's a good idea.'

'Oh, Mother!' Imogen said impatiently. 'Whyever not?'

'If my poor Ted was here' – a warning note in case any of us in the know had forgotten – 'he'd have voted the same way.'

'He's no longer with us, Mother,' Imogen said sharply. 'So why should he object to his story being told, along with the other Flowerdews?'

There was an awkward silence, as we all thought of just why he might resurrect himself from his so-called death to object.

'William wanted all the credit to go to his father and mother,' screeched Grandmother Violet (she is deaf and will never turn her hearing aid on). 'He never saw his own role as worthy of record.'

'It wasn't,' muttered Cecilia in a low voice calculated to miss Violet's ears.

This time it didn't, and by the time that had been sorted out more or less amicably, Quinn had lost count of who had voted for what. 'For or against, Stephen?' he asked wearily.

'I don't have a vote, not being a family member.' Look of longing at Columba. 'But I can't see any reason why you shouldn't go ahead, if you trust John.'

A chorus of 'but we don't' followed from Violet and Flossie.

'He's very nice,' Mum announced surprisingly. 'I trust him. I just don't agree with the biography, that's all. It would be different if it were one of the family writing it, but an outside historian is bound to be taken as the last word, and that may not be ours.'

'I could write it,' Imogen offered brightly, but was ignored by everyone, to my relief.

'Why don't you make it a biography of just Claud and his wife?' said Quinn despairingly.

'Dull,' came Columba's prompt reaction.

'It's been done,' came from Mum.

'Ask your chum John what he suggests,' was Quinn's next contribution for Columba.

'I am opposed to that,' came Grandma's shrill voice. '*Totally* opposed.'

'How many votes for and against?' Quinn asked mildly. 'Show of hands please, I've lost count.'

Wouldn't you know, it came out equally balanced.

'I don't know what you're all so worried about,' Columba said testily. 'Most people expect to *pay* for publicity. What have the Flowerdews got to hide, after all?'

Nothing save ourselves, I thought.

All in all, I was glad to get to Quinn's parents the following day. They too had family there, uncle, aunts, cousins.

'You don't know how lucky you are to be in a normal family,' I said feelingly to Quinn.

He said nothing. How could he? His family *wasn't* normal. He was adopted. It was one more sign that we were beginning to lead our lives at a polite distance.

And I had only one last hope of any clue at all as to where Richard was. John had given me the good news that he had traced the Fan Club lady. It had been surprisingly easy. He'd written to Peggy, since she had been a Mighty Rich fan. The Fan Club lady was no longer in Brentwood, but was alive and well and living in Maidstone.

Eight

Angela Parsons lived in a side street in a Maidstone suburb, a world and a half away from flower children and pop music.

Or perhaps not so far. John had elected not to accompany me on this mission, and when I rang the doorbell the door opened immediately and a dark-clad, doe-eyed girl of nineteen or so with pointy red hair rushed out with a 'Tara' for someone lurking in the background. Unconventionality was alive and well in Maidstone.

Her mother, a tired blonde in her mid-fifties, hurried to greet me, showing few signs of the raver she had presumably been in the 1960s. Perhaps it was my imagination, but she wore a defeated look as though she had given up expecting to change the world and had settled for marching with the majority. Or maybe it was just a bad day for her.

She ushered me in, chattering disjointedly about my excusing the clutter, and how was my journey, and wasn't it chilly today, and showed me into a carpeted uncluttered sitting room. She relaxed then, disappeared to make coffee, and when she returned with it, told me how honoured she was to have the Mighty Rich's wife's daughter here.

Was she joking? I peered at her suspiciously, but realised she was quite serious.

'Thank you,' I replied. 'Do you still run the fan club?' She had already told me on the telephone that she did not, but it did no harm to enquire again as an opener.

Angela grimaced. 'No. Time marches on. I work full-time

119

– and family, you know.' She glanced round at the almost non-existent signs of family, in this room at least. 'Anyway, there was hardly any point. I ran it for six years, but then interest fell off. Rich wasn't an Elvis. I announced I was giving it up in our newssheet – no web sites in those days – and no one offered to take it over. There was nothing new to fuel interest after Rich disappeared, save a few sightings . . .'

'Sightings?' I picked up eagerly. 'People actually *saw* him?'

'Well, yes and no. It's quite usual,' she explained dismissively. 'I use sightings in the Elvis sense – seen on remote desert islands, and so on. With us there were quite a few because Rich's disappearance was far less conclusive than Elvis's death.'

'So where were these sightings?' A clue, a clue at last, I thought.

'I kept a record of them for a few years until I gave up the fan club. I don't think there were any sightings after '75 or so. Only the occasional nutty one that couldn't possibly be true. There was one of him on Papua, garlanded with flowers, and dusky maidens all around. That's a standard illusion. And another in an Italian opera house. I can show you the list.'

She took me into another room which explained all. Cheerful clutter lay everywhere. 'My husband lets me have a corner of his study.' Big deal, I thought, warming to Angela and her sweetly old-fashioned idea that the parlour should be kept uncluttered for guests. A full-size poster displayed the face of my mother's first husband, whose twisted, rather sad smile seemed to be defying me to find out the truth about him.

Angela rummaged in a cupboard and produced an old record book – I almost snatched it out of her hands in my eagerness. I ran my eye down the list, which was composed of such helpful entries as:

1970, in a bar in Calais.

June 1972. Seen in Nepal.
June 1972 [the day after the Nepal entry] on top of a
double-decker bus in Piccadilly.

'Are any of them reliable, do you think?' I asked dubiously.

'Most are hallucinations. People seeing what they want
to see, putting ghostly images on faces that look somewhat
similar.'

'But suppose one, two – more? – *are* reliable? How can
one tell?'

'You can't,' she informed me brightly. 'If I know the
source, I pay more attention to it.'

There were at least a hundred or so in the first couple
of years, I judged, but it was the later years I was interested in.

'Everyone will have a sighting if they know other fans
have had them,' Angela added.

Everywhere from Hong Kong to Iceland seemed to figure
in the list. What did it tell me? Precious little, save that
Australia figured twice towards the end. This was interesting,
but what could I do about that? It wasn't much of an address
to go by, especially as it was getting on for thirty years
previously.

'I still dream about Rich,' Angela confessed.

'Why?' I asked curiously. 'Did you ever meet him? What
does he do for you now?'

'Oh yes, I met him quite frequently. But not as a person,
if you know what I mean.' She laughed nervously. 'He was
a god, and you don't ask yourself why you like idols. He was
always gentle. I think that's what impressed me, especially
since gentleness in the pop world was going out of fashion
fast then.'

I looked at the poster, of a lost man from a lost age, and
could see that it still had life, and meaning. And not only
through the memories of his fans. So where *was* he?

121

I walked back to my car with a sense of desolation. I would never find Richard. He was lost in an impenetrable past.

I had to face the fact that every door was closed, save the final test. For that I needed Quinn's co-operation. I had deliberately kept away from urging him to take a DNA test, to compare with one ideally from my mother, but more realistically from me. If ever I was to raise the suggestion, I needed more evidence than I had so far. Essentially I had achieved nothing. We were still back at Columba's 'Darling, the spitting image.'

Nevertheless, this was the only door open, even if it was blocked in my mind by the belligerent figure of Quinn and my reluctance to ask my mother. Then it occurred to me that there was another door open to check the story from Quinn's end, or rather his beginning – the French orphanage. If that led nowhere, I would nerve myself to tackle Quinn on the DNA issue. Checking the French connection would at least postpone that evil day.

Bang on cue my fairy godmother – or so she'd like to think of herself – reappeared on the scene. 'Darling,' Columba's voice purred down the telephone, 'I thought you might like a little break in Paris.'

Suspicions that this was no mere coincidence were put to one side.

'I'd love it,' I replied with mixed feelings. Columba has a flat on the Île de la Cité and I'd been there several times, though not since my marriage. 'What will I say to Quinn?'

'He'll never notice, Ellie,' she replied untactfully.

I doubted that, but since it fitted in so well with my decision to check out the orphanage, I agreed. It was a busy time at work, though, since couples setting their sights on summer nuptials were being galvanised by the prospect of spring approaching. First Jane had to be placated, which was easier than I had expected.

'No problem. I can cope,' she said.

I was surprised. 'But aren't you busy with the museum too?'

She shrugged. 'I'll manage. Off you go.'

I wondered whether she knew or guessed the real reason for my journey. She never mentioned it or showed any curiosity, and I was too thankful for her acquiescence to pursue it further.

Facing Quinn was much more difficult, and I didn't blame him. We'd talked blissfully on our honeymoon of how we would visit Paris in the winter. We would see it together through lovers' eyes, which would make of Paris a different world than the grab-a-chap bottle excursions.

I tackled him after dinner one evening as he lay on the sofa stroking Irving. 'We could go together afterwards . . .' I trailed off weakly, after breaking the news.

The stroking stopped. 'We could,' he agreed pithily, 'or I could come with you.'

Did the dismay show on my face? 'But—'

'But you want a free hand to poke your nose into my parentage,' he interrupted neutrally.

'Not if you'd co-operate,' I said desperately.

'I won't. You're on your own. I told you that. Come back with some hard evidence and we'll talk about it.'

'Then,' I said steadily, 'I'll need the address of your parents' friend who used to work in the orphanage.'

'Okay.' He shrugged dismissively.

That night the distance between us in bed was a wide glacier and neither of us even thought of crossing it.

He gave me the address the next day though, with no comment. All the same, it was relief to leap aboard Eurostar at Ashford and find Columba installed in her first-class seat, ready to sweep me into her embrace.

'Oh, what fun,' she announced happily to the entire carriage. 'Now darling, I have some shopping and a few people to see, but by night we'll see Paris.' She threw her arms open wide as though inviting everyone in earshot. 'John's very envious. He sent you his best wishes.'

'Didn't he want to come with you?'

She smiled mysteriously. 'He and I will have a separate weekend – perhaps.'

'Is—' I began impulsively and then broke off, but she guessed my thoughts.

'My darling, don't let's be inquisitive. Dear Stephen isn't here all the time.'

Was she teasing me? I could never tell with Columba, so I gave up thinking about it. It was their own affair, in all senses.

'We'll dine splendidly,' she continued.

With Columba, this was also never quite clear. One night it might be Lasserre or Maxim's, the next a tiny family couscous restaurant in a back street. One of the nice things about Columba is that they were both to her equally splendid. I only hoped she was paying if it were one of the former.

As the familiar sight of Montmartre's Sacré Coeur gleamed white on the skyline outside the Gare du Nord, a lump came into my throat. I felt I was betraying Quinn by coming here without him, even though I told myself my visit was to save our marriage. I got a grip on myself. I was here, so I was going to make the most of it.

Columba's flat was modest by her standards, with only one bedroom, so I had the sofa bed, which was amazingly comfortable. Perhaps being away from my problems – if only for a day or two – helped me sleep better than I had for weeks. Or perhaps it was the *moules marinières* at the local brasserie that achieved the miracle – or the bottle of Beaujolais that Columba insisted went well with it, despite the white face of the sommelier.

Columba disappeared on her errands the following morning after a breakfast of croissants and coffee in the café below her flat, and left me with Paris at my feet. I had no choice, however. I was expected in Vincennes, after several phone calls, to establish contact with Marie Lamartine. My reprieve was over. I had only been out on bail and now it was time for the gates of reality to clang behind me once more.

Marie was no longer living in Vincennes itself. She had migrated to the far side of the Bois de Vincennes nearer to the city. I walked down the dull side street of rue Claude Decaen, where tall apartment blocks shrouded the streets on both sides, keeping the sun shut out. Not that there was a lot around in mid-January. I found my way up to the third floor of the building in the typical minuscule lift installed belatedly in such old blocks.

Mme Lamartine was now white-haired and in her sixties, and there were few signs of her Irish origins, either in her appearance or in this flat. She told me, lilting in what was by now somewhat incorrect English, that her husband had died five years earlier. I expressed my sympathy and we smiled at one another, rapport established.

I conveyed the good wishes of Quinn's parents to her, and we talked of them for a while. It was left for me to get to the point, although I had made it clear on the telephone why I was coming.

'I'm sorry to take you back over old ground,' I began, 'but this is what Quinn's mother told me.' I related the story. 'That's how you remember it?'

'Yes.'

'Nothing more?' Surely there must be *something*. My voice broke, and somehow I found myself telling her the whole story and being comforted with Irish biscuits and *pain au chocolat*.

'This is important to you, Ellie?'

'My marriage means everything to me.'

'So I must tell you something I never told Bridget. It is true your Quinn was found in the chicken-house. But the cook who had befriended Quinn, and whose fiancé was one of the gardeners, added something else to the tale. Her fiancé had been returning to his home in the grounds late on the

125

evening Quinn was left, and in the roadway he bumped into a young man with long hair, walking quickly in the opposite direction. There was no proof that it was he who left the child, but the gardener had the impression from the fact that he had not spotted him earlier that he must have come through the orphanage gates. Whoever he was, no one like that came forward to claim the child. I thought it odd that the gardener should have remembered such a chance encounter, but the cook explained it was because he looked just like one of those pop stars.'

I licked nervous lips, and a crumb of the biscuit provided an anchor to take my mind from instant fear to impartiality. 'Just a general reference to his hair and outrageous clothes, probably,' I commented.

'No, my dear, he was quite specific. I'm so sorry. It is not good news for you. He thought he looked like the pop star from Britain who was often on French TV, the Mighty Rich. The gardener was a fan.'

She saw my stricken face. 'There was no *proof*, you understand, that he had left the child, or that it was indeed the Mighty Rich.'

It was proof enough for me. I walked the streets of a still wintry cold Paris, until at last I judged Columba would be home. I could not face four walls around me without company, and when I found her there, I nearly cried in gratitude.

'Darling,' she crooned when she saw my face, 'tell me, do.'

So I did. 'It's not proof,' I said brightly. 'It's just another sighting like the fan club lady told me. He was a fan, and they impose their idol's image on strangers who merely resemble their god.'

I looked hopefully at Columba for her corroboration, but I didn't get it.

'Oh, darling. I saw Jean-Paul Chesnais today.'

I recognised the name as someone who had once been big in French pop music.

'Didn't I tell you I was planning to meet him? I hoped I'd find out something,' Columba continued.

My heart jumped painfully. 'What?' I croaked.

'I knew he was interested in Rich because I remember talking to him years ago – he was so delighted when he discovered Rich was my brother-in-law.' She glanced at me, but if she was looking for approval from her doom-laden audience for this initiative, she was disappointed.

'Tell me, Columba.'

'Jean-Paul remembers doing a show with the Mighty Rich in Paris around that time, at either the Olympia or Bobino music halls. He couldn't remember which.'

That last nail wasn't going in, not if I could help it. I fought back. 'Around that time? You know what false memory is like, Columba. You specified the time to Jean-Paul and *then* he confirmed it. It's not evidence.' I realised I was shouting.

'Darling, we immediately checked with the music hall archives, and Rich and he are listed as appearing together at the Bobino in October '69.'

I made a last effort. 'But we don't know exactly when Quinn was abandoned. Only that it was autumn and chilly.'

'And Rich appeared there also in December.'

I wept all that night for my lost love and for my lost marriage. I went home alone the next day, leaving Columba clucking sympathy but planning her dinner for that evening.

What the hell was I going to do now? There was no point going on. No point in upsetting Mum with demands to know why she hadn't told me about the High Court case. No point in anything. Every muscle and nerve in me ached for Quinn, but the thought of being in his arms was torture now that I knew it was no longer possible.

When I got home – if that's what I could call this now loveless place – I could wait no longer. I broke every unwritten rule and went to find Quinn in his studio. The sight and smells of paints, papers and pads and easels, and cartoons pinned to walls or lying around in heaps greeted me, and I could hardly bear the thought that I was about to disqualify him for good from ever seeing it again.

He looked up and a shutter came over his face when he saw my expression.

'Good trip?' he asked apparently casually as he swept a pile of papers from his guest chair (only he never had any guests normally).

I couldn't sit in it, though. I just stood where I was. 'No.'

'You'd better tell me about it.' I saw him swallow.

'Columba has proved that Rich was in Paris that autumn, from October to December '69.'

'I wouldn't trust Columba's so-called proof,' he whipped back.

'You think she'd lie?' I fired up immediately.

'She wouldn't see it as lying. She'd see it as helping.'

'Over this? You're crazy.'

'Maybe.'

My voice was trembling. 'There's more, Quinn.' I told him the story of the gardener.

That shook him. I could see he was turning it over and over in his mind, looking for a loophole. When he spoke, his voice was surprisingly gentle. 'Hearsay, Ellie. Memories play tricks even at a day's distance, let alone thirty years.'

'Theatre records don't. Rich was there, Quinn. So there's no help for it.'

'Help for what?'

'We'll both have to have a DNA test to see if we have genes in common.'

He turned red, then got up very deliberately from his chair. 'No, Ellie,' he shot back at me.

I couldn't believe it, even though I'd half-expected it. 'Why bloody not?' I stormed.

'Because despite this so-called proof, you're *wrong*. We're not related. Young men seen in the dark near the scene of a crime is mere poppycock. Even if Richard was in Paris, I am *not* your brother. Just think about it for a minute. Why the hell would Richard put his son into an orphanage? Even if I were in his way, and he got fed up with me, only a monster would put a kid that age into an orphanage instead of taking it home to its mother. And there was no row between Richard and Margaret, unless your mother is lying, which having met her seems unlikely. You're just not thinking straight. You've no *faith*.'

'In what? In you? You're refusing to do the one thing that would prove it one way or the other.'

'And to have the test would remove all question of trust in our marriage. This story is nonsense, can't you see that?'

'No. What kind of a reply is that, Quinn? You're just ignoring what's plain as a pikestaff – that we're probably half-brother and sister.'

'If we have this test, what will it prove? Just think. If it's positive, we *still* won't know for sure, since we could be of the same family, but far distant branches. And have you thought what would happen if it's negative? You, my dear Ellie, won't believe it. You'll say in your heart of hearts that even DNA can be wrong. That the circumstantial evidence is enough for you. It would always lie between us even if you tried to believe it, like a naked sword in a marriage bed. We couldn't cross it. We'd be wedded to doubt, not to each other.'

'Then what's to be done?' I asked the fatal question.

'You have to trust. Can I make you see that I *know* I'm not your brother?'

'No,' I said hopelessly, 'because you can't or won't prove it with facts.'

'And you,' he threw at me, 'are intent on believing the worst *without* facts.'

It was an impasse. I knew I was right; I just could not imagine how Quinn could take the position he did. It was a nightmare to find oneself married to someone one didn't know, someone who put reason to one side and ignored the obvious.

'You're living in a fairy-tale world, Quinn.'

'No. *You* are.'

I couldn't understand him. Wherever that wavelength was that had once existed between us, we'd gone right off station. The airways were jammed.

'I can't go on,' I threw at him. 'I'll have to move out.' I meant it, but somehow I thought he'd come round to my viewpoint and plead with me. His face was ashen, but he had only to speak. When he did, I could see it was useless.

'Think about it, Ellie, please.'

'I have, and I'm going.' Say something, I silently pleaded. 'Stop me. Say you'll have the test.'

He didn't. 'You're on the wrong track, you know.'

I lost my cool. 'Are you just stupid, Quinn? Look at the facts. Just *look* at them. Don't say I have to trust you. Whatever use is that in the face of the evidence?'

'None, apparently. Anyway, I didn't mean that track.'

'What wrong track then?' I almost sneered. 'My thinking you were a rational being maybe? Can't you see—'

He buried his face in his hands, and I stopped abruptly. Tentatively I stepped up to him and put my arms round him. 'I love you, Quinn, but I have to go. You must see that.' I heard the words coming out. I meant them, but it didn't seem to be me voicing them. Stop, stop, said my heart, but it was engulfed by voices.

'Where will you go? What about your work? Are you going to take Irving?'

Now he was being practical. Why couldn't he be practical over the main issue? But I was past pleading now, and these chillingly matter-of-fact questions put it out of the question anyway.

'Maybe to stay with Jane. She'll take Irving.'

'You won't want me here. I'll leave this place and find somewhere else. Let's hope it's only for a time.'

The question mark in his voice was apparent, but I simply dared not let myself hope too much.

'Yes.'

As I walked – or rather stumbled – away, I still half-expected to hear the crash of the door as he rushed after me, begging me to stay. If he did so, I knew I'd cave in, and so it should have been with relief that I reached the empty house without a murmur from Quinn.

But it wasn't. I felt my life had come to an end.

PART TWO
QUINN

Nine

I was, to put it bluntly, gobsmacked. I watched Ellie walking out of my life – *our* life – but I couldn't move. I felt as if some wicked witch of fate had cast a spell over me. My legs wouldn't move, wouldn't help me run after her. I couldn't even shout after her to stop.

There was nothing to say, anyway.

She once told me she was frightened. So why couldn't she see *I* was scared? There she was, bleating on about DNA tests, but to me that was like inviting the victim to test the blade before the guillotine fell. I suppose I didn't recognise it as terror myself at the time. I was too busy coping with the fact that Ellie was determined to believe the worst, which for me was translating itself into the conclusion that she didn't love me enough to fight for me.

This was fairly stupid, looking back, but then not many men think straight when their wife of a few months marches out without a backward glance. They sing – or used to – pop songs about that, but it was no singing matter to me. It was real, and to freeze it like an aching tooth was the only way I could deal with the physical pain as well as emotional. Make no mistake, the fact that she was walking out on me didn't blind me to my own feelings. I loved Ellie, I loved every inch of her from her determined little backside to her steadfast loving, bubbling face and the joy for life that shone through it.

I'd had relationships before Ellie – a couple of long ones in fact – but never had I felt so 'at home' with the object of my desire, love, lust, whatever. Ellie curled up into the arch of my body in life, as she did in bed. We fitted, we belonged. We both knew that, didn't we?

So why the hell was she quitting? Why didn't or couldn't she understand my point of view? All this evidence of hers was entirely circumstantial, but she took it as proof. Then she came at me with this demand for a DNA test, and I just couldn't take it. I suppose I could see myself losing her for ever. But she just didn't think it through. To her it was already black and white.

I sat in my studio for two hours, numb with shock. I knew she must be packing, then I heard her car start up and drive through the gates, and after that came the silence. Emptiness. Night in the country can be a velvet glove, enclosing you in its gentleness, or it can be the menacing monster of the unknown. And the latter was at large in my studio as darkness fell. I couldn't even stir to put the light on, for the monster was in my mind as well.

'What would you do, Sadie O'Grady?' I asked my stalwart creation savagely. 'What's the answer to this conundrum?'

As usual, I had to answer for her. 'Sock it in the jaw.'

All very well for her, staring up smugly from my easel. She was right, however. Staying here would achieve nothing, and somehow this thing had to be resolved if I were to get Ellie back. It seemed to me I had three options. Option One, DNA test. Option Two, support Ellie and her blasted John in their hunt for Richard Hart. Option Three, hunt him down myself.

When I had said to Ellie that I thought she was on the wrong track, she misunderstood me. I had meant her search for the Mighty Rich was on completely the wrong track. So Option Two meant I would first have to persuade Ellie and John into my way of thinking. Not on, and as the idea of a DNA test still sent me screaming in the opposite direction, I was left with only one choice: Option Three.

Slumped in my studio that evening I couldn't imagine

where I would begin. Ellie calls me a Johnny Head-in-the-Air sometimes, which surprises me, for I know that my feet are usually firmly on the ground. Not tonight. The monster of night and fear crept insidiously through the windows of my mind. Was the fact that Ellie and I took such a different stance on this affair simply disguising the fact that we had married too quickly, and were incompatible – a fact that she was subconsciously acknowledging by leaving?

No! I pushed this away immediately. If I even thought about it any longer, I might help make it true, and it *wasn't*. At least for me, the monster whispered – you can't speak for Ellie. My God, I believed in us, and I would fight for us.

The monster slid away, but I knew he would only be waiting for an opportunity to return. I would not let him. I would start now on Option Three. And for that, there was something I could do tonight.

My resolution almost faded when I entered the Lodge, which felt all the emptier for the signs of Ellie left around. The breakfast dishes washed, but not yet put away. Two of everything. I wanted to smash the lot. I wanted to tear our appointment calendar off the wall when I saw her writing on it. I even missed her blessed cat, Irving. It would be worse when I got to our bedroom, and I decided I'd sleep in the spare room.

I pulled myself together, heated up a frozen lasagne and tried to think more rationally. There was no point in running away. I had to think positive all the time, and that meant sleeping in our joint bedroom – *after* I'd taken the first step in my hunt.

I went to the dining room where the pile of stuff John had given to Ellie early on in her search lay largely untouched. There were press cuttings, videos, records – a treasure trove. I was convinced that Ellie was on the wrong track in that she was concentrating on racing ahead to find out where Richard was *now*. In my opinion, we had to find out where he was coming *from*. The good old joke about the Irishmen giving directions applied to this too. 'If I were you, surr, I wouldn't start from here.' The Irish in me was right – I had to start from way back in Richard's life.

Was there any Irish in me, apart from upbringing? I acknowledged, not for the first time, that I had no idea. Nevertheless, I would only find out where Richard was now by understanding the man, on which Ellie, though mildly interested, had not spent much time. When she reluctantly told me of her endeavours, she had let tantalising bits of information drop but never seemed to see any significance in them. Perhaps there was none; but it was an area of study that would require some attention.

I went easy on myself and watched the videos first. In the sixties there wasn't much in the way of videos as we know them now, and so this pile was composed of compilations made up from early music clips or cine-recordings. The first two were of the Mighty Rich and the Coinmakers' gigs and a pop festival. Apart from giving the atmosphere of the times, they weren't a lot of help, though just to hear the music again helped me feel I was achieving something. The last one was more interesting. It was obviously put together by an amateur fan who had cine-recorded rehearsals and recordings, with a lot of 'behind the scenes' material. Ellie had missed something here. No doubt she hadn't even asked Angela What's-her-name whether she had any such material, being too busy with 'sightings'.

Complacently convinced I was at last doing something to help myself, I sat down to watch it.

Apart from the long hair, the Coinmakers and the Mighty Rich were reminiscent of the early Beatles, if not the Beatles of the late sixties. There was an innocence, an enjoyment of what they were doing, a bubble of enthusiasm for the new horizons of sounds that has been punctured, it seems to me, from the world-weary pop scene of today.

Whoever took the cine-recordings had done a good job in conveying the whole band scene, not just what the fans saw in performance. To see *Demolition Squad* in the making, to hear the banter and arguments between them over this chord or that, brought the songs alive. *Last Night, Next Night, Love Hits the Charts* – he'd recorded them all. It was fascinating – even if I'd had no ulterior motive in watching this video – to see how the well-known detailed effects were furiously debated and often had a near miss as to whether they were included.

Rich stood out from the rest of the band, and not only because the film-maker was clearly a Rich fan. He had an air about him that made him almost a solo figure even in concert with his fellow bandsmen. Colin Atley on the drums, Bryan Whatley on the bass guitar, and Michael Patterson, back-up vocalist and guitarist, had a unity about them in which Rich did not give the impression of taking part. He was an Ariel to their more earthbound spirits.

'Hey,' Rich called to the film-maker, who promptly closed in on his face. There he was, alive but lost in his own world. I recognised that look. Many of my artistic friends bore it while they were working, and probably I did myself.

'Listen to this,' Rich continued, and strummed a motif before his light but husky voice picked it up.

Finally the band recorded the entire song. I listened and watched *Last Night, Next Night* over and over again, for this had been their last hit before Richard went solo. It represented all the group's hopes and aspirations, which were never to be fulfilled. I theorised on what made Rich go solo after this hit. It could have been that the melody and the words were becoming too important to him to want to have to take the considerations of three other instruments into account.

And then I saw him – William Gossage. The film man had not deliberately filmed him, but the camera caught him as he slouched through the door. He threw his coat and scarf on a chair, and the band stopped rehearsal and gathered round. Except Rich. He went on singing as though whichever land he was inhabiting in his mind took time to leave, and when at last he laid the guitar down and came to join them, he still had that 'away' look on his face.

The film-maker ended that sequence there, so I never had a chance to hear William Gossage speak. I did see him, however. Arrogant-looking, I decided, conscious of his superiority – or maybe it was merely confidence. Whichever it was, I didn't like the look of him, and yet he was a missing corner piece of the jigsaw, or maybe even the whole picture. He, above all others, knew what made Rich the artist tick, and thus was the most likely to know where he was. He alone could tell us about that 'death' in Nepal – and about his suddenly increased proportion of royalties. Why Ellie had not tried harder to find him, beat me. Unless – the monster made a sudden determined appearance here – in her heart of hearts she was seeking an excuse to get out of our marriage.

By the time I felt I could face the ordeal of going to bed, I had got the general feel of Rich's musical life, at least for that particular year. Strengthened by a modest whisky, I went upstairs in confident mood. I faced that bed and addressed my absent wife: 'You'll be back, so you just make room for me. Okay?'

By the cold light of morning I also had to face the fact that I had to move out of the Lodge. It wouldn't be fair on either of us for me to remain so close to where Ellie was working. The flat I had lived in before our marriage was now rented out. I could go back to my parents, but that wasn't a choice for a man of thirty-four. I could rent somewhere in London. I decided I'd get my current commissions out of the way first, and then give thought to what was best.

I had just finished my work session when the phone rang. Normally I wouldn't have a phone in the studio to answer, but a craven hope that Ellie might ring made me take the cordless phone of our private line with me. It wasn't Ellie. It was her mother.

'Quinn? It's Margaret Peters.'

'Ellie's told you, I take it?'

'Columba's told us.'

Naturally, I thought viciously. Ellie was too proud to ring her mother herself, so good old Aunt Columba was doing the dirty work. But it answered one question for me. Ellie was staying with Columba – or at least had been. I wondered why she wasn't staying with Jane, as she had planned. Even Ellie wouldn't choose to broadcast our news to the world by deliberately phoning Columba.

'Did she tell you the reason Ellie left?' I asked cautiously.

'Yes. I was furious.' A pause. 'This Richard obsession of Ellie's. Why in heaven's name didn't you tell us this was still going on?'

'It wasn't my place to,' I retorted.

'Why didn't she then?' Margaret still sounded furious.

'Because she didn't want to worry or upset you.' My Ellie, my lovely Ellie, wasn't that just like her? Just like a Flowerdew too, I realised. Try so hard not to upset loved ones and end up with a real pig's dinner.

'Oh hell,' Margaret muttered. Then, 'Look, Quinn, can we meet? We've got to put this right.'

'You mean you want Ellie and me to stay together?' It was a crass statement on my part, but I was childishly pleased.

'Of course I do. We both do. We thought Ellie was safe for life married to you, and now look what's happened, thanks to Columba.'

'Why don't you . . . no, I'll come over.' I changed my mind. I wanted to be in Flowerdew territory, the house where Richard had once lived. Even though I realised all trace of him might have gone – except for Margaret herself – it was time to take the kid gloves off and find out from the one person who knew Rich as a person just what he was like and what might have driven him from his home. And this time Margaret must talk.

* * *

141

We agreed a time on the morrow, which gave me an opportunity to go up to Charham Place to speak to Stephen about
the Lodge. I carefully didn't go into the house itself in case
Ellie was at work, although the craving to see if she was was
almost irresistible.

I managed it, chiefly because I saw Jane walking purpose-
fully towards the stables – sorry, the museum. The plans and
planning permission had been whisked through remarkably
promptly – another tourist attraction for the area – and
building work on the extension was progressing amazingly
fast for winter conditions.

I hailed her and she spun round, flushing when she saw
who it was.

'Stephen about?' I asked pleasantly.

'He'll be down shortly. I wanted a word with John.'

'Is Ellie in today?'

'She rang in sick.'

'Very diplomatic. I take it she is not staying with you,
then?' I asked curiously. 'I thought she'd make straight for
Tunbridge Wells.'

'We thought it would be better,' she muttered. 'I'm
looking after Irving though.'

'So she did visit you first.'

'We agreed it wasn't a good idea to work and live
together,' she said awkwardly, 'even if it's only for a short
while.'

'Is that what Ellie said?' I asked eagerly.

'Yes. She talked about getting her own place again.'

My hopes deflated once more, and I decided on a bold
approach. 'Did she tell you why she left?'

'Yes. Look, why don't you talk to John? He's more
involved than I am.' Jane broke away with evident relief.
'He's in the museum now. I'll come back in half an hour
so that you can talk in peace.' She scuttled for safety back
to the house.

Talk to John? I never suspected Ellie of physical attraction to him, but nevertheless I was bloody jealous of their close association. Why couldn't she talk to me as she did to him? I hesitated, then remembered that I had a mission and must use all means at my disposal. I didn't like John Curwen, partly because Ellie seemed to think the sun rose with a gleam from his heavy spectacles, and partly because there was no point of contact between us. I tend to be outspoken, he's oblique. I don't like the feeling he's secretly laughing at me, either. Don't think I'm paranoid. It's his air of detachment, whereas I believe in involvement. I would take a long spoon to sup with this devil.

I pushed open the door and walked in. I hadn't been here for some time and I wasn't prepared for what I saw. I had to admit to an unwilling admiration for John's powers of organisation compared with my own. The open-plan rooms were already painted, and the reception area and loos looked well on the way to working order. It wasn't a museum yet, for there were no exhibits, but there was a sense of purpose and direction. Boxes, open and unopened, were piled everywhere. I wondered how John, with all his obvious drive, could have let Ellie go so far off track in her search for Richard, and it didn't endear me to him.

John looked up from the box he was working on, and came over to me.

'Columba told me the news. I'm sorry, Quinn. Guess it was bound to happen, the way Ellie was beavering away at the past.'

I considered whether this was depressing or cheering, and decided the latter – in a way.

'It won't be for long,' I said briskly. 'You can be sure of that. I'm going to root out this hallucination myself. Ellie' – (and by implication you) – 'has been pussy-footing in the wrong direction too long.'

'Yeah.' A long drawn-out drawl, unusual for him. 'I reckon.' A pause. 'Any plans?'

To hit your smug face right across the chops, I thought of

replying, but remembered my long spoon in time. Instead: 'Yes, but I'll keep them to myself, seeing that you represent Ellie and Columba. Just for the moment, I'm going my own way until I've something positive to tell them.'

He grinned, apparently taking no offence. 'You think Columba and I are an item?'

He was deliberately putting me on the spot and I saw it. Whether I said yes or no, he could make me look a fool.

'It's your life,' I replied with all the indifference I could muster.

'Um, detached viewpoint. I like that.'

'It's because I'm *adopted*,' I snarled, losing my cool right away. 'That's what Ellie would say and that's what you think. I'm depleted of identity. I grew up looking at folks from the outside instead of gut instinctive feelings from the inside.'

'It's an advantage for a biography. That's the way it works for me. And for a cartoon animator too, I guess. Roving imaginations are useful.'

'Okay, so we're both detached. So what?' I failed to keep the snarl out of my voice.

'You may have trouble believing this, Quinn, but I want to see this Rich thing resolved.'

'Why?'

He looked at me for a moment, then replied, 'I need Ellie and Columba to help with the biography, not to be in the midst of a family crisis.'

I had a feeling this wasn't what he had meant to say. Just as I suspected. He was just a self-seeking bastard. 'That's honest of you,' I said, with no admiration in my voice at all.

He shrugged. 'Crunch time for the museum is in sight. The opening's late May. I intend to parade the Flowerdews en masse and get this biography settled then and there. If Columba, Ellie, you and Margaret are still at daggers drawn, it won't be good for the museum or the book.'

'En masse? Won't that be hard, given the skeleton in the closet in the form of Uncle Ted?'

He ignored the sarcasm, and I began to think he was getting the better of this encounter. I was too bruised to compete properly.

'Think what you like,' he replied amiably. 'To show you I'm in earnest, though, here's something I picked up from Cecilia last week.' He delved into a box and removed a video from it.

I took it from him cautiously, and then saw to my interest that it looked like a pair to the last one I watched on the previous evening.

'It's of Rich when he went solo,' John explained. 'Ellie never said much about the earlier ones I gave her, but you might make more of it. And there's something else too.'

'Thank you,' I said awkwardly. 'What else?'

'Not material. Information about a visiting fireman.'

'A what?' I asked blankly.

He laughed. 'Easy to see I've got an artist in front of me, one who doesn't move in the music world. Visiting fireman equals VIP from HQ. In this case it's a record company in Denmark Street expecting their new supremo over next week from the States.'

'So?'

'His name is Augustus G. Williams.'

'So?' My spoon got longer by the minute.

'Augustus is the full version of Gus.'

I played along. 'And?'

'Think about it. Think about the G.'

I made an effort. Nothing. G. Williams. Then I saw what he meant. 'Gus, G, and Williams. William Gossage – a bit far-fetched, isn't it?'

'Certainly. But I checked. No one had heard of Mr Augustus Williams until 1975, when he arrived in the States from Australia and in due course applied for US citizenship.'

'Why are you telling me, not Ellie?'

'Ellie thinks she's reached the end of the road. You

don't. You're just beginning. Who would you pick, if you were me?'

'How do I . . .?' I began awkwardly, only half-convinced there wasn't some ulterior motive besides biographies and the fraternity of men.

John sighed. 'I've done the dirty work for you. I called him, and told him I'd set the Inland Revenue on him, not to mention a few disgruntled Coinmakers, if he didn't see you. Amazing what you can do with threats like that – if they're on target.'

'Come off it, John. How did you know you'd be seeing me?'

'It didn't take a lot of guessing you'd be up to see Stephen this morning. I came down early this morning and asked Jane to keep an eye open for you. If you hadn't come, I'd have strolled down to offer my condolences. Satisfied, pal?'

It was the first hint of antagonism from his side, and served to show me on what side my bread was buttered.

'Satisfied,' I said quietly, letting my drawbridge slip gently down. 'And I'm grateful. Very grateful, John. So I'll make a bargain with you. Continue working with me to get this affair solved, and I'll do anything in my power to make not only the museum opening a success but also to get that biography moving.'

'Agreed.'

'I still can't make you out,' I commented, just in case he thought we'd be bosom chums. 'Columba, Ellie, museum, biography, roving theatre commissions – they don't add up.' I had a feeling I'd missed something.

'Some day I'll tell you the story of my life, okay?'

I'd gone too far, and I backed off.

'Understood.' After all, I knew John meant what he said about our bargain, because he hadn't reminded me of the obvious: unless I did get the Rich puzzle sorted, I would be in no position to help him with the biography. I'd no longer be married to a Flowerdew.

*   *   *

That evening I sat down with the new video John had given me. Having a purpose made it a whole lot easier to face that empty house. The marital nest is not the same once the bird has flown, and the sooner I was out the better. I had seen Stephen, who merely said – no doubt primed by Columba – that he wouldn't be letting the Lodge for a while, and in any case why didn't I stay on?

Why not? Because I played fair. I'd get out of Ellie's way. She couldn't abandon her business, but I could leave the Lodge. And in some ways it would be a pleasure. Even my studio seemed infected with her – or, rather, with memories of our parting. I'd find somewhere else, and would start looking on the way back from Sussex tomorrow.

And then I watched the video.

To my immediate interest this was of Rich's solo career in the last six months before he vanished. Gossage was present, but musically only Rich counted: *Seven Wives, Hey You, A Man Can't Cry*. Oh, can't he? I remembered them all because they were still being played in my childhood. Even seeing them in rehearsal one sensed the power of the duo of Rich and Gossage. Musically Rich ruled, of course, but overall power was in Gossage's hands. He was the prime minister to Rich's splendid but impotent king. Just hearing Rich sing made the studio vanish into another world of magic, smoothed by Irish blarney.

Yet this was no magician, but a real husband and father, I reminded myself. How could a person who could sing like that abduct a child from its mother? How could he treat his wife so? And yet looking at him one could almost see the answer to that.

There were two Richard Harts: the Mighty Rich of his art and the one he became when talking and joking with his manager. Maybe there was even a third: the Richard Hart who lived somewhere between the two in his own lost land. I remembered that Cecilia had told Ellie he was a poet, and that when he went solo he wrote his own lyrics. Did that

147

come from the third Richard Hart? I felt I was inching my way to my goal, and that the roots of his disappearance lay somewhere in the year of '69, when he left the Coinmakers and went solo.

I ran the video a second time: if the magic vanished, I told myself, I could doubt its validity. The magic stayed. Rich's poetry, Rich's singing and playing, made a formidable team. And yet he threw it all up after six months and disappeared off the stage for ever.

I wondered if there was something special about the last gig in '69. The band had been there, Ellie had said, but didn't seem to have cottoned on to the fact that Richard had not gone home afterwards but vanished that very night. Was it by plan? If he meant to abduct the child, even he must have planned something. Had he taken spare clothes with him? His passport? Or had they met a terrible death on the way home, and no evidence been found? No – there was the postcard to Cecilia from Nepal. What about the passport? That I could not answer, but I was becoming convinced that the clue lay in that last gig.

I'd ask Margaret tomorrow, and if she did not know, I'd ask dear Gus next week. He above all must have known what happened on that July evening over thirty years ago.

Ten

As I drove to Sussex the next day, I wondered what the hell I was doing, doubting its wisdom. Yesterday, it seemed the obvious next step, perhaps the *only* one. Today I felt I would be betraying Ellie by discussing our private problems with her parents. In the end, reason managed its struggle to convince me this was the only way I could win Ellie back.

It seemed strange to be walking into Kingsgate House without Ellie. What had seemed an entrancingly original home when we first visited it after our marriage, now seemed dull and almost conventional in its Victorian gothicry. I pulled myself up short by reminding myself this was the house Richard had chosen to live in, and that meant I must have all my own antennae working if I was to understand him. That was objective number one and it was strictly no side paths from now on.

Gerald opened the door, looking strained. 'Glad you've come, Quinn. Let's get this thing settled quickly for all our sakes,' he hissed at me as I followed him into the warmth of the entrance hall.

'Including mine,' I reminded him. 'It's a tall order though. Richard could be anywhere in the world and until we have some clue as to where to start looking, we can't even estimate how long it would take.' Put this way I made myself feel, not for the first time, that my grand objective was impossible.

Gerald looked gloomy too. 'What about—'

'A DNA test? That's what Ellie wants, either herself and me or preferably Margaret and me. I thought—'

'It seems simplest,' he replied apologetically, 'but Margaret will take some persuading.'

'To do what?' Margaret came rushing through from the garden door. She put her arms round me and hugged me, which cheered me up. 'Coffee?'

I followed her into the kitchen while this preliminary ritual was carried out. 'Ellie wanted me to have a DNA test.'

'She didn't ask me.' Margaret banged down three cups vigorously. 'Probably because she knew I'd refuse.'

My heart lifted. There is safety in numbers. 'That's what I did. After all, what if it's negative? Worse, if—'

'You turned out to be my long-lost son,' Margaret replied helpfully. I couldn't even frame the words. 'I can't believe that, Quinn. I believe the likeness that Columba claims she can see between you and Richard simply stems from the Irishness in you both. I don't *feel* any bond with you, save as my son-in-law. Do you?'

'No.' Relief poured off me in bucketfuls. 'Not that that's proof, of course,' I added. 'I don't even know whether we could be expected to.'

'Surely we would feel something in common?'

'I'd have thought so, but then lots of parents and children don't. I see having the test as a last resort. How do you feel?'

'I agree. If it's the only way, I'll do it, but I'm not too sure how Ellie would take it if it was positive. Or how *I* would, come to think of it. Suppose your parents and Richard's were related, for example?'

'Just what I said.'

'So we do think the same way,' Margaret quipped.

'No joke, Margaret.' Gerald put in his oar. 'If you're unhappy about the test, then we had better find out what happened to Richard, *quickly*.'

'That's what I'm planning,' I said.

'I hoped you'd say that. Not' – Margaret said a little too gaily – 'that I'm expecting you to produce my long-lost son, but it seems to be the only way of solving my daughter's problems. But how do you propose to do it? After all, I put years into the search.'

'A stranger on the scene could help,' I said more confidently than I felt. 'But I can't do it without you.'

'Ah. Somehow I knew you'd say that. What do you think, Gerald?' she asked. 'Do we unlock the closet and let the skeleton march out?' Despite her light-heartedness, I noticed her lips trembling – and so did Gerald.

'I don't see how raking up old heartache can help,' he said firmly. 'Margaret is quite sure she knows nothing more about the disappearance than she told the police at the time and countless other people since. The band is the only line worth pursuing. Maybe Ellie didn't ask the right questions.'

'There's one difference. Margaret can tell me what Richard was like in his personal life. The band would know him as a colleague and maybe a friend. Cecilia is the only other person who could tell me a little about the real Richard, but even she would be limited, compared with Margaret's views.'

A silence. Then Gerald went into protective mode. 'But what the blazes is going to be the use of knowing that he was kind to cats, but left the top off the toothpaste?'

'I don't know . . . yet,' I admitted.

'I don't see any harm in it, Gerald,' Margaret said. 'In fact, re-examining it with someone new might help me as well as Quinn.'

Gerald shrugged, but I could see and understand his fear. Fine, if memories could be taken out, aired, and then replaced – or better still, deleted – but what if taking them out reawoke old monsters, old dreams, old desires?

Margaret must have noticed it too. 'You're wrong, Gerald,' she told him gently. 'Whatever was there has gone, except for' – she made an effort – 'Marcus himself. Richard was part of my youth, what I thought I wanted from life. But I know now, and perhaps even then, that if Richard hadn't disappeared, the marriage would have broken up in time.'

Gerald gave reluctant way. 'Ellie comes first, I suppose. If you really think it would help, Quinn . . .' A last appeal to me, but I couldn't let it influence me, especially after what Margaret had said.

'I don't know that it will help. But it's my last hope – or rather hunch.'

'I'll take myself off then,' Gerald said gruffly.

Margaret and I spoke together. 'There's no need.'

He chuckled at that. 'You'll get on better *à deux*. My opinion won't count for much.'

'Did you ever meet Richard, Gerald?' I asked.

'No. I remember seeing him on television. Going to pop concerts wasn't my scene.'

'You don't get the right impression from television,' Margaret said frowning in concentration, reaching back into the past.

I gathered hope that I'd been right to think there had been two or three Richards.

'I'll get the lunch,' Gerald offered.

'Done.' Margaret accepted gratefully.

Margaret and I retreated to her studio, which was a purpose-built one-storey brick building divided into two. One half was purely work, with kiln, pots and supplies; the other half, as I recognised from my own working space, was a nest where pads, pencils, books and ancient computer jumbled happily together, ostensibly untouched by organisation. In fact, there is always organisation, however unlikely it seems, but it is sometimes known only to its owner.

It was the first time I'd seen her working area, although I'd seen Gerald's when Ellie and I had first visited. At Christmastime it had been too cold to cavort in the garden unnecessarily, but, although it was only January now, it was one of those days when the crisp sunny weather gave hope of spring. This, together with heating, made the studio come into its own again. It had a small garden to itself consisting of a tiny lawn and semicircle of shrubbery border around it.

'Was this built when Richard lived here?'

'Oh yes. It was his studio in fact. I hadn't taken up pottery then. It was one reason we bought this house. It and the studio were far enough away from other houses for him to make as much noise as he liked. The band would come down here to rehearse sometimes. There was a piano here then, of course.'

She followed my surprised gaze. It was hard to imagine this as ideal for musical creation. 'I've changed it completely.'

'At least Richard thought of something so mundane as neighbours. Not many pop stars would do that,' I commented.

Margaret snorted. 'He just didn't want the bother of dealing with them if they came to complain. He liked to keep himself at a far distance from his public.'

I thought of the video clips I'd seen, many of them showing Richard surrounded by fans and apparently loving it. There was no sign of distance there, and I told her so.

'He kept his emotional distance all the time, and physical distance except when wearing his public face. That's why we didn't make friends in the village.'

'He surely didn't keep *everyone* at arm's length?'

Margaret thought back. 'When we first married he was relatively unknown. The band was just starting up – they'd only released a few singles and some of those bombed. Then it began to gather pace and it became a question of how to preserve some private life for ourselves. Most famous people have this conundrum; Richard took it to extremes. The village was curious when we first moved in, knowing Richard was a pop star, but they weren't fans. On the contrary, we were highly disapproved of locally. In the sixties, pop stars only had approval from the younger generations; the older ones saw them as a threat and were still hoping all those weird sounds and singers would quietly vanish and we could get back to real music like Richard Tauber and John McCormack.

'When Richard and the Coinmakers became more famous, they disapproved of us even more in the village, but by then the younger generations were beating a rock path to our door. Richard didn't know how to handle it, so – typically – he left it to me. I did a great job handing out signed postcards and posters and advertisements for gifts, but Richard was never around. Macavity the Mystery Cat wasn't in it when it came to his capacity to vanish. Once a year I persuaded him to have a village fête in our field – that's attached to our garden and it's let for grazing now. You'd think its success was his dearest wish, he put on such a good show on those afternoons. The band came down, he sang, he mixed, he circulated, he almost kissed babies.' Margaret stopped. 'Is this what you want?' she asked doubtfully.

'Yes.' My doubts as to whether this visit had been the right move had already vanished. This was just what I wanted to know. 'Do you mean he was scornful about fans and villagers most of the time?'

Margaret was horrified. 'Oh no, Richard wasn't like that. He thought fans were great. He even liked the Colonel Blimps and Disgusteds of Tunbridge Wells. It's just that he was wrapped up in his own world, and didn't want to share it with anyone more than he had to. That's why he went solo, I believe.'

'What about sharing it with you?' I caught my breath, thinking I'd gone too far.

She gave a twisted smile. 'I thought he wanted to at the time.' The words jerked out. 'When he walked out on me, I had pause for thought. Richard would never hurt anyone, you see, particularly not those near to him – although I qualify that by saying he didn't want to *see* them hurt. If he could distance himself from the pain, it was another matter. He could simply cut himself off then.'

'He didn't love you? I'm sorry.' I saw her face change.

'No, it's all right. It's a fair question. I would answer yes, he did love me – insofar as he could. There was always this inner core in which nothing mattered but Richard and some dream of his own. I suppose much the same could be said of anybody, but in Richard it dominated his life.'

'And the dream was?'

'I never quite knew. When we married he'd talk of how many kids we'd have, what he wanted to do in his musical life and so on, but looking back, I don't think they touched him deeply.'

'You must have some idea.'

She thought for a moment. 'I'm not sure I have. I'm not even sure *he* had. Have you ever read that H.G. Wells novel, *The History of Mr Polly*? It opens with Mr Polly, failed husband, failed haberdasher, sitting on a gate, where he came to the conclusion that if you don't like your life you can change it. Not that Richard was a failed anything. He was a good husband, Quinn, despite everything I've said, and obviously not a failure in his career. Quite the opposite. Yet like Mr Polly he had this dream, but neither of them knew what it was. Mr Polly found his dream by accident; he simply became anonymous, gave up the life in which he was always expected to achieve, and settled down as a barman and handyman in a country pub by a stream run by a jolly easygoing woman. I think that's the kind of life Richard would have liked, one of complete anonymity, no responsibility – he never took kindly to that – and just doing the sort of things he enjoyed doing.'

I remembered what Ellie had said. 'Cecilia said he had lots of interests.'

'Oh yes. He liked not exactly dabbling, but investigating. He painted a bit, wrote a bit, acted a bit, liked cooking, even liked gardening – all sorts of things besides music.'

'But can one turn a dream into real life?'

'Mr Polly did, and even though it's a novel, I would think it's possible – if you've the right temperament and can believe that there's something else in the world other than mortgages, work, complaining wives and so on.'

'Did *you* complain? I can't imagine that.'

'I would have done if the marriage had continued. I was too much in love and too starry-eyed at first, of course, and a woman's role wasn't defined in those days. It was okay to work, but it was also okay to stay at home and raise a family. Richard didn't encourage me to come to gigs, though I insisted on going to some when we were first married. He said it was because he wanted to sing and play for me alone. And it wasn't just talk. He actually did. That's why I wasn't too surprised when he told me he wanted to go solo.'

'Do you think he left in intentional pursuit of this dream of his?'

'Mr Polly didn't, because he didn't know what his indigestion with modern life translated into. Perhaps it was the same with Richard – I don't know.'

'But Marcus . . .' I began hesitantly.

Margaret flinched. 'Go on.'

'You said Richard didn't like hurting people, but to abduct the child, isn't that strange? It's weird even though you say that if he wasn't there to *see* the hurt, it didn't matter to him.'

'I don't think I said it didn't matter,' she replied instantly. 'I said he could shut it off. He need not take the responsibility of someone else's pain if he wasn't present.'

'But to *plan* to do so. That's devious. Was he?'

'No. That was the most hurtful thing about it. He wasn't. He would do something and not tell you, but not through deviousness. He would simply forget to tell you because he wanted to do something, and that took precedence. Responsibility didn't stretch to telling others around you.'

'Did he take extra clothes for the child or himself when he left on that last gig?'

'Not for Marcus, and I don't think for himself either, though in his van he kept spare clothing. Sometimes he'd sleep there after gigs, if he could not get home or wasn't up to driving back. Taking clothes for Marcus wouldn't occur to him, though, whether he planned to disappear with him or not. He just didn't think that way. He'd buy more stuff as he went along. The gypsy rover, that was Richard.'

'Do you think he's still roving?'

'Not if he's found out what he wants. I wasn't it, but some other woman may be. And before you ask, he wasn't gay or bisexual. That's not just my opinion; I discussed it with the band, and they knew me well enough, and liked me little enough, to tell me the truth.'

'What do you know about that last gig? It's my hunch that something happened there to make him go away.'

Margaret thought this was funny. 'Like the old song – "Twenty-Four Hours from Tulsa" stuff?' she asked drily. 'Love at first sight?'

'Unlikely, I'd have thought. And presumably someone would have told you if there was a woman in the case. Did you have a row before he went?'

'No. That was what was so odd. I remember it crystal clearly because of what happened. It was a Wednesday night and it was our wedding anniversary at the weekend. Richard said we'd leave Marcus with his parents or mine, and go away somewhere; he'd booked a hotel in Cornwall, down at Mousehole. Dylan Thomas spent his honeymoon there, he said, and that's why he wanted to take me.'

I felt I was making progress. With no row, it focussed attention on that last gig.

'So when he didn't return that night or later,' Margaret continued, 'and I'd made sure there'd been no road accidents or hospital admissions and so on, I went into everything. I turned every detail inside out for hidden meanings. I talked to Colin, I talked to Mike, I talked to Bryan – separately, so I'm convinced they hadn't invented a joint story. Nor did I get any impression they were keeping anything from me. All three of them said they stayed on for a drink in the pub and Richard said he was leaving to take Marcus home. They were so mad with him for ditching them, as they saw it, they'd have spilt any dirty water they could. I'm sure of that.'

'What about William Gossage? Did you see him? I'm told he disappeared that autumn from the London pop scene.' Encouraged, I wanted to move towards spongier ground: those royalties, and the presumed death that Ellie had held back from asking her mother about.

'No hope there either. Yes, I did see him. I didn't like him. I always sensed he resented any time Richard spent with me, or any affection he showed me or even Marcus. He was completely wound up with Richard's music, so determined to get him to number one when he went solo. He began to manage the Coinmakers quite soon after they formed the band, and came to regard them as his own creation. Richard always seemed happy to let him do so, and even allowed himself to be bossed around by him. He was a good manager, although I was constantly surprised that Richard let him get away with so much. Looking back, I think perhaps he only did so as long as their interests coincided.'

'You mean if Richard pursued his dream, and that dream wasn't music . . .'

'Precisely.'

'I'm seeing him next week,' I said abruptly. I hadn't meant to tell Margaret about Gossage, and it came out badly.

'Richard?' she almost screeched at me.

'No, no, I'm sorry. I'm seeing the man John believes is William Gossage.'

'Well done, him.' Margaret calmed down. 'I don't like the idea of this biography – far from it – but he's doing a good job with this museum, and he's been a great help to Ellie, I gather. I like him, too . . .' She caught sight of my expression, which I'd rearranged too late. 'Ah, you don't.'

Honesty is the best policy. 'No, he's too thick with Columba, for one thing.'

'Don't be too hard on Columba. She means no harm.'

158

'As the steamroller said to the ant.'

'What are your views on the biography, Quinn?' Margaret asked hastily.

I came clean. 'I've agreed to help John if I can and if he comes up with information leading to Richard.'

'Honest of you. And what does Ellie think about that?'

'I don't know.'

'You should, Quinn. Ellie needs you to understand her way of thinking.'

Not so unusual, I thought. I could do with a bit of understanding myself.

'It's early days,' she continued. 'You have to work it out somehow.'

'Unfortunately, there may be no later days.' My turn for dry humour. But it didn't cheer me up. Instead, I used the opportunity to plunge into the deep end. 'After the High Court presumption of death case,' I continued casually, as though it had been a constant subject of discussion between us, 'Ellie said Gossage's share of the royalties shot up.'

Margaret grimaced. 'I knew you'd find out about the case. I didn't tell Ellie because it would have convinced her I was barking mad in believing Richard still alive. And I'm not.'

I was relieved it was in the open. 'You must have given evidence?'

'Yes, but not personally. I turned over what the court ordered, and swore a statement that I had not seen Richard since July '69. I had as little as possible to do with it.' She saw my puzzled look. 'And before you begin to think that's because I wanted to keep my illusions about Marcus, it wasn't.'

'Why then?'

'I loathed their guts. Father and son alike. They didn't give a damn about Richard, only the money. They did their best to get hold of my share too, but I fought them off. It's still in trust for Marcus, until my death.' She saw my look. 'And there are arrangements in my will in case

Marcus really is dead. As for Gossage's share – you know what I think?'

'I can guess – but tell me.'

'It was payment for services rendered. A false oath that he'd seen Richard die.'

Over a lunch of trout fillets, salad and sautéed potatoes, Gerald looked hopefully at us both. 'All over?'

'I've finished my interrogation-in-chief of the witness,' I said. 'Margaret was very patient.'

'And you still don't think she's your mother?'

'Gerald!' Margaret said warningly. 'Don't tease him.'

'Pity. It would have made the household a family again. Did you ask him, Margaret?'

'I thought it would be better coming from you.'

I looked enquiringly at Gerald. What on earth was this about?

Gerald cleared his throat, reminding me of my own father who always did that when he wished to be jolly decent to me, and didn't like me to notice this feeble-mindedness in him.

'What are your plans, Quinn?' he asked gruffly. 'Are you staying in the Lodge for the time being?'

'No, it's not fair on Ellie.'

'Got anywhere else to go?'

'Not yet.' I was surprised at this interest in my welfare. 'I was going to start looking on the way back today.'

'We'd like you to move in here.'

For a moment I didn't take it in. 'With you?' I asked stupidly.

'We're not proposing to move out ourselves.' Margaret laughed. 'You'd have to put up with us here. We have a lot of space around, so you can be all but self-sufficient. You can have the attic room – it's huge. There's room for you to sleep and work. Easy enough to put in another telephone line for your computer.'

I simply stared at them. 'It's very generous of you. But why on earth are you suggesting it?'

'Firstly, it would keep us in touch with what's happening,' Margaret said honestly. 'Through our own fault, we've been too much in the dark. Secondly, we think it will help to keep you in the family and to keep it together.'

'It's more likely to blow it apart,' I said bluntly, 'if Ellie finds out. What's she going to think?'

'Let's hope she doesn't find out. She's obviously decided not to burden us with the news of your split herself. Columba isn't going to know you're here either.'

'And John? If I'm working with him, even to a limited extent, I'm going to have to give him some address.'

'You can tell him or anyone you like. He won't split to Ellie and Columba.'

'Sure?' I wasn't.

'I shall tell him not to.'

'And you trust him?'

'Yes. In any case, he wants to get me to co-operate on the biography, remember? Keeping his mouth shut is a small price to pay for the privilege of coming to beard me in my own home. He'll leap at the bargain if I change sides.'

'I bet he will,' I said savagely. 'I still feel I'm going behind Ellie's back, though.'

'You said she went behind yours.'

'Yes, but in order not to hurt me.'

'Yet she did,' Margaret pointed out. 'Go for broke, Quinn, that's my advice. Come here for a while. Don't write off Ellie's family yet. Stay part of it. It will help everyone in the end.'

I turned the problem over in my mind. Put that way, I could hardly refuse. The offer of a family. Once I'd had none and now I had two. Pray God, I'd have a third sometime – mine and Ellie's.

Getting the train to London from Crowborough the following

week seemed a whole different experience than from Kent, and I don't just mean the Connex rolling stock. Somehow, having settled into Kingsgate House and travelling up from Sussex gave me a new outlook on what had happened. I was detached, able to cope with what lay before me. It gave me more purpose, unhampered by ever-present signs of our brief marriage. Now I had a plan of the road ahead.

When I reached the Denmark Street offices, I wasn't shown up to the Great Gus's office. Instead he appeared from the lift almost immediately after I was announced.

'I've booked a room at my club,' he informed me loftily, after we'd introduced ourselves.

Could this really be William Gossage? I wondered. Usually, twenty or even thirty years later, people are still vaguely recognisable, especially if you know who they are. This man wasn't, and for a moment I doubted the Mighty John's diagnosis that this was my quarry. Where William had been tall, lanky, supercilious and over-eager, this man was burly, broad-faced, closed-in and suspicious. Only the height hadn't changed, although at first it seemed to have done so because the frame had broadened.

Nevertheless, the fact that he had elected to take a private room for our discussion made me think this must be him, and I determined to hang on to that if he tried to deny his identity.

'What makes you think I'm this joker you're after?' Gus Williams obligingly put his cards on the table as soon as the waiter departed after delivering coffee and biscuits to the room, and the ritual casual conversation, during which both sides appraised each other, was over. So far as my appraisal of this devil was concerned, I intended to keep my long spoon firmly in hand.

'Your name. It fits easily into a transformation of William Gossage.'

'Listen, my friend, if I was this Gossage, don't you think I'd have made a more thorough job of changing my name?'

162

'Possibly,' I conceded. 'But it might have amused you to keep the same name turned around.' Wouldn't that be what an arrogant man like William Gossage would think?

'What else?' he asked.

'The fact that I'm here.'

Coffee was busily stirred. 'This Curwen fellow had a touch of blackmail about him. I don't like that. I thought I'd take a look at you.'

'I think Michael Patterson and Bryan Whatley would like to take a look at *you*.' I decided to omit the Inland Revenue, since it smacked of deep waters and I didn't want to find myself in them with a brick tied round my neck. This man looked all too capable of arranging that with the greatest of ease.

He considered this. 'What do you want from me?'

'Not much. I've no interest in anything about you, and nor has John Curwen. We want to find the Mighty Rich, and quickly. You might have some information.'

'Why go to this Gossage about that? The man went off and left his manager in the lurch. The Mighty Rich are dirty words in my business.'

'As are William Gossage to the Coinmakers' band. Did you know one committed suicide?'

'I heard.'

'And that Michael Patterson is still shooting his mouth off about what he'd do to you?'

'You terrify me.'

I changed tack. 'Why shouldn't you tell me? You've nothing to hide, presumably. No one's accusing you of making anything out of his disappearance, or that of the child.' Yet, I added to myself, there was still the trump card of his commission.

'Child?' he picked up.

'When the Mighty Rich disappeared, he took his child with him. He hasn't been seen since either.'

'But he wasn't—' Surprise made Gus Williams go too far.

'Let's drop the pretence,' I suggested. 'It's quicker. I don't have a tape in my pockets or in here . . .' I pushed my briefcase towards him.

He didn't bother to glance at it. 'Okay. So I'm William Gossage. Now what?'

What changed you so much? I wondered, but didn't think it polite to ask.

Having taken this giant step, Williams became more approachable. 'Don't look like my early pictures, do I?'

So I did ask my question. 'What changed you?'

'The Mighty Rich did.'

I made a giant leap of my own. 'You had a row at that gig in Richmond.'

He stared at me. Impossible to tell what he was thinking. 'A mother and father of a row,' he eventually said, only that was paraphrasing his language. He eyed me speculatively, as though weighing up how far to go.

'Can you tell me what about?'

'Why not? It was a straightforward business matter. I told him about this terrific deal I'd signed for him in Paris for dates from August through December. He could get home to see his blasted wife and kid in between. It was a sweetheart tour for him, but he turned me down flat. I nearly exploded. He gave me no reason, except that he had other plans. He was murmuring about being a spectator and not a participant for a while. That made me go berserk. Then the kid started yelling and Rich followed his example. I said if he didn't take up the Paris offer he was a fool and could forget me as a manager. He just walked off and that was the last I saw of him until . . . Every time I rang his home after that he was out, and then his wife eventually told me he'd never come home that night.'

'He didn't give you a hint as to what those other plans were?' It was a long shot that he'd confided in good old Gossage.

'He wouldn't do that, would he? I did see him talking to

164

someone, a young hippie singer, but I've no idea whether that had anything to do with Rich's disappearance.'

'You never saw him again?'

'No.'

'What happened to the "until" you tried so hard to swallow just now? It wouldn't have finished with "Nepal", would it?'

Another silence while he stared at me arrogantly. Another thing that hadn't changed. He was smirking, daring me to push this any further. I did. 'You swore to the High Court in 1977 that you'd seen Rich die in Nepal. How come you say you haven't seen him since '69?'

He still smirked.

'You've nothing to lose by telling me,' I continued. 'We've no witnesses to this conversation, and all I want to do is trace Richard Hart. You could make a fortune as the man who rediscovered the Mighty Rich if I do.'

His short laugh dismissed that idea. '*If* I happened to be mistaken about his death, he probably hasn't sung a note since we last met.'

'Which was when?'

He brooded, then decided he might as well come clean. 'I heard a rumour in December '69 that Rich had been seen in Paris, so off I went to see if he'd taken up the tour after all, and was quietly forgetting my commission. He had, but the commission was waiting for me. In cash. I managed to book a couple more dates in Paris for him on the same basis, only to have him blasted well disappear again as soon as they were over. I found out he went to Nepal.'

'You followed him?'

A scathing look. 'Not much of an address, is it? Who knows if I would have run into him there, and if I did, I might well have put paid to his looks for good. No, I stayed in Paris and began a new career. I know Nepal so it wasn't hard . . . Well,' he switched hastily, 'a few years later I went to Australia with another band and ran right into Rich,

who was working his way round under the name of Frank
Penrose. It was him all right, and not delighted to see me.
He was busking, doing okay, and as far as I was concerned
he could carry on doing it for good. I'd had enough.'

I thought of Ellie's story of the sighting in Tahiti and
wondered if it were true.

'I offered him everything,' Gus said, aggrieved. 'I even
offered to build him up under his new name. After all, he'd
wangled a passport under it. He turned me down. He said
he was quite happy doing what he was doing. I indicated he
could be sure his voice would be recognised sooner or later,
and his wife would find out where he was.'

I bet you were blackmailing him, I thought.

'So he upped and disappeared, *again.* Haven't heard a
whisper since. Seemed to me he owed me for that. I reckoned
he could well be dead, so why not do his family a service –
and myself too?'

'No comment,' I replied. I decided it would be politic
to overlook that hefty commission. Now for the important
question. 'Did he have a child with him?'

'No way. I'd have seen him, or heard about him. I
didn't.'

Bad news. By December '69 I'd been in the orphanage. It
didn't help my case one bit. And worse, what the hell was
I going to tell Margaret? I decided I could only tell her the
truth. She knew I was coming here. She knew I'd ask the
question. There was no evading the issue. There was one
thing I could do, however. I could remember my objective:
what was Richard Hart like as a person? Whatever William
Gossage said would be interesting.

'Did you like him?'

'The kid?'

'No. The Mighty Rich.'

The answer I got surprised me. It was preceded by a slow
but unmistakable grin.

'Listen, buster, I'm a manager. Liking gets in the way

of common sense, and I let it do that with Rich. Like him? I thought he was the greatest thing since sliced bread until . . .'

Here we go. That 'until' again.

'He went solo. I bloody well urged him to do it. Too good an artist to be chained to those three deadweight strummers and drummers.'

To whom, according to them, you begged to return, I was tempted to add.

'Then I realised I'd unleashed the monster from his Frankenstein,' Gossage continued. 'He broke free. He was using his own lyrics – fine, I urged him to do that – but he wanted to experiment, to push further. Too far for the public, which was into violence at the time, not how beautiful the world was. Bring him back now and he'd be great, but then, forget it.'

'But he had several hits then.'

'Because I was managing him the best I could. When he broke away, he forgot that. That's why everything went silent. Happens all the time. Think they can do without a manager. Can they, hell. He was finished, kaput, and I always know.'

I couldn't resist it. 'But you liked him.'

'Great guy. One of the best. Just one thing . . .'

'Yes?'

'If you find him, I won't be sending red roses.' A pause. 'And if he or any of his chums finds *me*, you'll be off the list too. Understood?'

I could already feel the brick round my neck. 'Understood.'

Eleven

The weeks went by, crawling through the bleakness of February and the cold winds of March, and April, reluctant to concede that spring might be near. I saw nothing of Ellie, and heard little. Margaret and Gerald went to London to meet her for lunch and reported that Ellie was going away with Columba for Easter.

Still my mind remained blank on where to search next for Richard Hart. I watched the videos endlessly, but he seemed almost to be mocking me.

It was May before the breakthrough came. I was glad to be sleeping in the attic studio room at Kingsgate House, for outside I could see the velvet night sky. I wished my path to Richard Hart was as clear. I had begun to feel he was all around me, just as I do when I'm working on a series, the imaginary world inhabited by Sadie O'Grady or the Rab-Hits.

For whatever reason I dreamed of Cornwall that night, probably because we had been listening to a recording of *Under Milk Wood* and my mind connected with Margaret's mention of Dylan Thomas's honeymoon in Mousehole. I'd been there several times on holiday or on walking trips in my life and the publication and animated film of *The Mousehole Cat* had sent me scurrying back a few years ago.

It is a grey-roofed fishing village tucked into granite cliffs, a village that has risen above the danger of becoming solely a tourist attraction and retained its strong character, as has St Ives. Strip the visitors away, and what lies underneath is as solid as the granite of Cornwall itself. To me it is a village of birds rather than of cats. There is a bird hospital high above the village on the road leading (eventually) to Lamorna, and seagulls are wheeling and diving, or standing on the roofs and chimneys, swooping into the harbour, and calling, calling, all the time.

It was that sound I heard in my dreams that night. It was almost as if they were summoning me, and when I awoke it was that sound I could still hear in my imagination. It was so vivid, so clear, I will never forget it.

As my feet hit the floor in the first stages of greeting the day, it occurred to me to wonder if Richard Hart had been able to forget that sound. He clearly had some connection with Cornwall. After all, he'd chosen a Cornish name for his new life. Whether in Nepal or in Australia, had he lain lazily under the blazing sun or sleepless in the humid nights and heard that plaintive summons? *Had he obeyed it?*

Ridiculous, I decided. England was the last place he would have come. False passport, danger of being recognised – the idea was out of the question. And yet as I tried to work, the mocking sound of seagulls' cries kept replacing the laughter of the Rab-Hits. They grew so shrill, I eventually put the idea to Margaret.

'Would he do it, do you think?'

'Oh yes,' she replied. 'He's crazy enough, if he wanted to come back that badly. But the sound of seagulls doesn't sound a strong enough reason to me.'

'You said he wanted to visit Cornwall on the weekend of his disappearance.'

'True, but coming back years later for a missed weekend doesn't make sense. No, I'd have to have a stronger reason to believe he wanted to throw up the security of Australia for a possible hornet's nest back here.'

I wasn't going to give up my one idea so easily now that I'd warmed up to it.

'*Why* did he suggest Cornwall as a venue for that weekend, though? It's a long way to go for a couple of days.'

169

She shrugged. 'Maybe he'd been reading a Dylan Thomas biography. But I'm sure if Cornwall was important to him, if it had significance, then he'd have given a sign of it somewhere, if not to me, then . . .'

'To the band?' I suggested helpfully when she paused.

'No, but I think perhaps in his work.'

'In his music?' Even as I said it, I realised that was wrong. Not the music, but the words. The lyrics for his music after he went solo, the lyrics he wrote himself. *Seven Wives.* I shouted the words in a triumphant clarion call to Richard Hart, wherever he might be.

'That was based on an old nursery rhyme: "I met a man with seven wives",' Margaret said. 'Doesn't it go back to Greek and Roman times?'

'Maybe, but what was the first line? "As I was going to *St Ives*".' Richard's lyric had nothing to do in content with the old riddle rhyme, but this to me only strengthened the notion that Cornwall was deeply imbedded in his subconscious mind.

'I still don't buy it,' Margaret objected after I finished explaining my idea. 'If you're right, *what* brought him back?'

'The dream, perhaps,' I threw out at random. The problem with sharing one's inspiration is that it either sparks off new heights of brilliance or knocks the first spark dead. This one wouldn't die though.

'Even the dream has to be based on something.'

I thought for a moment. 'St Ives equals the Tate, it equals the St Ives art colony, Nicholson, Hepworth, Leach, Heron, and lots of others. In the sixties it had a new lease of life in the number of its artists achieving world fame. And much earlier there was the Newlyn School of Painters. Cornwall was riddled with artistic connections . . . and didn't you say Richard dabbled in painting?'

'It's possible you're right,' Margaret admitted cautiously. 'But don't pin your hopes too high on a lot of bricks without straw. He could be using yet another name. How would you find him there? Wander round, hoping to spot an ageing eccentric? You'd find your work cut out for you.'

Her doubts served not to depress me, but to urge me on. Those seagulls were still in my mind, calling me down there. I had to go, and I had to find something to go for.

'I can start with the telephone directory.'

She did not reply, which made me the more obstinate. 'The worst that can happen is that I come back with a number of fleas in my ear,' I continued, and she grinned, realising there was no stopping me.

I collected quite a few fleas until I perfected my telephone approach. It was a tricky job, for if Richard was there, he wasn't going to respond to my eager request. I had to put up more antennae than the Rab-Hits.

'I'm trying to track down someone I met in Australia some years ago by the name of Frank Penrose.' The reason I gave was a wishy-washy story about his knowing the whereabouts of a good friend. Mostly I was treated as a harmless idiot, and by the time I'd pared down my shortlist a week later, I was down to three.

Frank Penrose Number One refused to give me any information at all over the phone; he was nicely secluded out on the moors near Zennor. The wife of Frank Penrose Number Two said he never talked about Australia, which was hopeful. He was in St Ives itself. And Frank Penrose Number Three, who lived in Paul near Mousehole, said he didn't believe in the past but admitted he'd been to Australia. I quite warmed to this one, since it was a strange thing to go to Cornwall – where the past is all around one – if one didn't believe in history.

I was all for leaping in the car and taking off immediately, but Margaret and common sense persuaded me to wait for a few days to think my theory through. I reluctantly agreed, since my work load was heavy, and used the time to digest everything I'd been told. A week later, I was still hooked on Cornwall, so I headed the car westwards.

I decided that Paul was as good a place as any to start, and until those seagulls got out of my ears, I wasn't going to be able to take anywhere else seriously. Half of me itched to stay, in case Ellie suddenly appeared; the other half was determined to get this nightmare over and done with first.

The drive to Cornwall is a long one from Sussex and I had plenty of time to reflect on my foolishness in chasing seagulls who would probably turn out to be wild geese. I was committed, however, and as I drove over the Tamar and Cornwall lazily greeted me, I relaxed into the slower pace of life. I decided to take the longer route past St Austell rather than the A30 in order to savour the full atmosphere of Cornwall. It was the same difference as avoiding the autoroute from Paris to the Riviera and taking the old N7 instead, with the wonders of Provence gradually creeping up on you.

I'd booked a room for the first night in Mousehole. I parked in the large car park at the entrance to the village and walked down the narrow street, following its ninety-degree bends until suddenly the whole panorama of harbour and village was displayed before me like the unveiling of a painting. I strolled around the village, gradually becoming reacquainted with it. I wasn't seeing Frank Penrose Number Three until tomorrow morning – indeed I'd had to use all my powers of persuasive charm to get any kind of permission to see any of my three shortlisted targets. With one of them I'd had to call in Sadie O'Grady to clinch the deal. As her creator, I sometimes got street cred from unexpected quarters.

I walked up the hill to the bird hospital, and in through the iron gate to its enchanting garden. Since it was first founded in the 1920s by the Yglesias sisters, this bird hospital has always been a tribute to life. If an injured bird's flying days are over, it can find sanctuary here for the rest of its life.

After I walked round the hospital, I stood on the steps looking out over Mount's Bay towards the fairy-tale St Michael's Mount. In my ears was the sound of birdsong – not seagulls and seabirds alone, but blackbirds, robins, sparrows, all joining together. It did not seem fanciful then that, if Richard

Hart had heard this song as he walked the wilds of Australia, he could have come back to this place, seeking his own sanctuary.

The next morning I woke up heartened for the day ahead, assuring myself that one of the three jokers *must* be Richard. I walked up the steep hill to Paul, so steep that all the glorious views of Mount's Bay couldn't hide the fact. When I reached the village, I strolled past the church and pub and down the road where my fellow who didn't believe in the past lived.

How could that be? The old church bore testimony to past centuries – outside it was a memorial to Dorothy Pentreath, the last speaker of the Cornish language, and Celtic cross and stones lay on the quiet farmland around. How could one live here and not believe in the past? Maybe, I decided, it was because past and present were indistinguishable in such villages. Or, more likely, I admitted, this Frank Penrose was just a jerk who couldn't appreciate what he'd got around him.

When I met 'FP3', as I mentally dubbed him, I understood exactly why the past and he did not agree. He was a morose man in his forties who'd left Australia after a divorce five years ago.

The weak points of my campaign were that I could not say exactly when I'd been in Australia, since I had no idea when, if at all, Richard had left the country. Putting my visit back too far would necessitate reasons for wanting so urgently to contact someone who was merely the friend of a friend. Making the visit too recent might obscure a major contender for my quarry if Richard had departed from Australia before that date. Nor could I ask my FPs how old they were. Richard was born in 1942 and so would now be nearly sixty – yet my targets might well be much younger.

I walked back down to Mousehole feeling pleased, nevertheless. At least something was settled, even if negatively. I would drive on to St Ives for the night. This is easier said than done, for the roads in St Ives itself are not conducive to heavy tourist traffic, so I found a room on the edge of the town on the road to Carbis Bay. Then I walked down into St Ives to see FP2.

Instead of FP2, however, I only met the wife, a slow-moving, rosy-cheeked Cornishwoman in her late forties, who apologetically explained that her husband had had to have a tooth pulled out urgently and could I come back some other time? I managed to elicit from her that her husband was six feet tall and had been born in Australia sixty-eight years ago. I made my excuses and left.

So my only hope was FP1, he of the open moors. It sounded promising. Zennor is a small village and its position, tucked inland from the sea and surrounded by moors, was ideal for those who seek solitude. FP1 fitted in with that. The fact that he had refused to see me at first, and had only agreed to see me because he was a cartoon fan, also made me optimistic. Artistic tastes, I noted, trying to ignore the obvious corollary that he also had something in common with me.

My first impression when he opened the door was hopeful. He was short, fair-haired, and about the right age. There was no sign of any family, nor was there a piano. Still, that didn't mean he didn't have – or had – musical tastes. I worked the conversation round to pop singers.

'Classical man myself.'

'Have you ever performed on stage?'

He found that very amusing. 'No, I paint a bit though.' It wasn't an answer, and so I persevered, my reasons for doing so gradually wearing very thin.

Finally, he lost his patience with me, opened his mouth and launched into 'Your Tiny Hand is Frozen'. There was no doubt about it – he was tone deaf and it wasn't faked. We got on quite well after that. I even considered telling him the real reason I wanted to find Frank Penrose. I held it back, since one whiff of that, and Richard Hart would slip away before I could get to him.

I went back to St Ives in a savage mood. Margaret said it was a daft idea to come, and it was.

It was only as I was halfway through my fisherman's lunch in the pub that I made the connection I needed. *Margaret said.* Margaret had also said that she had spent her married life fending off unwanted visitors. Just like the wife of FP2. And – I almost choked on a mackerel bone in my excitement – I only had Mrs Penrose's word for FP2 being six foot tall and sixty-eight years old. What if . . .

I would call again. I tried to curb my impatience, however. If FP2 was not Richard, he wouldn't want to have visitors too soon after having his tooth pulled out; if he was, he might well have gone out till tomorrow to be on the safe side. His wife had said to call again, but clearly the stage was set for him being 'out' for good.

To hell with patience, I would strike while the iron was hot. I went down several flights of the steps characteristic of St Ives and into the town centre again. There are numerous studios in St Ives, many now adorned with hanging baskets and fancy name plates. The fact that FP2 had none was an encouraging sign. I rang the bell by mistake. No answer. I remembered that this morning I couldn't hear it ring inside. That fitted Richard too.

I used the knocker and once more Mrs Penrose came to the door.

'I wonder if your husband's feeling up to seeing me now?' I asked blandly.

'He's not, me handsome.' Her soft Cornish accent seemed a direct challenge to me. Placid she might look, but daft she was not.

'Could I call back tomorrow?'

'You can that, but very busy is Frank. May be out. Why don't you write to him?'

'Have you an e-mail address?' I wasn't giving up this easily.

She laughed at that. 'What would we be doing with that for – we don't even use postcodes down here.' Suddenly her manner changed, and from good humour she became uneasy. It was none of my doing, so what could have caused it? Her eyes had shifted from me; I was aware that there were footsteps in the narrow lane and that a man was walking not to the house, but past it, whistling. So what? Save that whistling is unusual nowadays.

Of course he was going *past*. He could see a stranger at the door!

I spun round and took a leap into his path, blocking it and seizing his hand with every ounce of the Irish in me (or not). 'Frank Penrose, to be sure. I know it to be you.'

Unhappy eyes in an unremarkable middle-aged face looked into mine and away again.

I was face to face with the Mighty Rich.

I leaned on the railing and gazed out to sea. The harbour looking over towards the Island was to the left; to the right lay grassy cliffs towering over the blue sea. I wondered if Robert Louis Stevenson had ever been to Cornwall. 'I will make a palace fit for you and me/Of green days in forests and blue days at sea.'

Richard Hart was at my side, at least physically. It was hard to tell where he was emotionally, and it had been difficult to get him even this far. I had said, not wishing to scare him off, that I wanted to talk about Australia. We had acquaintances in common, and I thought he might know where one of them was. It was only a slight embellishment of the truth.

He had just stared at me. He was several inches shorter than I am, and his thinning fair hair was greying fast. The face was lined, which usually gives clues to personality, but somehow his did not. It was probably because of the grey eyes that, even when looking at me, seemed to be keeping their distance. His clothes – chinos and a field jacket – didn't help pin him down either. Yet for all the anonymity of his looks, I think I'd have been aware of a personality behind that face, even had I not known who he was.

I had assumed that I would be invited into the cottage. I wasn't. 'Let's walk,' he said.

I belatedly realised that he would feel trapped in the four walls of his cottage. Here, there was at least the possibility of escape. We walked through the lanes to the Market Place and past the parish church, and I assumed he was making for the harbour. Instead we twisted round another few bends and down to this tiny tarmacked opening to the sea between buildings. To the right a cluster of cottages on a steep one-track road called the Warren looked far more interesting to me. But it was space Richard Hart liked, not quaintness.

There, leaning over the railing, with the rocks and sea below us and the sea and sky beyond, we listened together to the sound of the seagulls calling in the mild May air. To me they had a triumphant note in their calls now. I couldn't go on with tales of a friend of a friend. Voices are important though, and so I made mine unthreatening.

'I know who you really are.'

'Were.' He replied without surprise or anger.

'The past is always there.'

'Not so far as I'm concerned.'

I believed him. I don't know what I expected, but he asked me not one word about why I wanted to find the Mighty Rich. He left it to me to make the running and now that I was here, the running was slowing to a crawl. 'It no longer seems so urgent,' I said. 'We can take it gently.'

He turned to me for the first time with some interest, but not enough to make me feel that I could continue onto the quicksand right away.

'What do you do now?' I asked.

He seemed amused. 'I look, I am.'

'Nothing more?'

'Yes. I listen.'

'And make sound yourself, presumably. You still sing and play, even if not under your real name?'

'There's no need.'

'Because' – I grappled my way to the light, trying to understand – 'you have it all here?'

'Something like that.' There was music in his voice as he answered.

Rightly or wrongly I brought the conversation down to earth again. 'And your wife? Do you have a family?'

'Jessie? Yeah. There's a daughter.'

'But how—' I wanted to ask how he supported his family, how he could speak so impersonally of his daughter, how, presumably, he could blank out his own family past. For all he knew, he was still married to Margaret. I stopped, because we were not yet at the point where I could ask such questions.

'How, what, where, and when/Are the most annoying of men.' He seemed to sense what I was thinking. 'They disturb everything, don't you agree?'

I did, but most of us haven't the luxury of ignoring them.

'Is, now, here and you/Are tried and trusty, strong and true,' he continued.

'Is that one of your lyrics?' I asked drily. 'I don't think it would make number one.'

'It should,' he said seriously. 'Anyway, I just made it up.'

I was waiting for him to ask who I was, what I wanted, was I a fan? I waited a long time and would wait for ever, I realised, if I slipped into the enchanted wood where Frank Penrose had built his log cabin. A seagull, busily attacking half a sandwich thrown onto the rocks by some passer-by, glanced up at me proudly, as if to point out the sluggardly nature of my progress compared with his. I silently informed it that I had a different problem. The Mighty Rich let fall no crumbs to gobble. I had to gamble, and I did.

'Cecilia says you painted, as well as writing poetry and singing. This is a fine place for both.'

The knuckles of the fist that grasped the railing grew tighter. He could be in no doubt now that I had come out of the past he had left behind, and whose existence he denied.

'That's really past life,' was all he observed, however. 'I dabble, that's all.'

My frustration grew. This stone-walling had to stop. 'I'm an animator, a cartoonist. Fantasy worlds.'

'Want me as a model?' The first glimpse of humour I had seen in him.

'I'm here on personal business. *My* personal business, which unfortunately is mixed up with yours.'

'Blackmail?' he asked without venom. 'No point. I'd just move on.'

'And leave all this? Leave the dream you've found? I envy you,' I added sincerely. 'Not many of us achieve that.' I thought I had when I married Ellie, but it had cracked wide open.

Slowly Richard uncoiled himself from his hunched position. 'Dreams are in the mind.'

He smiled for the first time, and I saw immediately why everybody had liked the Mighty Rich. His smile, which began in his eyes, wrapped you round with tenderness and warmth. It was genuine, or so I told myself. I couldn't believe he laid this on for all his fans, although maybe that's exactly what each and every one of them thought too. As Margaret had. That thought steeled me. He owed her, and he wasn't going to slip from my grasp.

'And I take my dream wherever I go,' he continued.

'Once I've found out what I need to, I shall go for good . . . and keep your secret. So don't leave here – there's no need.'

'I'll judge that.' A pause. 'How's Margaret?' he asked casually, having obviously made the leap some while ago.

'I'm married – technically – to her daughter Ellie.'

He looked up sharply at me, and I realised I had unwittingly shot an arrow through the armour. He was wondering if Margaret might have been pregnant when he walked out.

'Not your daughter,' I reassured – or, who knows, disappointed – him. 'She married again. You're divorced in case you don't realise, not to mention presumed dead.'

'I read the papers. Richard Hart is dead.'

'To you, maybe.' A definite snarl crept into my voice, which I could not keep out. 'Unfortunately he has a way of cropping up.'

'Forget him. I have.'

I couldn't hold on to my temper any longer. 'I wish I could, damn you. It's you who's responsible for my wife having left me.'

He looked puzzled, as indeed he might. 'Explain, if you please,' he asked politely.

'Your son, Marcus Quinn Hart. My name's Quinn and I'm adopted.'

Now that it was out, I could hardly bear to watch his expression. Not that I appeared to have given him a mighty blow. He looked disturbed, but unlikely either to seize me in an embrace or burst into tears. Perhaps that was because he knew Marcus *hadn't* been adopted. Why, he might be wondering, did Ellie and I think I might be his son? On the other hand, perhaps he just didn't care, crazy though that might seem. I had to play fair.

'*I* don't think I'm your son. Margaret doesn't think so either. The problem is that Ellie does.'

He turned those unreadable eyes on me again. 'Let me think this out. I'll meet you here tomorrow—'

'No way,' I said firmly. 'I don't want you upping and leaving St Ives to forget all about it.'

He shouted with laughter. 'Me? What have they been telling you?'

'Quite a lot. And you admitted the same yourself earlier.'

'Then I daresay it's true. Point taken. But let's get out of here.'

'We could go to a café, or your home, or my hotel.'

'The moors. They put things in perspective. Got a car?'

'Yes, don't you?'

'An old banger. I fancy you drive a BMW or a Porsche. Might as well do it in style.'

'I've a Honda Civic.'

'Okay.' He grinned. 'That'll do. At least we'll get there. Remember that song, "You'll never get to heaven in a beat-up wreck"?' He chatted amicably about life in St Ives as we drove out to Zennor again where my other FP lived. I described my cartoon work, and added some information about the Coinmakers but not, mindful of my undertaking, about Gossage. He didn't seem interested in how I found out about his being in Australia, though I had a story ready about sightings by his fan club. I deemed it not tactful to discuss Margaret – and, more to the point, Marcus – too soon, but I was waiting. Oh yes, I was waiting.

The tourist season hadn't yet begun, and before we went on to the moors he insisted on showing me the famous pew end in Zennor church with the carved mermaid.

'The mermaid of Zennor,' he murmured. 'Just right for you. Fantasy world of folklore. Sang her siren song to lure young men into the sea with her, and then for love she came out of the sea one day. And died. Like the Mighty Rich.'

I tried hard to see a parallel but failed, and it struck me that perhaps there wasn't, and that it was merely a device to build up his armour again.

At last we were on the moors, miles of gorse and bracken, and in the distance the sea. Stones lay all around us; each one of them might have come from a prehistoric beehive-shaped home, or from a cross or cairn. We walked in history here, and whether Frank Penrose believed Richard Hart dead or not, was but an infinitesimal speck in the annals of time.

'I have to know – and I have for humanity's sake to tell Margaret and Ellie – what happened to Marcus,' I said at last. 'Is he dead or alive? Margaret told everyone that Marcus was dead.'

He was hunched up in his field jacket, whether against the wind or my barrage of questions.

'It was the only way she could deal with it,' I continued.

'She hopes against hope that he's alive, well, and that you're in touch with him.'

'Why should I rake all this up?' He frowned, talking, it seemed, to himself as much as to me.

'One very good reason.'

'Your marriage?'

'No. Margaret's kept all this to herself all these years, and she deserves to know the truth. So does Cecilia.'

'Ah. How is Cecilia? I'm glad she's still going.'

I took his unspoken point to give him breathing space. With great restraint on my part, I entertained him with stories about the Flowerdews, the museum and the biography. He thought highly of Uncle Ted's extravagances.

'I liked Ted.' Pause. 'Do I come into the biography?'

'Only as Margaret's husband. According to you, the Mighty Rich is dead anyway. No problem. You're Frank Penrose. How did you manage it, by the way?'

'Bought a passport in Nepal.'

'But how does that tie up with pension records, work permits . . . ?' The complications seemed endless.

'I don't bother with all that.'

'You're fortunate.'

'Jessie works. I work.'

'At what?'

'Here and there. Cooking in the season, helping, arranging art shows, whatever I fancy. Sold ice creams last summer. All right, I'll tell you about the boy,' he added with no change of inflexion.

Whatever came now, at least it was the end one way or another, but I was screwed up with tension.

'I took Marcus to this gig – forget where it was. The band was there too, and I didn't want to get in a hassle with them, so I was going straight back home. This manager of mine was around too, and he was coming on too heavy. Telling me what I should do, where I should play—'

'That's what managers are for,' I pointed out.

'My soul's my own. So I thought I'd avoid him. Then as I was coming out I started talking to this flower-child hippie. He was a fan of mine, he said. Anyway, I couldn't get away, and he started talking about Woodstock, which was due to take place in a couple of weeks' time in the USA. I'd been reading about it in magazines, but that's not the same as having someone light you up face to face. He talked and talked about it, said it would be the biggest party of all time, a microcosm of the world as it should be, all peace and happiness. I missed Monterey in '67, and even though no one could guess then how big an event Woodstock was going to turn out, I knew I had to go. I knew it was something Marcus should see.'

'So you went there to contribute your bit?'

'No. I just wanted to be there. Part of the experience. To listen. Joan Baez, Ravi Shankar, The Who, The Grateful Dead, Jimi Hendrix. It seemed as though it might be the nirvana of sound – see what I mean?'

'I think so.'

'All the sounds of the world coming together. I knew I had to go, and *now*, and this fellow asked me for a lift. His van had broken down and he had a cheap passage already booked, which we could make if we set straight off. It took a week or two to get there by this sea route, and it was already the end of July. It was too good a chance to miss.'

'But what about Marcus? And what about passports?' I began to feel a real fuddy-duddy in this story.

'I meant *Marcus* shouldn't miss it. He would get the experience too.'

'He was three years old, for heaven's sake. He needed his mother.'

'The right time. Immerse a child in peace at three and he'll never make war. Marcus never took to the gigs much, though I never told Margaret that. But this was different. A big musical party in the open, junk food and music – a kid's dream. So we went. I always carried a passport in case I went straight off to a gig across the Channel, I already had a visa for the States, and the passport had Marcus on it, so no problem.'

I was literally open-mouthed. 'You didn't even ring Margaret.'

'I told – I thought I did anyway – Will Gossage to ring her. I knew she'd understand.'

'He didn't. And she didn't.'

'Ah. I had this row with Gossage. Maybe I forgot to tell him about Margaret, or maybe he forgot to tell her. He was mad at me for not falling in with his latest plan. I wanted to follow my soul in music, not climb a Jacob's Ladder to Gossage's idea of paradise, which was perching on top of the hit parade.'

'So you went. And what was it like?'

I tried to keep irony out of my voice. I had to try and see it on his terms. It was a banal question, but views on Woodstock ranged from its being a nigh criminal activity – a threat to world order as we knew it – to an experience that changed participants' lives and the world itself. Some saw it as a *Götterdämmerung* to the passing of the flower children's dream of a better world. At the next pop festival in December '69 at Altamont Speedway, which was meant to be another Woodstock, the heavy brigade moved in. The end of innocence.

It was then I remembered something, in all its sickening clarity. I'd had this recurring nightmare when I was young. It began before I was left at the orphanage, or I think it did. As I grew up, I'd had vague images of animals, of toys, of people around in my very early life, but nothing concrete – except for this one glaring image of a huge crowd of people and noise. In the nightmare the people came closer and closer, the noise louder and louder, until I ran. Then there was a dark hole, and outside I could hear the noise coming nearer. I always woke up then, screaming. It must have gone on till I was seven or eight or so; then the security of my home made it disappear, and I forgot it. Until now.

The frightening thought now came to me that the noise was

Woodstock, but I banished it. I *knew* I wasn't Marcus, and I had to hang on to that at all costs, or my marriage was finished.

'Like?' Richard picked up my word, but not the irony. 'As if all the dreams of the world united together and said "Sing, man, sing". It began at five o'clock on the Friday – just as we were finally parked – and never stopped for nearly three days. Time didn't mean much, only the music. It all synthesised into one glorious sound.'

'Did you sing, after all, when you got there?' I knew a little about Woodstock, and couldn't remember the Mighty Rich. I schooled myself to keep this conversation at his pace and not demand to know about Marcus until he chose to tell me.

'No. I was going to fill in when they had gaps in the programme, but I decided I wouldn't. From the first moment we arrived, on the Friday in a great traffic jam, all of us trying to get parked, to sort ourselves out, you could already hear the music. Richie Havers it was; the other performers couldn't get there in time because of the jams. It was like that poem, *The Pied Piper of Hamelin*. We were like the children of Hamelin – we couldn't follow the piper's music quickly enough. And those of us who managed it, who kept up with the music, had the mountain door shut fast behind us, and we never did go home.'

'You certainly didn't.'

'I'm trying to explain how it was,' he said mildly.

'Sorry.' I'd slipped there in my exasperation. 'Go on.' All this must have a purpose, I assumed, and fascinating though it was in its own right, I was intent on what came next.

'So there was music day and night; we slept, ate – if we could find any food.'

I longed to ask about the welfare of a three-year-old boy, but managed to hold my peace this time.

'We got friendly with one of the food van ladies, so that was okay,' he continued.

'You and Marcus?'

'I joined up with some folks from the States and we messed about together. There was a kid around for Marcus to play with, so he was happy. We were all on the same wavelength.'

He couldn't be stopped now, and I didn't interrupt him as he talked about the music, the rain, the mud, the squalor and the splendour.

'Massive crowds, half a million – the planned organisation never happened. Ticket booths never got set up, so it was free entrance, food was rushed in as emergency supplies, and all the time the music. The whole place stank of pot, but that helped us forget the mud. There was Janis Joplin screaming out all the joy and pain of life, like we all want to do but keep bottled up. I tell you, we saw the road ahead was for the young, and we were put in the driving seat at Woodstock.

'On the Monday we tidied up. We couldn't believe it when the music stopped, and we had to join the traffic jam trying to get out. Mile after mile, and we didn't give a damn.'

It was time to ask the question. 'How about Marcus?'

'Oh, he loved it. Cried a bit, got a bit scared, but the music . . . Oh, he took to that particularly – he was listening. He liked living in the same clothes and not being told to wash his face. Loved it. I'd hopes of his taking up music in a big way. Woodstock would change everything, his life and mine.'

Too right, I thought sadly. I'd been patient enough, and I asked the question:

'So what happened to him?'

'I lost him.'

Twelve

'He *lost* him? That's all he said?' Margaret repeated my words incredulously.

'There was more, of course. I made him explain.' It sounded inadequate even to me. Being face to face with Margaret was harder by far than with Richard, and the result was that what in Cornwall had sounded outrageous enough now seemed completely ludicrous.

I had had a long time while driving back from Cornwall to consider how and what I should tell Margaret. After all, I had no direct line to her private feelings. For all she'd said, did she perhaps still hold a romantic dream of her first husband, which was bound into her anguish at losing her child? However much she loved Gerald, such feelings could remain dormant until disturbed – which, by tracking down Richard, I had done.

Back in Sussex, it seemed hard to believe, firstly, that I'd actually met him, and, secondly, that even after I'd met him, I was still not sure who the devil I was. The probabilities of my being Marcus were reduced, but far from annihilated, and that childish nightmare recalled from the distant past was always there to remind me of the fact.

Fortunately Gerald was nowhere around when I drew up at Kingsgate House, and since I only wanted to deal with one of them at a time, I was glad. Two pairs of accusing – or hopeful – eyes would be too much to take on so soon. Margaret came flying to the door at the sound of my car – it has a distinctive roar of its own – and five minutes later we were closeted in her studio and I was recounting to her what had happened. I

187

could hardly delay telling her, much as I'd have liked to get my bearings first.

'It wasn't in itself unusual,' I began. 'In that scrum it apparently happened to a lot of kids.'

'Lost for ever?' Margaret chipped in, straight to the heart of the matter.

'No,' I admitted.

'Tell me the whole story, Quinn.' She was keeping herself under control but it wouldn't take much, I realised, to tip her over the edge.

'It happened on the Monday morning. It was just one continuous party, and sleep and food were incidental, he said.'

'Even for Marcus?'

'I suppose so. With the half a million people swarming around, the children had to stay with their parents throughout. It was all part of the experience, Richard said.'

Margaret made no comment, but her thoughts were crystal clear.

'On the Monday morning the music eventually stopped.'

I remembered how Richard had described it. 'That was the moment,' he'd said, 'when the whole thing climaxed. Jimi Hendrix singing *The Star-Spangled Banner*. After that, the music stopped, or if there was any more, I don't remember it. It was the end and the beginning. We packed up and made for our transport, with a kind of optimism for the world again. The party wasn't over; it would stay right with us, for it had eaten into us, deep down.'

To try to describe Woodstock to Margaret as Richard had seen it would sound like an apology for his actions, however. I had to be neutral, and to the point.

'The problem about the end of Woodstock was that no one knew where their cars were. Richard was lucky in that his van wasn't too far away and he was able to make his way there on foot, even with Marcus. But it was a scrum, as cars were all jammed in together, everyone was carrying gear with them, and a great many people were simply lost, milling about hoping to see someone or something they recognised. Marcus had been complaining he was hungry, but there was no going back to the food stall, so Richard ignored him. Then suddenly he realised Marcus wasn't with him, and reckoned he must be trying to get back to the friendly food stall. Richard dropped everything and fought his way back, but there was no sign of him.'

'Was he on drugs?' Margaret asked fiercely.

'He says only pot, and the stuff they were selling there was mostly bogus anyway.'

'He'd tried acid, you know.'

'He says not there.' Helplessly, I watched her bleeding inwardly for her lost child. I'd known it would be bad, but not this bad, and the worst of it was there wasn't a thing I could do about it.

'So what did he do then?' she asked quietly.

'He just waited until the crowds cleared, telling anyone he came across to look out for Marcus. The food stall hadn't seen him. He wasn't with any of the organisers. He reported it to the police—'

'And then he drove off?' Margaret interrupted bitterly.

'No. He said he hung around for days – nothing. The police did everything they could, but eventually he had to face the fact that Marcus was gone.'

'Oh.' From that terrible strangled gasp, it was clear that Margaret realised all the implications. Even in those days there were paedophiles around, though they had a lower profile.

'He couldn't face coming home to tell you.' It was hard to say it so bluntly when I myself had hurled fury on her behalf at Richard. He had taken it without comment, which had frustrated me even more.

'No, I see that. He wouldn't,' she said dully. 'So he just went. How bloody, bloody, *like* him. I understand now. I should have understood a long time ago.'

It was more than I did. I still found the whole story mind-chillingly inexplicable.

'What did Richard do then?' she continued. 'Forget about Marcus? Tell me about him – Richard, I mean.'

'He said he thought he'd take up Gossage's offer of the French tour after all. It would give him time to think things out.'

'I doubt if Richard ever thought anything out in his life.'

'Then Gossage turned up in Paris,' I continued doggedly, 'banging on about Richard's future and so on. It was all too much for Richard. He couldn't tell Gossage the full story, of course.'

'Of course not.'

'But he said he was back in the trap,' I explained hurriedly. 'Caught in the race up the ladder of fame. Woodstock had made him see how empty a goal that was, and merely to be back on the stage in Paris reminded him of the past. I suppose he set out to find himself by going to Nepal, and finding the path to a new life.'

'Pity he hadn't devoted more time to finding his son,' Margaret said sadly, though without venom.

'I think – I *honestly* think, Margaret – that he tried, but, as you said yourself, he couldn't take responsibility.'

'You said he has a daughter now. Presumably he does for her.'

'More probably his wife does it for him.'

'Does she know who he is?'

'Yes, but not the daughter, apparently.'

'Poor woman, poor girl,' Margaret said feelingly.

How could I tell her the wife at least looked happy, and that Richard himself was happy?

'Did you tell Richard that we'd keep his secret from the press?'

'Yes.'

She sighed. 'I suppose that's right. I wouldn't put it past him to up and run again now that we know where he is. Not that I care if he does. We've found out what happened now. Thanks to that, I know that even if my son is still alive, I have no chance of ever finding him now.'

'Unless,' I said bleakly, 'I'm he.'

Margaret looked startled. 'Surely you don't still think you can be Marcus?'

'The chances are reduced,' I conceded, 'since Marcus was lost in New York State and I was handed in to an orphanage in Paris a few months later. But we know it wasn't Richard who stuck me in there. His being in Paris was mere coincidence, which they say happens more often in real life than one could ever get away with in fiction.' I wasn't going to tell Margaret about that nightmare lurking around, the menace of the music. Putting voice to it would give it credibility.

'Surely once Ellie knows what happened, she will come back to you? The bounds of possibility can only go so far.' She still looked shaken at this new dimension I'd thrown in.

'I hope so, though the uncertainty would always be there.' There was a pit of ice in me as I faced this desolate fact. Ellie dancing on the fringes of my life for evermore, and never truly in my arms again – never, as the poet wrote, glad confident morning again. What lay ahead was a marriage built on shifting sands, and that could only lead to one ending. All the joyousness with which I had tracked down the Mighty Rich now evaporated, as I realised what it had brought.

'I'll talk to her,' Margaret said firmly. 'I refuse to see your lives ruined because of this.'

I'm afraid, I thought to myself; you'll need to talk to me as well. The problem with quicksand is that when you try to pull someone else out, you get sucked in yourself.

'How was he?' Margaret asked abruptly when I did not reply to her.

'Who?' I asked stupidly.

'Richard.'

So there were hidden depths, old memories. 'I liked him. I saw what you meant about his charm.'

'But what about *him*?'

191

'I can't answer that. He looked like his photographs plus thirty years, I suppose. Except . . .'

'For what?'

'That hungry eager look in his eyes. It had gone.'

'He's found what he was after.' I could not read her expression.

'I would think so.'

'I'm glad.' She laughed when she saw my startled expression. 'I really am. After all, *I'm* happy, despite all this. I found Gerald, and thereby I found my niche in the Flowerdew hierarchy – which is out of it, and into my own thing. Just like Richard. Why should I begrudge him happiness when I suppose even he must have suffered over Marcus?'

She was silent for a moment, then burst out: 'The fool, the *idiot*. Why didn't he tell me? Stupid question. With anyone else but Richard, we could have seen it through together. Instead, Johnny Head-in-the-Air decides to create a new life for himself.'

'You're generous.'

'Realistic is the word I'd use. Are you surprised?'

'Not many women could separate their regard for the man from the suffering he caused them.'

For a moment I saw tears for the first time, but she blinked them away quickly. 'You must help me, Quinn. I've got to see Ellie happy and only you can do that. You want to, don't you?'

Another stupid question. Of course I wanted to. Separation was tearing me apart, and only the thought that I was – or had been – doing something to put it right kept me going. Now that dark fear inside me was holding me back too.

'What do you propose to do next?' Margaret asked. 'Accept it, or follow it up?'

I hadn't thought beyond telling Margaret about my encounter with Richard. That hurdle was over. What came next, apart from the greater hurdle of Ellie?

'Let me make it easy for you, Quinn.' Margaret read my

expression correctly. 'We need to check Richard's story. You can follow that up. Let's just be sure he really did lose Marcus there.'

'You think he lied?'

'No. That wasn't his way, but nevertheless it's worth checking the police records.'

'You're right.' I thought for a moment. 'Stephen or John?'

'Both.'

'They're heavily involved in the museum at the moment.' The opening was less than two weeks away.

'I haven't told John yet that I'm thinking of changing sides over the biography. He can work for it.'

'Would you give in if he does?' I asked curiously. I was all too willing to see the Great Cur worsted over the biography, but I was mindful of our agreement – he had played his part, and so far I'd done nothing.

'Yes. To hell with Flowerdew hang-ups, say I, and let's get priorities straight. Ellie is ours.'

'Do you have hang-ups over your family?' It was naive of me, but I'm still surprised, even at my age, to find that childhood battles can continue throughout life.

'Washing lines full of them,' she replied cheerfully. 'Why did you think I was so against the damned biography?'

'I thought it was because of Marcus and Richard, and the truth emerging.'

'Small chance of that, even now.'

'Or because of the famous Uncle Ted.'

She snorted. 'It's time Imogen grew up, in my view. It's also high time my dear older brother got his deserts.'

'In the shape of three women chasing him and managing to catch him?'

'Certainly.'

'What's Ted like?' This was safe ground compared with Marcus.

She considered this carefully. 'He is eleven years older than me, and five years older than Columba, which for me made him a hero when I was a child. Columba has never been into hero-worship. She and Ted were the great white hopes to carry the Flowerdew torch. My father saw in them all that he tried so valiantly to achieve but couldn't. He trod the respectable middle way on the stage while vainly trying to live up to the reputation of his father. I adored my father, though. I suppose it was because we were on the same side in the Flowerdew battle. Edmund and Columba were grandfather's favourites, and I think my mother's also.'

'Was she disappointed in your father? Did she put pressure on him?'

'If she did, she never let us see it, but she was always urging Ted and Columba on – and me, too. My father didn't urge us to do anything. I was a great disappointment to my mother, and you may have noticed we're not that close even now.'

I had. At Christmas I had got on better with Cecilia than with Violet, who, though kind enough, wore a faintly supercilious air, as though she was used to better things than the charades currently on offer. Cecilia was in her element, of course.

'You probably know about Ted's early career – goodness knows what he's doing now. He went on the stage in the post-war boom of theatre, the days of the five-year plan at the Old Vic to present the entire First Folio of Shakespeare. The days of Richard Burton, Paul Scofield, John Neville, Peggy Ashcroft – all the greats. Ted was, I suppose, a sort of Richard Burton in a way, an *enfant terrible* who was tolerated because of his talent. He was cut out for the *Look Back in Anger* type of drama and the kitchen sink school, came to fame in those, went to Hollywood to make a film or two, and then disappeared in 1972. Poor Flossie wept on my shoulder a lot, since we had disappearing husbands in common.'

'Did Flossie do the same for you?'

'She would willingly have done so, but I preferred my own pillow to her shoulder. Anyway, you asked what Ted was like. To look at . . . Well, you've seen the pictures, no doubt. A shock of black hair, tall, Olivier type. Not a touch of Gielgud about him. As a person he was an enigma – at least to me, probably because I didn't see a lot of him. He was Richard gone mad in a way. He did what he wanted to do and was truly amazed if anyone got hurt or if the law got in his way. I suspect, as he saw it, taking on new wives was a way to keep them happy, and not bothering to divorce the old ones kept them happy too. They could all live in the fool's paradise that Johnny would come marching home again someday.'

'Why hadn't Flossie been called as a witness in the court case?'

'They didn't discover about her, that's why. Two of his other wives had pride of place in the Charles Merridew proceedings.'

'But wouldn't he have been recognised as Edmund Flowerdew?'

'Only by ardent London theatregoers and a few press pictures. The case wasn't heard in London. It was in Manchester, I think. Anyway, television wasn't the instant publicity machine it is today.'

'When did he take to the road?'

'When he was released from prison in the early eighties.'

'Does he sell *The Big Issue* now?'

She laughed. 'Ted would never be homeless, believe me. If he's still travelling, it would be with a Gucci suitcase, a nice little car, and a touch of the private enclosure at Ascot about him.'

'It seems incredible that he should escape notice by all his families.' It seemed more like a French farce than real life.

'It seems incredible to you and me, Quinn. But then that's because we don't see things in the Flowerdew way as do Columba, Cecilia, and even my mother. That's where my hang-ups come in. I was the child who acted so dismally that she could only be given a walk-on part. "A Flowerdew," I remember my mother saying, "*never* walks on. They stride, Margaret. Metaphorically as well as physically." I was ten years old, and I hated the stage. Even so, I was put through drama school – misery. It was hardly surprising I married Richard as soon as I could. I married at nineteen, and Richard was three years older.'

'How did you come to pottery and sculpture?'

'Through Gerald, actually. He watched me handling a statue in the garden once, and suggested I take it up. I had sculptor's hands, he said. I laughed him to scorn, but he was right. I remembered the plasticine I used to play with for hours as a child, and decided I'd give stone and clay a go. I'm no Hepworth, but I have a feeling for materials and shapes. The funny thing is, I think that comes from my mother's side of the family. Shall I put that in the biography?'

'I'll tell John you intend to play fair.'

So did I. I drove over to Charham the next day to see John, and discovered that Stephen was in the States but was expected back a few days before the grand opening.

My phone bill went up quite a few pounds that evening. I told Stephen I would ring the police myself, if he preferred, but he might carry more clout. Even in classless America, status counts for something. He agreed, and indeed it was a simple enough task – if the records still existed. I wasn't asking him to research into the annals of Woodstock, only one specific question.

It had been John's suggestion that Stephen was the best person to tackle the police, and I don't think he was just trying to escape a tedious job. He was preoccupied with museum details. Jane was looking after the catering arrangements, but he was coping with catalogues, press, new staff, credit card arrangements, souvenirs – the lot. So it was reasonably good of him to take time off to listen to me.

In return, I told him all about the Mighty Rich, under strict seal of confidence – and not telling him where Richard was living, a point that didn't escape him.

To give the creep his due, he listened attentively as I told him about Woodstock and the loss of Marcus, and I was forced to grudgingly admire his patience at such a busy time.

'When's Columba arriving?' I asked.

'Next Wednesday. She wants to be in on the final details.' John kept a straight face, though it must have been clear to him that Columba checking final details would be as much help as the bull in the proverbial china shop. 'That's the day Stephen's back,' he added.

I wondered again about John's sex life and how he and Columba fitted in with Stephen. A threesome? I banished this irreverent and irrelevant thought, and concentrated on the grand museum opening. What was my position? I'd had an invitation, but there was a problem.

'What about Ellie?' I asked. 'Is she coming on Saturday?'

'Yes.'

'Then I won't.' It was a simple decision, and one I'd made some weeks ago. Nothing had changed – or so I convinced myself. I wouldn't speak to Ellie until I was *sure*.

John frowned. 'You told me the kid was lost at Woodstock. Paris is one hell of a long way away. You can't still think you're Marcus Quinn Hart. Or is it something more?'

I ignored the latter. 'Richard was in Paris at the time I was dumped.'

'If you still think it was he who did the dumping and you're Marcus, then tell me why he should lie about it.'

'That's obvious. It would save his admitting that he took me to the orphanage.'

He considered this. 'Wrong, Quinn. Think about it. If Richard dumped you there all those years ago, why didn't he tell you and get the brownie points for restoring Margaret to her long-lost son?'

I hadn't thought of that, and a weight cautiously lifted itself from me. I wasn't going to admit that to him though. 'Who knows with Rich?' I answered. 'There could be any number of reasons.' One of those reasons I was definitely not going to share with the Mighty John.

'After this museum's launched, and depending on what Stephen finds out, I'll do some scouting around.'

'Thanks.' Time ticked away, and although Ellie was tantalisingly nearer, she seemed even more unreachable.

'Don't mention it. Margaret rang me last night to tell me she'll co-operate with the biography if I help you.'

In his polite – smarmy – way he was telling me that I could go to hell. He was doing this not for me, or for Ellie, but for the bloody biography.

'Come to the opening, Quinn. There'll be a mass of people besides Ellie. You never need meet.'

Some hopes. Wherever she was, I'd sense it, and I'd be drawn to her whether I liked it or not. But once there, once face to face with my lovely Ellie, what would I say? What *could* I say?

I hoped that Stephen would ring before he arrived but feared he wouldn't, since he isn't a great telephoner. This time, to my relief, he did oblige. His voice sounded light and breezy, obviously because he was about to leave to join his beloved Columba.

'Stephen here. How are you, Quinn?'

We got through the formalities, which I thought would never end.

'Have you news?' I was able to ask at last.

'I don't know whether it's good or bad for you, Quinn, but I can tell you your information was right. On the police records there was a three-year-old child who was never traced. A boy. Name of Quinn.'

We were at the end of the road. I could in theory reclaim my Ellie – save for that one dark shadow of uncertainty.

Thirteen

'Have you told Ellie yet?' Margaret demanded for the umpteenth time. With the museum opening looming only two days away, she had ample justification.

'Not yet.' A feeble admission to have to make. Fortunately Margaret didn't, as most people reasonably would, immediately say, 'Why not?' or 'Then I will.' Instead she asked – perceptive woman that she is – 'What's wrong, Quinn?'

I couldn't even answer that. How could I say there was still a doubt in my mind, simply because of that damned nightmare about music that had resurrected itself? Rationally it could have been anything – a pub jukebox or an over-loud car radio that had been frightening to a child's ears. But there it was. I tried to convince myself that it was due to false memory syndrome, but it was too specific, too unheralded for that. It had not grown gradually during the months of uncertainty over my background, but come unannounced, reawakened by a few careless words from the Mighty Rich.

All I could reply to Margaret was, 'I'll be seeing Ellie on Saturday.'

Once I had said it, I realised I was trapped. I could no longer play with the idea of avoiding confrontation by not going to the museum opening. I had to go, and Ellie would be there. What would she be expecting? Not me, that was for sure. She obviously had no idea I was living with her parents, although she rang them from time to time or met them in London. Would she be hoping to see me? Or would she dread the mere possibility that I might be there? On the

199

few occasions I'd seen Jane, it had been hard not to ask after Ellie, but I saw no reason for involving Jane in our private mess. John was a different matter, though I hadn't let on to him that I'd heard from Stephen. I was postponing that till Saturday as well.

And now Saturday was today. I decided I'd travel separately from Margaret and Gerald – just in case, I told them awkwardly. Located somewhere between sweet dreams of packing a reconciled Ellie into my car and driving into the sunset and nightmares in which we were parted for ever was the knowledge that I needed to be on my own and not with Ellie's parents.

When I arrived at Charham Place I drove past the Lodge quickly, looking ahead and not at our former home. Once I'd parked it was easier, and to my surprise my own two feet carried me forward to whatever lay ahead.

Stephen, or rather John and Jane on his behalf, had set up a marquee on the lawn as a hospitality tent, and by the time I arrived quite a crowd was enjoying Stephen's best champagne. The museum itself and its tea-room weren't big enough for today's spree, apparently, which had all the hallmarks of one of Ellie's weddings rather than a museum opening.

The sun was out, and looked as if it was going to stay around to see what was going on. Spring flowers were just giving way to early roses, and Charham Place was doing its utmost to remind everyone that this was Old England at its best.

I couldn't appreciate it to the full, however, because I had my Rab-Hit antennae tuned in to spot Ellie at three hundred paces. I knew I had to get myself into that tent, but all the 'supposes' in my head were fighting me. Well, I was still almost a Flowerdew, so I decided to stride in, not walk.

Once inside the marquee entrance, I felt more able to cope. It was a mixed crowd – I knew that every Flowerdew plus spouse or partner and offspring who could be contacted had been invited, as well as leading critics, local press and theatre stars and directors who had a direct link with the Flowerdews. John had told me there was even an ancient wardrobe mistress coming who, as a young girl, had had the privilege of attending Sir Claud in his final years in the 1930s at his beloved Albion Theatre; there was also an old thespian who had played Mamillius to Sir Claud's Leontes in *The Winter's Tale*. Columba's television cronies were well in evidence, of course, for Columba – who else – was formally to open the museum at two o'clock, by which time all the non-drivers at least should be in rip-roaring form on champagne.

Waiters were speeding around with trays of drinks and buffet tables groaned at one end of the tent under platefuls of food, whose style I recognised. It was that of Ellie's chief, much-prized caterer. The waiter who served – almost threw – a drink to me was straight out of *Fawlty Towers*: dark hair, moustache, and air of anxious incompetence. It crossed my anxious mind that Stephen might have hired him specially, but he merely looked puzzled when I joked about 'Manuel'.

Stephen had detached himself from the group he was with and come to greet me. I appreciated it.

'Thanks for your help in the US, Stephen.'

He looked pleased. 'Glad everything's all right between you and Ellie now.'

He must know more than I did. 'Is she here?' I tried to sound casual.

'I thought you'd come together.' He was surprised. 'I've seen her somewhere.'

'She doesn't actually know yet,' I admitted.

Stephen's surprise turned to worry. 'I guess she does now. I told her – anyway, I referred to it. I assumed she'd know.'

I should have realised that could happen. 'I haven't told her the good news yet. I was keeping it till today.' It sounded fairly feeble even to me. Why the hell had I come? Stupid even to think that. Of course I had no choice. Sometime, somewhere, I had to tell Ellie about the Mighty Rich and Marcus Quinn's loss in the US, regardless of whether we got together again or not. Now she knew, but not from me. I could blame no one but myself.

Margaret waved to me across the tent and I gave her a thumbs-up to show I was on top of the situation. It reassured her if not me. She was with her mother, who was holding court in one corner of the tent on one of the dozen or so comfy sofas thoughtfully imported for the occasion. Cecilia was in the other corner holding her own court. Occasionally one or other of their voices could be heard holding forth over the general noise level, and then the other one, determined to keep in the race, would raise hers even higher.

'Hallo, Quinn.'

I jumped, distracted from my hunt for Ellie, as I was accosted by a stalwart brunette of forty or so whom I didn't immediately recognise. She was clad in an old-fashioned two-piece and staring at me with earnest eyes. I made up for my belated recognition with heartiness.

'Good to see you, Imogen.'

She surveyed me for a few moments and then told me helpfully, 'Ellie's here.'

The word had obviously gone round the clan. Now I was back in the game of who knew what, and I had to play it.

'Splendid. Where?'

She turned round and waved vaguely in the direction of the museum. 'Last time I saw her she was going off with John. I think she wanted to talk about the biography.'

'How's it going? Any further forward?' Anything to get off the subject of Ellie.

'A shift towards the ayes,' she answered. 'That's good. I can sell it in the shop. For once I'll be able to wave the Flowerdew flag myself as bookseller-in-chief.'

'Were you forced through drama school like Margaret?'

She snorted. 'Not a bit of it. Mum was already telling

me the stage was no place for a lady – she should know. And in the next breath she informed me I had to uphold the Flowerdew tradition. I lumbered across the stage a few times, and decided I'd support the great old tradition in other ways.'

'With Cecilia? You do a good job.'

'It works both ways. We don't get in each other's way emotionally. I have my life, she hers, but when I'm at home I look after her.'

'That makes good sense.'

'But shows I'm not a true Flowerdew. There's not an ounce of common sense in one of them,' she said scathingly. 'Except Aunt Margaret perhaps, and even she's a little odd – fancy marrying a pop singer.'

'Maybe he was to her what Great-Aunt Cecilia is to you.'

She thought seriously about this comparison. 'I never thought of that. So that's why she's against the biography.'

'She's not now. Margaret's switched sides.' I hoped this was for public consumption.

I'd been tutored by Margaret in the Flowerdew family tree – which was extensive, since Sir Claud had seven children in all. If seven Flowerdews had seven spouses, that made a healthy number of people who could claim a stake in this biography, so I was glad someone appeared to be keeping an official tally of those for and against the biography.

'Has she? Oh, good. I am pleased.' A large grin spread over her face. 'That's one in the eye for my mother, isn't it?'

'One can see your mother's point of view.'

'Can one? How?'

I realised I was on the point of putting my foot in it with my idle comments. One could only see Flossie's point of view if one remembered she was protecting Imogen from the true story of her 'dead' father. I did my best to scramble back to terra firma.

'Some people like to keep memory green. Your mother probably sees her marriage as a memory for herself alone. She would want . . .'

I rambled on. Imogen gave me an odd look, but seemed to accept this at face value.

'I don't see it as a problem. John can write as little as Mother likes about Father. He can keep to Father's contribution to English theatre and that's that. If Flossie puts her foot down firmly with him, she can co-operate and keep her hallowed memories intact.'

'Were they hallowed?' I asked rashly.

'Don't ask me. I was only twelve when I was left father-less—'

'Excuse me,' a familiar voice interrupted us. Cecilia had left her corner and had waltzed up to spar in fine form. Today I suspected we had Lady Teazle from *A School for Scandal*, judging by the wig. I wouldn't have recognised her save for her obvious age and the fact that every two minutes she whipped off the wig to give her head an airing.

'The lavatory, if you please, Imogen,' came next in her majestic ring as she projected her request to the entire gathering, complete with a grand sweep of Lady Teazle's arm. I watched Imogen as she metaphorically scooped up Lady Teazle to conduct her to the discreet Portaloos.

'I'm glad,' followed Violet's slightly mincing but no less projected voice, 'that I have more *control* than some people.'

The light relief from Violet and Cecilia heartened me, and I deposited my glass with Mr Fawlty Towers to go in search of Ellie. There was no point in delaying it now. I would tell her . . . what? Was it premature to talk of getting together again? If I told her I still had doubts, what reason could I give other than the truth?

My tension level rose. Where would I find her, what would I say? Should I look in the new museum, or in the house itself? I found her in neither, so I retreated to the rose garden to gather the emotional strength I needed to carry on searching for her. And that's where I ran into her, by chance, marching determinedly back towards the gathering. She had been to the Lodge and this was the most direct route back to the party, she told me.

Was there a more ridiculously romantic place to meet than a rose garden? Even if the roses weren't properly out, even if the sun did choose that moment to go behind a cloud. She was dressed in pale blue, reminiscent of the dress she'd worn on our wedding day – or perhaps it was her wedding dress. I didn't spare it a second look. I shouted after her, and as she turned, the look in her eyes was enough for me.

'Quinn!'

A cannonball hurtled into my arms and stayed there, gently heaving. Or was that me? I didn't know. I didn't care. All I knew was that she was back where she belonged. With me. All my doubts flew out of that rose garden like petals on the wind.

After a while, the gentle heaves became a struggle to back out of my arms and glare up at me. 'Why didn't you tell me? Why did I have to hear it from Stephen?'

Bereft of words, I could only reply, 'I don't know.'

The glare became anxiety. 'You do want us to get together again? You do want me?'

This time my arms held her a great deal tighter in case she had any thought of slipping out of them again without my permission.

'Yes. Does this convince you?'

I rearranged my arms and face so that I could find her sweet lips again. Not only did I find them but they came to meet me, more tenderly and lovingly than ever before – or so it seemed to me at that enchanted moment.

When at last we separated she whispered, 'Do we have to?'

'*I* have to,' I said honestly. 'Rose gardens are for kissing – I can't show you here just how much I want you.'

'We could run,' she said thoughtfully.

'Run? You mean jog to get it out of our systems?' It didn't appeal.

'To the Lodge. It takes five minutes.'

I shouted with laughter. 'Only four if we run fast.'

We did. I caught her hand, pulling her in the ridiculously tight dress and high heels over the paving stones of the garden, then the grass of the lawns that divided us from the Lodge.

And then we reached our front door, our home, our paradise again.

'The key. I didn't bring my key,' I howled in anguish.

'I did,' she shouted, fumbling at the door.

We fell inside and the closed-up smell of an unloved home began to vanish as Ellie pulled me upstairs. The pulling was not through reluctance on my part – I was merely tearing my tie (formal occasion, see?) and shirt off as I went.

The bed that I'd seen as a monster all those long weeks ago now looked like a tempting paradise . . . and so it proved.

I caressed Ellie's dearly loved body as though on my way through a familiar road map to bliss. After I exploded all my passion and adoration inside her and felt hers in return, I wept on her breasts in sheer joy.

'Quinn, it's quarter to two,' Ellie yelped in my ear after an immeasurable amount of time had passed.

'Which day?' I murmured drowsily, then '*Quarter to two?*' and fell out of bed prancing around on one foot trying to get my underpants on. Ellie whipped into the bathroom and by the time we were both presentable, flushed cheeks and all, it was five minutes to the hour.

'Will we make it?' she asked in a panic.

'We'll have to run.'

We ran with considerably less enthusiasm than we'd run with in the opposite direction, and made it with half a minute to spare. When we arrived outside the museum, Columba was already at the rostrum, scissors in hand to cut the ribbon across the door. A gleam in her eye told us our arrival had been noted.

I hardly heard Columba's speech. I was still in a daze. All my resolutions had been broken and I didn't regret it for a moment.

Odd snippets of what Columba was saying came through to me: her modest reference to her own work being entirely attributable to the Flowerdew in her (for the benefit of the press); words of praise for Cecilia (genuine *and* for the press); praise for her departed father and for her departed brother (the nature of his departure being left suitably vague). Ellie squeezed my hand as Columba continued with glowing words first for Stephen and then for John the Creep and Jane. (I was almost willing to reconsider the word 'Creep', conscious that through John's help Ellie was back with me.) Then there was an announcement of the biography, and I felt Ellie's hand tighten – the starting pistol had been officially fired. And finally: 'The Flowerdews,' Columba proclaimed in ringing tones, turning to cut the ribbon. 'May the spark live on from generation to generation.'

'That's a bit much,' Ellie whispered to me. 'There's only Imogen and me in the direct line to inherit this spark. Whom do you reckon? Her or me?'

'I think she means our children.'

Ellie giggled. 'Wouldn't it be nice if we've just conceived that little spark?'

'There were a lot of them flying around,' I hissed in her ear.

The white ribbon was duly cut, and Columba walked in on Stephen's arm, followed by the élite of the theatrical profession.

Not everyone could get round at once, so the majority of us milled outside while Mr Fawlty Towers and his mates emerged from the marquee delivering glasses of champers or orange juice. I was still in a happy glow of my own, so much so that I didn't even mind when Ellie said she ought to finish the rounds of the relations. It was enough for me that we were together again, and we'd sort out the details later. Somewhere there had to be an answer, and we would find it together.

I wandered around chatting to people, and a ridiculous silly grin plastered itself on my face and refused to move. When at last the crowd had died down sufficiently for me to get into the museum, Columba collared me in the reception area. 'Take care,' she hissed at me, fingers over her lips as if she were in a 1920s drawing room comedy.

'What about? Ellie? We're fine.'

'*They're* here.'

'Who are?'

'The bastards,' she pronounced in her stage-projected voice.

'I'm lost,' I apologised. What on earth was she on about?

'I wish *they* were. Poor Flossie.' Columba was indignant. 'I want you to take care of them, Quinn, make sure they don't get near Flossie. The women are all right – she doesn't mind Joan or Patsy. It's the children. *Pooooor* Flossie.'

This repetition was having its effect. Slowly it was penetrating through to me: the other wives had turned up and presumably brought their children with them. I'm supposed to be good with children, so I asked where they were.

'There . . .' A dramatic finger pointed to a group in the video and audio room who were listening to an early recording of Sir Claud as Lear. 'Howl, howl, howl, howl, howl,' came his deep, measured Edwardian delivery.

I could see his point. I felt like howling myself. These 'children' were now in their twenties, four girls and a young man. One of the girls was nursing a baby on her knee, who was howling in sympathy with King Lear. It was the man who caught my attention however. I'd seen photos of Uncle Ted in his youth, and there was no doubt that he was more than a chip off the old block. If I were Flossie, he was the last person I'd want to see. In the girls, the likeness was less obvious, but in him the late (or not so late) Edmund Flowerdew was reborn. After the recording had finished, and they all strolled out, I collared him, and then realised I had a difficulty: was I supposed to know who he was or not? I decided I did.

'I'm Quinn. I'm married to Margaret Flowerdew's daughter Ellie. Your Aunt Margaret, that is.'

He looked superciliously amused. '*My* aunt Margaret? This really is reconciliation day. Wouldn't have anything to do with a biography, would it?'

I'd dropped a clanger. Did he think his father was dead or merely missing?

'Everything,' I replied gloomily, 'has to do with that blasted biography.' I was about to ask him whether he had been approached to help, but realised John wouldn't have gone that far before he knew the biography was viable. Or would he?

'I wouldn't know. We haven't been asked to contribute. We're only here as grace and favour, courtesy of that American guy John. Maybe he can see an angle in us and is softening us up. He had a go at Mum – that's Patsy Harding to you – and Joan and her daughters. I'm Jasper, my sister's Alice. We all got quite chummy after the court case.'

I was aghast. 'You do realise Flossie's daughter thinks he's dead? She has no idea about the court case or who you are.'

He grinned. 'Nice to have the whip hand for once.'

'Flossie's a nice woman. So's Imogen.'

'They're *all* nice women. Flossie came first, that's all.'

What the hell was John playing at inviting them here? Yes, of course, the Creep (he was back) was hoping the whole story of Edmund Flowerdew would come out at an early stage – but not be lodged too closely to his door – so that any remaining objection to the biography would automatically be removed. Was that Columba's idea or John's? I could guess, and I was going to do a damage limitation exercise.

'I'd play my cards close to my chest if I were you,' I said.

'You are not.'

'I'm like you, though. Although you have the luxury of at least knowing who you are. I don't. I was adopted and there's a query over my parentage.'

'Better than being spat on by Flowerdews.'

'In your imagination, or in fact?' I asked mildly.

'The former,' he conceded.

'Which Flowerdews? Have you talked to them? Have a word with Cecilia and Margaret. I don't think there'd be spittle flying around, even though they'd be nervous about Imogen finding out. Why don't you wait to see what John does with the biography? Just think – if he *doesn't* approach you and sits on the story, you'll have him on toast. If he plays the line that your father is dead, you'll have all the Flowerdews where you want them.'

'Yeah. Maybe.' He eyed me keenly. That face could go far, I thought. 'What's your stake? Why are you so eager to advise me?'

I explained briefly, then asked, 'Are you on the stage?'

He mimicked my voice. 'Yes, I'm on the stage. I've taken the boards by storm at the Little Piddling amateur dramatic society. We're almost professional, you know.'

'Under the name of Flowerdew?' I continued doggedly.

By accident I hit the right nerve to see the real Jasper Harding. 'I'm not going to work my way into parts by saying I'm a Flowerdew. Harding is good enough for me.'

'What's your line? Comedy, drama, musical comedy?'

'All of them.'

'Any West End plans?'

'I walk on splendidly as Third Lord. That sort of thing.'

'I'll introduce you to a few people, if you like. Critics and so on.'

'I'm not a Flowerdew, remember.'

Good, I thought. Then he couldn't be planning to break the story. Nevertheless, if this young man was The Spark, I didn't want it on my conscience that he was never recognised.

I fulfilled my offer, left him with a Sunday newspaper critic, and departed back to the tent. I was suffering Ellie withdrawal pains.

Back in the tent, Columba smiled beneficently at me. 'Thank you, Quinn, dear, for looking after that little problem. By the way, Ellie was looking for you.'

'Yes.' I hadn't a care in the world. 'All's well now.'

'I think not. Something seems to have upset her,' Columba said airily. 'I hope it wasn't something I said.'

Fear clutched at my heart. What had the old besom done now? The rose garden floated away, leaving behind a bed of nettles. I glimpsed Ellie at the far end of the marquee talking to her father, and alarm bells flashed immediately. I couldn't think what had happened – or could I? I had a terrible suspicion that my cowardliness had landed me here.

She noticed me, said something to Gerald, and came towards me brushing off several people en route. Her eyes were no longer full of love.

'You didn't tell me,' she yelled unbelievingly. '*Why* didn't you tell me?'

'Tell you what?' I knew. Oh, I knew.

'I managed to overlook the fact that you didn't tell me about the Mighty Rich. For days I was left in the cold, while you knew that everything was all right and I didn't. But' – there was deadly venom in her voice – 'now I understand my parents knew too. Why didn't you tell me that, Quinn? Why did you never bother to mention you were *living* with my parents? I feel shut out, betrayed.'

'Why?' I asked inadequately. 'It was their idea. I didn't foist myself on them.'

'Leave them out of it. The point is you accepted, and never told me you were ganging up with them against me.'

'No.' I was appalled. 'How can you think that? Your parents and I were uniting to try to save our marriage.'

'Pity you didn't think of uniting with me to save it in

211

the first place. Oh no, the only uniting you have in mind is in bed.'

I went white. 'That's below the belt, Ellie, and you know it.'

'Maybe, but answer my question. Why were you so keen to accept my parents' help when you wouldn't help me?'

I couldn't speak. Not even to save this frightful situation. It was too soon, too unexpected, after our reunion. How could I explain everything that had led to it, and tell her about the music too? She was in no mood to listen, and we were back to square one.

'I thought we'd learnt something from being apart,' I eventually managed. 'Yet you won't even give me a chance, just like before.'

Ellie simply walked back to her father's group.

I couldn't understand how she could just turn away from me. Not Ellie. Not now. I couldn't stand the tent sides around me any more. I had to get outside, and stumbled on my way there. Maybe I looked as sick as I felt, for Columba asked concernedly, 'Are you all right, Quinn?'

'Yes, no. I'll leave. Don't worry about me.'

'Is it Ellie?' Her words floated after me as I headed for an indoor bathroom in Charham Place where I could be alone to disgorge the champagne, the pâtés, the canapés and the heartbreak all in one fell swoop.

When I emerged, there was a fresh delight awaiting me. The music, hitherto a bland muzak, was familiar sixties music, Woodstock music, and Mighty Rich music. If there was anything I didn't want to hear it was that, and I headed for the car park. I had to get out of this place, get away from the music dinning into my ears. Always there, reminding me.

I reached the car, still besieged by noise on all sides. Dear God, did nightmares never end?

'Quinn, what's the matter? Columba said you were ill.'

Ellie raced up towards me before I could get into the car. 'I'm sorry,' she blurted out. 'Maybe I made too much of it. If only you knew how lonely it was without you, and I didn't even have my parents around. And all the while you were with them, having a jolly time without me. Can't you understand how I felt?'

I stared at her, still shaky, that music still pounding at my ears. 'Perhaps.'

'I want to try again, Quinn. You know how I feel and how you feel. It wasn't just the sex this afternoon. It was more than that. It was *us*, wasn't it?'

'Yes.'

'Then we must try.'

'We can't. I can't.' Just saying that made me retch again.

'Why not?' she asked when I'd finished. 'Now that we understand each other.'

'*You* don't understand.'

She put her arms round me as I turned away. 'Then make me understand. Talk to me. You never did.'

'You never listened.'

She swallowed. 'I'm listening now.'

'I was scared.' Out it came at last. 'Just as you were when all this began.'

Ellie was taken aback. 'Scared of whom? Of what?'

'Of losing you.' Wasn't that obvious? It was to me, but perhaps it didn't seem that way to her. I made a further effort. 'If I'd had that test, suppose it had been positive? That would have been the end of us.'

'It nearly was anyway,' she said quietly, 'but it's all right now.'

I removed myself from her arms. This was the hardest part and there was no escaping it. 'It's not all right. This afternoon I thought it was. But it's back again.'

She was trembling herself now. 'What is, Quinn?'

'The doubt, the question mark.'

She looked bewildered. 'I don't understand. From what I heard from Mum and Columba everything's checked out with

Richard's story. His losing Marcus Quinn at Woodstock, the police being notified and you being in Paris make the long arm of coincidence far too long to take seriously – even for me,' she tried to joke.

I couldn't speak. I tried but failed, and then the amplifiers blared out their message of doom for me: Jimi Hendrix singing *The Star-Spangled Banner*. It was the end of the ceremony here, and the end of my marriage as that music closed in around me.

'Quinn, please tell me what's wrong. You look terrible.'

'The music,' I blurted out.

'What about it?'

'This nightmare I had as a child. Music closing in around me and I couldn't get away. I wet my bed – it's all come back to me. I had forgotten all about it, but now it's crystal clear again. Music. Noise. People. The smell, the mud. Suppose it was Woodstock, Ellie?' I whispered. 'Or even just one of the gigs Richard used to take me to. It must have been one or the other.'

'Coincidence. It could have been anything.'

'Too many coincidences, Ellie.'

'But we know it wasn't you.'

We stared at each other, helpless, on reversed sides now.

'I *don't* know, that's the problem.'

Ellie gazed at me. I could see tears glittering in her eyes. 'You won't come back to me until you do. But will that ever happen?'

'I can't answer that.'

'Well, I can. The answer is yes, and then you'll come back.'

'How can we ever find out the truth now?'

'*We* can't. *I* shall. It's all a question of auxiliary verbs, Quinn.' Ellie tried to grin encouragingly but failed.

'There's nothing more to find out. How can there be?'

'There can be because there must be. Leave it to me, Quinn. I'm taking over now.'

Part Three

ELLIE AGAIN

Fourteen

I must have sounded so confident to Quinn; I even sounded confident to myself. As I watched him slide inside his car and drive away, however, confidence was a million miles away.

I'd managed to pull myself together sufficiently to urge Quinn to go back to Sussex and continue staying with my parents. That seemed important to me, though I couldn't analyse why. Later I realised that it was because I was desperate to hang on to what might otherwise be flying coat-tails intent on disappearing for ever. If he were staying with my parents, I was still in with a chance. He'd agreed, albeit very reluctantly.

'Okay, Ellie,' I said to myself in that soulless car park. 'You told Quinn you'd take over. So *do* it.' If I hadn't heard Quinn announce so clearly that he still believed he could be Marcus Quinn Hart, I wouldn't have believed the irony of it. First it was me intent on digging a heffalump pit for myself, now it was Quinn. Then I amended this. No, first had come Columba to dig the pit. *Then* I'd jumped into it of my own free will.

I had to force myself to walk back to the marquee and the party. I wanted to drive away and howl out all my frustration and tears. Quinn had been near to breaking point, and I was full of remorse and guilt that I hadn't seen it earlier on. I hadn't appreciated that Quinn, my darling Johnny Head-in-the-Air, might simply be pushing this worst problem of all to one side through sheer terror. It was time

217

for me to pay for my insensitivity, however much I felt like following his example.

I tried to sort things out in my own mind as I drew closer to the noise of the party. Was there a sound basis for Quinn's continued concern? Was it more than mere coincidence that he and Richard Hart had been in Paris at the same time in '69, and that someone like Richard had been seen walking away from the orphanage that night? I felt panic rising inside me, and fortunately realised I was in no state to make rational judgements alone.

A few people were probably still lingering in the museum, but most people seemed to be back in the marquee, where tea was being served; some were even sitting on the lawns. It was a peaceful scene, hats and floaty dresses mingling with stylish stark female trouser suits, male blazers, a few suits, a cane or two, and strawberries and cream. No doubt the tea was Earl Grey, and Manet would be coming along at any moment to record the picnic in paint for posterity. I wondered savagely if I was the only person in this tranquil party in turmoil. I felt more like the ghost of Christmas past than the spirit of present summer as I marched steadily towards the party. How could fate have restored Quinn to me, only to let me lose him again within an hour or two?

A plan – or the beginning of one – was forming in my mind, but I needed to talk it over with someone before I approached Mum. There was of course only one candidate, since talking over was not an accomplishment that either my grandmother or Great-Aunt Cecilia possessed. And I certainly couldn't talk to Imogen – this was way out of her league. Her life moved on main-line railway tracks with no branches. That left Columba. It wasn't easy to talk anything over with her either, but she owed me. This first step decided, I felt somewhat better.

Plaster a smile on your face, I ordered myself. I thought at first my face would rebel, but finally it obeyed, though it probably wore the grimace of a Notre Dame gargoyle rather than the happy grin I had in mind. I quickly surveyed the crowd in the tent to see if Columba was there, but could see no sign of her. As she was distinctively dressed in red from top to toe, she was fairly distinguishable today.

I tracked her down to the museum, where she was talking to John. This unexpectedly threw me, especially as they hardly registered the fact that I was joining them. They were deep in their own discussion.

'I can't do it, Columba,' I heard John say.

'Nonsense,' Columba said briskly. 'I'll deal with them.'

It was only the biography they were talking about, so I decided to intervene. 'Can I have a word with you, Columba?' I gave John a brilliant smile, to indicate I meant alone. I didn't want him there, for it would seem like letting Quinn down, since I knew he disliked John.

'A quick one, darling Ellie. We're in crisis.' It was true she looked agitated, almost annoyed.

'What's happened?'

'The worst.'

'It's my fault, apparently,' John admitted, not looking in the least sorry about anything.

'He would insist on inviting *the other parts of the family*,' Columba hissed, as though the press or, worse, Imogen were peering over her shoulder. I was lost for a moment, till I vaguely remembered my father pointing out the famous ladies, they of the bigamous marriages. On a normal day I'd have been entranced at this spectacle – but today was not normal.

'Joan and Patsy?' I asked.

'Worse.' John could hardly stop grinning, which did not please Columba.

'I'm beginning to think, my darling, that you actually wanted this disaster to befall us.'

'I don't believe in secrets being unnecessarily hidden.'

'Who decides necessity?' Columba whipped back. 'And I don't want those' – she paused for a politically correct word and then decided not to bother – 'by-blows dogging my footsteps. Surely they don't count as Flowerdews?'

'In the eyes of God, they do.' I entered gravely into the spirit of it, perhaps because it took my mind off the ache in my stomach when I thought of Quinn.

'The Flowerdews have higher standards,' Columba retorted loftily and entirely seriously.

'Bigamy, desertion, adultery?' I murmured.

'My dear girl, you may not be *quite* Flowerdew, but I gave you credit for family loyalty.'

I came near to disliking Columba then, and she saw it.

'But then you're not yourself at present.' The charm came back. 'Let me tell you what's happened.'

I had no chance to tell her what was upsetting me, and there was clearly going to be no opportunity to get her on her own.

'I have, as you know, just announced that the Flowerdew biography will proceed.'

'I told you not to.' John still appeared highly amused at the crisis, whatever it was.

Columba ignored him. 'I knew my mother would be furious, and so would Flossie, but it was obvious – or so it seemed – that we had enough Flowerdews on our side to proceed. To take the front rank' – Columba blithely dismissed a hundred or so other Flowerdews – 'in favour are Aunt Cecilia, myself, Imogen, yourself Ellie, and now Margaret. That only leaves my mother and Flossie against it. However, there are enough to make the biography viable even if they do object. I am quite certain of that. Or I was. And now look what a pickle we're in – thanks to John.'

'What's happened?'

'Jasper has.'

The wicked Sir Jasper of Victorian melodrama? Even in my mood, it seemed farcical – enter stage left, to ruin Columba's day, the villainous Sir Jasper in black cloak and top hat. 'Who's he?' I asked.

'The ghastly Patsy's son. John would insist on inviting not only Joan and Patsy but their children, on the basis that they are all Flowerdews. I knew it would lead to trouble. And the press here too. If I didn't know you better, John, I'd assume you deliberately engineered this to cause trouble.'

'What on earth did you invite them for?' I asked him. For the first time I began to have doubts about John. It just seemed an incredibly crass act to invite them with Imogen and Flossie here – unless of course, as Columba suggested, he had just one thing in mind: publicity. The great family reunion. And great material for the book. It would certainly bring the Flowerdews into the headlines again, even if it was not in the way my grandmother would wish. Or poor old Flossie.

'How could you, John?' I continued indignantly, full of fire on the Flowerdews' account.

'*Et tu, Brute?*' he enquired, clearly disappointed in me. 'Just think, both of you, what would happen if we went ahead with the biography and it was published with the clear message that Ted is dead and that his life after leaving Flossie never took place, and that his marriage to Flossie was one of perfect harmony.'

'She claims it was,' I pointed out.

'Don't you think the press would leap on that with great gusto? It would discredit my book. Remember that Jasper is on the stage himself.'

'Is he? The London stage?' This was interesting. I decided I had to meet this Jasper.

'Oh yes. Small but meaningful parts. He's reckoned to be a rising star – or so John Halliday said.' He was a leading theatre critic, I knew, so there must be something to it.

'But he is *not* a true Flowerdew,' Columba trumpeted.

'There seems ample proof that he is,' John said. 'But he isn't using the name Flowerdew on stage. To get back to the point, the biography would be the laughing stock of London.'

'Of course,' Columba sighed, 'if you're merely thinking of your own reputation . . .'

'I am,' John answered. 'What's equally important is that I'm thinking of the Flowerdews' reputation too. If that book were published without the full story, and the press discovers what it is – as they will – then another book will follow on the footsteps of ours, containing the dirt. The full unauthorised story.'

'Ah.' Columba, to do her justice, saw his point instantly.

'I came to the conclusion that it's the full story or nothing,' John said gently. 'It seems I'm right now.'

'Now?' I picked up when he stopped. Columba filled me in.

'Jasper, the dear little soul, has said that if the biography is published without the full story, then he will oblige by writing the unauthorised one, ensuring that it's serialised in the Sunday press at the same time as we publish. We could of course sue for libel.'

'Not for the truth, Columba,' I said. I was fully absorbed in the pickle by now, although aware that – as usual – my own problems were being distanced by the Flowerdew predicament. At the moment this seemed a good idea. 'So what now?'

'We lean on Jasper,' she answered. 'I'll fix his goose.'

'No, I told you. I won't do that. We must lean on Flossie to tell Imogen the full story,' John argued.

'Now?' I almost shrieked at him. Nothing like a gentle awakening. How on earth was Imogen going to react to the news that her father was presumably alive and well, probably married to a further three or four women by now, and that far from being an only child she had a whole new family to meet? In all his preparations for today, even Stephen wouldn't have thought to lay on trauma counselling.

I did some very quick thinking. 'John, my guess is that this Jasper is gently blackmailing you into doing just that. After all, he's had ample opportunity to make his relationship to the Flowerdews known today, but nothing seems to have happened yet.'

'Oh darling, you're right.' Columba sighed with relief. 'He's a mischief-maker. So like Ted.'

'Aren't you both forgetting he's an actor?' John asked drily. 'He's awaiting his moment to enter the stage. That may or may not be today.'

We froze. 'Where is he?' I asked.

'In the marquee.'

'With everyone still there? With *Imogen* there?' My mind boggled. 'Let's go.'

Columba saw my point. 'My mother will never stand the shock.' She began to run towards the marquee.

'I think she'll love it, actually. It's Imogen I worry about.' I panted after her, remembering I'd done rather a lot of running that day, and pulling my thoughts resolutely back. Not a moment too soon. Some people had left now, leaving a hard core divided between Violet, still in her corner, and Cecilia in hers. In between were the tables with the remains of tea and staff still serving tea and champagne to a few who preferred not to join either of the groups.

Flossie's ample, placid body was comfortably ensconced near to her mother-in-law, Violet, completely unaware that her world was about to be shattered. Flossie knew about Joan and Patsy of course, but they, as Columba pointed out to me, were in Cecilia's group. I instantly saw it was the group round Violet that held trouble. There was a striking-looking young man I'd seen earlier, who must surely be Jasper. Of course he was a Flowerdew. I wondered that no one had marked the resemblance already. I presumed that only aficionados of Flowerdew history would be acquainted with Uncle Ted's looks. To my relief there was no sign of Imogen.

Columba, John and I strolled towards Violet's group, doing our best to look casual. We obviously failed, for Jasper turned round and grinned as we approached. 'Miss Flowerdew, Mr Curwen, excellent. Just in time to hear what I have to say.' I was ignored, but I didn't mind, for I was too caught up in what was going to happen, despite the fact that I had greater problems than a Flowerdew biography. Here it was possible to kid myself that there could be nothing more important.

Jasper had projected his voice well and both groups fell silent. Into that moment of quietness, he dropped – with admirable technique – his bombshell: 'Ready for the family photograph?' He looked around. 'We *are* all family, aren't we? Except for Jane and Mr Curwen of course . . . and Stephen.'

'Young man,' screeched my grandmother, exactly as he must have wished, 'the only family here is the Flowerdews. Are you a member of it?' Violet obviously meant this as a scathing put-down. Why the hell had no one put her in the picture?

Jasper bowed. 'I have that honour, ma'am. The bar sinister, of course.'

His first mistake.

'What does that mean?' Flossie asked, puzzled, thus giving him back his opportunity on a plate.

'It means we're all born out of wedlock, dearest step-mother. Flowerdew wedlock, that is.'

I wished there were a photographer handy, but naturally they'd all gone just when the fun started, and Flossie realised who these other ladies were. She'd never actually met them before, only seen their pictures in the newspapers (thanks to Columba). They had the advantage of Flossie, since they would be looking out for her, whereas apparently John had forgotten to warn her of the new family coming today.

Cecilia began to play a Lady Audley scene of high drama, then changed her mind and did a Noel Coward comedy instead. 'Darlings, it isn't often one comes to open a museum and goes home with three glasses of champagne and several new great-nieces and nephews.' She'd obviously been well primed by John.

Flossie rallied gallantly from the shock and came back to the main issue: 'Imogen. Imogen must not know,' she moaned.

'Darling Flossie, don't worry.' Columba galloped to the rescue on her white charger. 'I'll tell Imogen this young man and any siblings he might have are mine.' I realised that Columba must really be rattled to be prepared to claim she had managed to give birth to four daughters and a son in her late thirties without anyone noticing.

Flossie realised it too. 'Imogen? Where is she?' She looked like a beached whale, but there was help on the way. The two groups were now one, and with one accord Joan and Patsy rushed over to her in a great example of the sisterhood of women. I couldn't hear what was going on and firmly dissuaded Columba from intervening. Jasper stood on one side with his sisters – whole and half – looking somewhat bemused.

And then I saw Imogen. She was strolling up to us without a care in the world, and there wasn't a thing I could do about it. Jasper saw her too, and a gleam came into his eye as power was restored to his hands.

'Imogen,' he called brightly. 'Just the person I wanted to see.'

'Shall we faint now or later?' Columba hissed in my ear.

'Later.' I had to go down with the ship, I decided.

The sisterhood of women had different ideas. Casting a scathing look at her son, Patsy rushed forward, her high heels catching in the coconut matting and sending her headlong into Imogen's arms. Once disentangled, she beamed at Imogen. 'How pleasant,' she cried. 'Joan and I are old acquaintances of your father's, my dear. We've just been swapping tales of the old days. Poor old Ted.'

Imogen looked somewhat startled, but allowed herself to be dragged into the sisterhood, every member of which began to talk of the old days with great gusto.

I tried not to look at Jasper, knowing him outwitted – provided the 'old acquaintances' remained that way, with closer ties unrevealed.

Jasper was made of sterner stuff though. When the group

at last made way for him, he tackled Imogen immediately.

'Nice to meet you, Imogen.'

'Oh yes. We must have a chat some time. I gather you met my father once,' Imogen said brightly. 'Perhaps you could come to tea with Aunt Cecilia and me one day?'

I froze, but, without knowing it, Imogen had hit on the right line.

Jasper was taken aback. 'I'd like that.'

'I really do have to get Aunt Cecilia back home now,' Imogen explained, 'and I expect Grandma Violet has had enough too, Columba.'

Columba, cowed for once, meekly acquiesced. She wasn't used to Imogen as a major player in any game, and I knew very well that Columba was booked to take Violet home today.

Flossie gazed anxiously at her daughter and made a gallant effort in her role as Imogen's protector, addressing Jasper in strangled tones. 'Perhaps I could come to tea too? I should like to hear your tales of my poor late husband.'

His face darkened. 'My mother—' he began, but I stepped in quickly.

'Why don't we all come? Joan and Patsy too. Cecilia would love it.'

'Tea then,' said Imogen chattily. 'I'll give you a ring, Jasper. John has your number, I expect?'

It struck me that Imogen might have his number too, whether she sensed any danger or not. My tension over this crisis began to recede, and the pain in my stomach began to make itself felt again. I had done nothing about the latter, and it was time to face the music.

I decided not to bother with Columba, but to talk to my parents straightaway to put them in the picture. They had been in Cecilia's group, and I made my way to them once Imogen had departed. John had gone to the museum with Jane to clear up and close down for the day, and with everyone now leaving it was the perfect opportunity to talk without distraction.

'Can we go into the house?' I asked. 'I need to talk.'

'What's wrong, Ellie?' Dad asked when we found a quiet corner in my office. 'You're looking terrible. Not still this Jasper fellow, is it?'

'No. My marriage.'

'I thought it was all right.'

'No, Mum. Quinn's left. It *was* fine and then . . . then . . .' I took control of myself again. 'It unsorted itself. Now it's Quinn who thinks he could be Marcus Quinn Hart.'

Mum went pale. 'But why? He met Richard and got the story. Weren't you convinced by it?'

'Of course I was. It was heaven for me, but, Mum, he doesn't believe it himself.'

Mum glanced at Dad. This had clearly shaken them both. 'Why not?'

I told them about Quinn's nightmare, and they took it seriously. 'It depends whether this is just the result of his anxiety. Perhaps he's made up this dream to fit in with it – unconsciously, of course.'

'Or whether the nightmare's a bona fide recollection,' Dad added. 'Knowing Quinn, I'd say the latter.' My heart sank. 'Where is he now?'

'I made him promise to stay with you. I hope that's okay with you. He needs to be in touch with us, or we'll lose him.'

Mum frowned. 'Then you must come too, Ellie.'

'Me? But how can I?' I longed to, but it was impossible.

'I'll give you the spare room. You have to be under the same roof so that you can work together on this.'

I turned the idea round in my mind, remembered the hopelessness I'd felt all these last months at being on my own, and knew she was right. I couldn't bear to be apart from Quinn any longer than I had to, and the closer we worked together, the better it would be.

What would Quinn think about it though? It wasn't going to be fun, sleeping in separate beds – especially after today's experience. Yet now that his doubts were out in the open, Quinn wasn't going to share a bed with me again until they were resolved.

'I'll talk to him,' said my splendid mother. 'Now, Ellie, what's your next step?'

'I haven't thought it out.'

'Then you must. *We* must. After all, I'm in this too. I've got to get to the bottom of it for my own sake as well as yours.'

'I know.' I felt a dismal failure. That photograph by the bed had been just that, a photograph of a memory that hadn't vanished, but had not obtruded either. Now it coloured every facet of our lives. I racked my brains for a new angle. The band, Gossage – no hope there. They couldn't help on this. 'Marie Lamartine might remember music at the orphanage,' I suggested.

'Hardly likely to be playing loud pop music in a convent-run orphanage,' Dad pointed out.

'It's a starting point,' I insisted. 'I could also ask Quinn's parents more about him as a three-year-old. They might have played pop music. But if that fails . . .'

'What next?' Mum asked. 'Quinn has tackled Richard and the American end.' She glanced at me, and in one of those splendid instances when people are on precisely the same wavelength and sparks fly, I knew what she was thinking. 'Ellie, it seems to me there's something unsatisfactory about the American side of the story. Paris is tied up neatly, thanks to Columba—'

Dad growled. 'No thanks to that dratted woman at all.'

I ignored him, and leapt on to what my mother had said. 'Yet it all adds up: the police, the records, Woodstock, Richard's irresponsibility. Mum, you know Richard . . .'

'I did, and I feel I still do.' There was a rising excitement in my mother's voice. 'Ellie, I don't think he told Quinn the full story, do you?'

'You mean he lied from start to finish?' Dad almost howled.

'No,' Mum answered hastily. 'He wouldn't do that; that's not Richard's way. But my goodness—'

'The truth, the whole truth, and nothing but the truth,' I interrupted.

'With Richard you get the first, and maybe the last.' Mum took the point.

'But not necessarily the whole truth. Oh, Mum, would he try to spare Quinn bad news? Would he omit the vital factor that would prove he *is* Marcus Quinn?' I could have wept at this terrible thought, and later I did.

'I wish I could say no,' Mum admitted dully, 'but I can't.'

'If he did,' I said slowly, 'you gain a son and I lose a husband.'

I thought Mum was going to cry. But she didn't. She's a Flowerdew and made of sterling stuff when the going gets tough. 'We're going to find out, Ellie. Gerald, do you mind?'

'No,' said Dad heavily. He realised what she meant immediately, but I didn't. What she meant was that we were both off to Cornwall to see the Mighty Rich. And what *that* would do to Mum I didn't dare to think.

The party was over. Sometimes the sight of dirty dishes, remains of food, and staff clearing up and packing stuff into boxes can have a positive feel, and so I suppose it must have done to most people there. But to me, when I returned to the tent to make my final goodbyes, it looked desolate, a brave attempt that had ended in failure. Like my marriage. I couldn't even say it was through no fault of my own. If I hadn't investigated I wouldn't be in this position. The truth – if it was the truth – would have remained hidden. Now despite my brave words to Quinn, I was going to need my mother's stalwart help to get through this.

The staff were packing uneaten food into doggy boxes and dirty glasses onto trays for washing at the house. One particularly inept man was doing a Fawlty Towers imitation with a tray of uneaten pastries, which he managed to tip all over the floor instead of into its box, and was busily scraping up the mess under the stern eye of his boss.

The last revellers left, and with them my parents. I arranged with them to pick up some clothes and drive straight down to Sussex.

'Don't leave it,' my mother advised. 'Come this evening. I won't warn Quinn.'

'That's not fair.'

'I know. Do you want this to work or not?'

'Yes.'

'Then do as I say. We'll leave for Cornwall as soon as we can both manage it.'

I felt slightly more heartened after Mum had gone, but stayed in the tent for some reason, waiting till the car park would be clear. Then I remembered something in the office that I had to pick up, and that I also needed to say goodbye to Stephen. I performed the first mission, but failed to find Stephen.

Champing at the bit, since I was anxious to get away, I rushed back to the marquee. To move back under the same roof as Quinn – even if not into the same bed – was a step forward into the unknown. It was, however, the most important step, because it denoted will. I needed to get going.

There was no Stephen in the marquee either.

What there was was Imogen talking to the Fawlty Towers waiter. She always did like lame ducks. I supposed I should say goodbye to her, so I walked towards her. Thus it was that I had a good view of Imogen throwing her arms round Mr Fawlty Towers and kissing him vigorously several times on the cheek before he left the tent through the rear staff exit.

I must have looked as gobsmacked as I felt, for Imogen stopped to speak to me on her way out of the tent.

'Ellie, I'm glad I've seen you. Goodbye. I'll be in touch about that tea.'

I was still speechless, so she added, 'What's the matter?'

'Nothing. Yes there is. Why on earth were you kissing the waiter?'

She looked faintly puzzled. 'It was only Father. He always turns up at these Flowerdew gatherings.'

Fifteen

It was an odd feeling driving up to Kingsgate House late that evening. Mum had wanted me to arrive in time for dinner, but I needed to see Quinn alone, not face him across a dining table.

In any case, I'd had to go to the Lodge first – and that took some emotional doing – to pick up some clothes, since I didn't want to drive all the way to Columba's London flat where I'd been staying. Moreover, I was still reeling from my encounter with Imogen, and wondering how or indeed whether I was going to break the happy news about Uncle Ted to my mother.

I think that Imogen genuinely had no idea what a bombshell she would throw into the Flowerdew family. She either deliberately wears blinkers through life, or has extremely restricted fields of vision. She had looked almost pleased when I explained to her in no uncertain terms that most members of the family had been doing their best to keep the news of her father's post-Flossie career from her – and that her mother had tried especially hard. It occurred to me that even now Imogen might not know about her father's criminal record, but I needn't have worried.

'Well, of course,' she had replied indignantly, 'I wasn't going to tell mother about seeing my father. She's so conventional.' (This was Imogen with her sensible-shoed attitude to life, remember.) 'She'd have been shocked to hear he'd done stir, as well as upset about Joan and Patsy, *and* their families. Anyway, Father asked me not to tell anyone about his visits.'

'He would, wouldn't he?' I commented, wondering whether to mention that Flossie had thought exactly the same about her. I didn't though, deciding that discretion is the better part of valour. 'How long have you been seeing your father, Imogen?'

'Oh, ages,' she answered brightly. 'He used to turn up once a year or so, except when he disappeared to Australia after he came out of jug. He even came when he was married to Joan and Patsy.'

'Or not married,' I couldn't resist putting in.

She looked rather hurt. 'You don't understand my father, Ellie. How could you, after all? You come from a two-parent family.'

I couldn't believe this was straight-as-a-die Imogen speaking. 'You mean you didn't *care* that Uncle Ted did time for bigamy?'

'When you know Father, it seems quite natural. He can't bear to upset people by telling them the truth, and he liked to please the ladies he was fond of by marrying them. You can see that he succeeded, from the way that they are still chasing him. That's why Father couldn't tell anyone where he was.'

'And where,' I enquired innocently, 'was he?'

She shot a glance at me. 'If I knew I wouldn't tell you, but I don't.'

'Of course not. He just hears about these family events by osmosis, I suppose.'

'There's no need to get narky, Ellie.' At this reproof from Imogen, I subsided with a muttered apology.

'You must get into the twenty-first century,' my cousin continued kindly. 'I get in touch by e-mail. And before that, he just used to turn up at school or at work.'

'Did anyone else know about this? Cecilia? Grandma?' Surely he would have told his own mother?

'No, I've already explained that he didn't want to upset them.'

'But don't you think it's upsetting for them that he sees you, but ignores them?'

'They don't know he's around,' she replied pragmatically.

'Then why did you tell me?' I asked reasonably enough. 'You could have made up some story about having a fetish about kissing waiters with moustaches.'

'I don't think you would have believed me. Anyway, I like you, Ellie, and I trust you. Actually, I thought you'd guessed long ago that I was seeing him from the very fact I never mentioned him.'

Ridiculously, I glowed at her praise, which outshone her drawing attention to my lack of discernment. 'That's nice of you.'

'So now,' Imogen continued implacably, 'you're going to keep silent, aren't you?'

I thought about this. It would be easy enough to agree, but I wasn't sure. 'It's not as easy as that,' I replied at last. 'There's the biography, after all. Everyone's attitude to it was coloured by the need not to reveal to you that Uncle Ted was still alive and a convicted bigamist.'

Imogen looked sombre. 'I thought that damned biography would never get written, since Aunt Margaret and Grandma were so against it. If it is written, I don't want my father's full story included. It would upset my mother.'

'You supported it yourself,' I pointed out drily. 'Didn't you think of that little wrinkle? Why on earth were you so enthusiastic when it was suggested?'

'Father wanted it,' she said. 'I went by his wishes. After all, Mother knows quite well that he's alive. So my father was going to meet John and give him a truncated version of his life story. He said John would be so thrilled, he wouldn't enquire too deeply into his present whereabouts.'

'I think it's you who's not living in today's world,' I replied forthrightly to this innocent explanation. 'Firstly, John knows the whole story – with the exception of your association with Uncle Ted – and John has a regard for the truth. Secondly, there are Joan and Patsy to consider.'

'Father said he could square them.'

'Can he square his son, Jasper?'

'What's he got to do with it?'

I remembered Imogen hadn't overheard the wicked Sir Jasper's big moment. 'He's a moral blackmailer. It's to be the whole story, or he goes to the tabloids on publication day to tell the unauthorised part of the story.'

'Oh!' Imogen was taken aback. 'I suppose,' she said resignedly, 'I'd better tell Mother I've been seeing Father all this while.'

'Yes,' I agreed unsympathetically. 'And if I were you I'd do the rounds of Joan, Patsy and their families so that everyone is prepared for the full story coming out. You can look on the bright side, Imogen – you'll have a best-seller to sell in the shop.'

She was rightly indignant, but she got her own back. 'And you can tell Columba.'

'But—' I stopped, aghast. I could hardly object. How could I have forgotten Columba? So much was happening nowadays that even Columba was temporarily outstripped in the competition among all my preoccupations. True, it would be no news to Columba that Ted was alive and well, but how was she going to react when she realised that she, the queen bee, had been unaware that her own brother, in some guise or another, had been attending every single Flowerdew family or theatrical event? Imogen had told me he attended first nights – often as a barman, sometimes even working behind scenes – and he would even nose his way into private parties. 'It's his form of acting,' Imogen explained. 'He likes playing different roles in real life as well as on the stage.'

'Is he still acting?'

'I don't know, Ellie, I really don't. All I know about are his own visits to me. It used to be a game, to see whether I could recognise him before he made himself known to me. He used to whisper in my ear, "Flowerdews floreant." '

This was not easy to convey to Columba, who fancied that she was in charge of the entire Flowerdew clan when it came to family get-togethers. This was another reason I postponed my visit to London to pick up clothes. I simply told Columba I was going back home for a while, and stuck to this simple announcement despite the gleam in her eye indicating she guessed something more was afoot.

As I drew up by the garage at Kingsgate House I could hear conversation from the terrace in the back garden, although it was almost dark. The flowers were giving off their night scent, which added an unreality to the scene but seemed to stiffen my resolve. I could hear Mum and Dad's voices, but though I listened carefully I could not detect Quinn's. I let myself in to the house, feeling more like a burglar than a family member.

All was quiet as I lugged in my bag filled with an odd assortment of clothes grabbed at random. I walked through to the kitchen, which was in darkness and through whose windows I could confirm that only Mum and Dad were on the terrace. As it was too early for bed, I knew I would find Quinn somewhere in the house, most probably in his attic bed-studio. This was one way Quinn would try to find escape: drawing cartoons. His sketches could express thoughts he could not face himself. With luck, he would not have heard my arrival up there, and I had advised Mum not to warn him.

'Quinn!'

I had been right – he was there, though doing nothing except staring at the easel and computer screen. He whisked round and his face closed up as he saw me.

'What are you doing here, Ellie?' he asked without anger.

'I'm coming back home for a while.'

'Then I should leave.'

'No. That's just what you mustn't do.'

'If you think' – all the weariness of the world in his voice

236

– 'I can sleep with you while we're in this mess, you're wrong.'

'You don't have to. It's all arranged. We'll sleep separately.'

'Arranged? You've fixed this up with your parents without telling me?' Anger now. 'Let's box poor old Quinn into a corner and everything will be all right? Don't I even rank a consultation? How could you foist this brilliant scheme on your mother?'

'It was her idea. Listen, Quinn, don't go overboard before I've explained.'

'There's no explaining to do.'

'It was time to take a stand. I had my chance of seeing the solution to this problem, you've had yours, and we're both still in a mess. Now my mother must have her go – it's only fair to her. She's as much concerned with this story as we are, perhaps more. We owe it to her to work together, Quinn.' It all came out in a rush, and I couldn't tell how it was going down.

He said nothing, so I tried harder. 'We've taken it as far as we can go, and we're still in limbo, married but not married. Isn't it worth going the extra mile to see it through?'

'It depends.' At least he was listening. 'What are you proposing to do?'

'Mum and I are going to see Richard.'

'What the hell for? Is this your doing, Ellie? Have you thought what it would do to your mother? He's happily settled in St Ives and he's told us what happened.'

'Has he? She doesn't think so, and moreover she doesn't have any romantic feelings left for him.'

'It's her child at the heart of this.'

'Then she has the right to investigate all she wants.'

He sighed. 'He told me the story, Ellie. The truth.'

'But perhaps not the whole truth.'

He saw the point immediately and went white. 'You mean

he *knows* I'm Marcus Quinn Hart but left out the vital factors to avoid hurting me?'

My stomach turned over. 'Or . . .' My voice didn't sound my own, for it was obvious he had made up his mind that he was my half-brother. 'Or,' I repeated more firmly, 'he knows that you are not Marcus Quinn, but for some reason didn't want to tell us the defining factor that would prove it. After all, if you're Marcus Quinn, you're his son, and that must mean something to him.'

'You can't get over the fact that I was in Paris at the same time he was. Nor that I had those nightmares of music and people. Are you going to say it's false memory syndrome? Because I can tell you, it's not. I checked it out with Madame Lamartine on the telephone when I got back here this evening, and she admitted I had terrible nightmares at the orphanage, and that I would scream at the sound of music for a while. Especially singing.'

I tried to pull myself back from the brink of giving in, for he'd made his mind up. Yet how could I? What lay ahead for me was worse – much worse – if I surrendered. Divorce would be the inevitable result. Anything was better than that, so I had to shut my ears to the possibility of defeat.

'Are you going to throw in the towel, Quinn? Just like that? Split up for good? I thought you were a fighter. Why don't you send Mum and me like the Rab-Hits to sort it out? You don't *want* a divorce, annulment or whatever?' Sudden devastating doubt.

'You know I don't.'

'Then whatever the alternative, it has to be better.'

He shrugged. 'You're right, Ellie. But how can I live in this house with you, in separate beds?'

'That's your share of the fight,' I replied, relieved. 'You think it's any easier for me?'

'Yes, because you're taking the next actual step.'

'Oh no, my friend, not that,' I said cheerfully. 'There'll

be plenty of action. You can come with us to Cornwall if you like.'

His face brightened, then he reconsidered. 'No, I don't think that's wise. Richard is a fellow who's easily scared. It will be bad enough for him to meet your mother again, so you as an extra is quite enough. In the interests of our joint fight,' – he gave a twisted grin – 'I'll stay here.'

The train ride on the tiny branch line between St Erth and St Ives must surely be one of the prettiest in Britain, and while watching the sea, the cliffs and the June sky, I was so entranced that I almost forgot the urgency of our visit.

Mum appeared cheerful too, and it was impossible to tell what she might be thinking. I didn't want to intrude more deeply than I had to, but I was relieved that she was showing no outward signs of tension. By the time the small train drew in to St Ives and we had walked up the hill to our hotel, it was early evening, which only gave us time to get our bearings and have dinner. We could pretend we were on holiday and face the truth tomorrow.

'I remember coming here with Richard once,' Mum said, staring out of the restaurant window at the view of endless bays and cliffs stretching into the distance. 'He took to it immediately, and spent the whole time we were here prowling round studios – Hepworth, Wynter, Hilton, Leach, and so on. It was clever of Quinn to seek Richard out down here; I should have thought of it for myself. It was just like Richard to gravitate to the art community here even if he had no serious talent himself. I remember the hippies chiefly. We came in the winter, when regular tourists were few and far between, and the town was a different place to the one it seems now.'

She seemed so relaxed I dared to ask her the question I most wanted to: 'How do you feel about seeing Richard again, Mum?'

'The truth?'

'Yes.'

'I feel nothing but a passing curiosity, Ellie.'

I realised the reason at last. 'Because you're thinking all the time about Marcus Quinn.'

She licked her lips nervously. 'Yes. Seeing Richard is a major stepping stone to the truth. I couldn't have left it any longer. I feel we're so near, although we still haven't a clue what really happened. All I am sure of is that Richard isn't in touch with Marcus now, and therefore the story about his being lost must be true.'

'In which case my Quinn is highly unlikely to be yours.'

'Unlikely, but it's still possible, darling. Suppose Richard lost Marcus in France, not Woodstock?'

I hadn't thought of that, and stared bleakly at my strawberry cheesecake. Mum reached out and patted my hand. 'Very unlikely, Ellie, and you know it.'

'We don't *know* anything,' I pointed out.

'Until tomorrow, thank heavens,' Mum said fervently. 'I think I'd go off pop if it was any longer.'

We sorted out a plan of campaign. Quinn had warned us what it had been like to engineer a meeting with Richard. If he would run a mile to avoid meeting someone who had ostensibly been a stranger from Australia, what lengths wouldn't he go to to be shot of having to meet his first wife, for at the very least he must feel a certain guilt for having abandoned her and taken her son.

We therefore reasoned that if we simply rang the doorbell, we weren't going to get any admittance past the Cerberus wife who guarded him. If we waited till she left the house and rang the bell, it would undoubtedly remain unanswered, for Richard still didn't like strangers. There was only one way to go: he didn't know me by sight and he was unlikely to recognise Mum immediately after thirty years, so we would wait until Richard left the house himself. On a summer's day – even if we had to wait the whole morning – he must come out sometime, and we would get there early enough to see him if he had a job to go to. We had booked the hotel for two nights, so we had a little leeway in case we fouled up the first time round.

We needed it. We did wait the whole morning. We patrolled the area singly for an hour or two, then took up station in a café near enough for us to spot an opening door. We saw two people emerge, one of whom was undoubtedly Cerberus and the other a girl of about seventeen. His daughter, we presumed.

But no Richard. The girl in the café was beginning to eye us meaningfully as lunchtime approached, and as we were extremely tired of cups of coffee, we sauntered out and past Richard's door. Mum, I noticed, was growing tense.

We saw the wife come back, then first I and afterwards Mum did a tour of the block. Still nothing. We repeated the process. Still nothing.

'I've had enough of this,' Mum said decidedly. 'I'm going to knock on the door.'

She did, with me at her heels, and Cerberus appeared at her summons. She was, as Quinn had said, a large comfortable-looking woman, but implacable in her determination not to give an inch. It was left to us to make the running.

'Mrs Penrose?' Mum asked hesitantly.

'That's me.'

'I'm Richard's first wife.'

If this direct approach was meant to bowl her over, it didn't work, and we'd blown our cover. Mum must have got something right, however, for although Cerberus stayed right where she was, she didn't look hostile.

'Could I see Richard please?' Mum continued. 'I won't upset him, and I won't keep him long.'

'What's it about, me handsome?' Not hostile. Almost sympathetic. But still implacable.

'Our son Marcus. I don't want to upset him; I just want to know. You can understand that.' It was risking a lot to assume the wife knew all Richard's past history, but again it paid off.

'You'd best come in,' said Cerberus.

This was progress, but I didn't get such a good welcome. 'Just her, my lovely.' An amicable rejection.

'I'm her daughter,' I ventured. 'Quinn Connelly's wife.'

'I guessed that. No offence, but it's just your ma I'll see. She'll only be a minute or two.'

I was left kicking my heels in the street, torn between frustration and impatience. What did she mean by *I'll* see? Was Richard still to be kept from us? When the door opened a few minutes later, my mother was thanking Cerberus sincerely, but her face was bleak after the door closed behind her.

'What is it?' I asked. 'Was he there?'

'No. Oh, Ellie. He's gone.'

'*Left* her?' After all this? Fate was not kind.

'She says temporarily. Richard guessed I would be down here once I heard what he told Quinn. He knew that I would realise he only gave Quinn part of the truth.'

'But his wife must know where he is?'

'She doesn't, I'm sure of that. From the little we talked it was obvious he treats her just as he treated me. If he goes off, he leaves no address. All she is sure of is that he'll come back to St Ives when he thinks the coast is clear. She says he's too happy here to want to march off into the blue.'

'He was happy with you, and yet he left.'

'He's older now, Ellie. I think Jessie – that's her name – is right.'

'So what now?' I was growling in frustration. 'Do we hang around St Ives for ever, hoping he'll turn up?'

'No. We'll go back home. I think I've told Jessie enough to have her on our side, within reason. When Richard comes home, she says she'll tell him what we want and make sure she gets the whole story. Then she'll contact me, so Richard need not see me at all. I convinced her I wasn't after revenge; I just wanted to know what really happened.'

'Did you get the impression she agreed he probably hadn't told Quinn everything?'

'Yes. Unfortunately, Ellie, Jessie didn't know the full story either – he'd also told her that Marcus was dead. She could sympathise with me, even though she seems tolerant of Richard's little ways. I could never have been so forbearing. Richard's been lucky.'

'So where does that leave us?'

'I don't know. I asked Jessie whether she had any idea at all where Richard might have gone. She convinced me that she hadn't.'

'So that's that.' Dejectedly, I looked at all the holidaymakers, the jolly T-shirts and the screaming children, and I wanted to scream right along with them.

'Yes. It's just you and I, Ellie. Me with my knowledge of Richard, you with your bright intuition.'

At the moment my bright intuition seemed extremely dim.

'What is it,' I remarked savagely, 'about our family that makes it so prone to sudden disappearances?'

We both felt defeated. We discussed endless possibilities – could he be with the band? his former manager? his family? – but nothing seemed to offer any hope. I suggested paying another visit to the father, and even thought about the brother, although he was unlikely to be a candidate for Richard's confidant.

The atmosphere in Sussex was tense when we got back, with both Quinn and Gerald agog to know what had happened, but not liking to push us too quickly. Mind you, our faces told the story for us. I didn't know how to break it to Quinn, but he was surprisingly supportive when I eventually did. He even offered to come to see the ghastly brother with me – or rather with us, since Mum insisted on coming too. This was her quest now, she said. So I dropped out of that party. Mum went to see her former father-in-law, getting no further than I did except to get the brother's address. She had never got on with Philip, she confessed, and Richard couldn't stand the sight of him, since they were like chalk and cheese. Richard, Mum said, took after his mother. Having met his father, I believed her.

I tried not to show how much I minded not being included in the party, though I had the sense to realise that Richard's brother might respond better to Quinn than to a mere woman like me. Mum was a special case, of course.

When I arrived home from work they still had not returned, and Dad was in the midst of preparations for supper. He thought a nice *coq au vin* might suit, and I agreed.

Funny how things turn out. In the end it was me who came up with the only progressive idea of that day – and all because of Columba. She was staying with Stephen in Charham Place – there was no sign of John, but whether these two factors were linked, I didn't like to ask – and so I had every opportunity to bend her ear about the biography and explain about Imogen.

I made sure Stephen was present too, although it was obvious he'd rather not have been. Jane was also there – Columba had a lot of respect for her, since the museum idea had worked so well. The point is, Columba wasn't going to lambaste me in front of these two. Cunning, eh?

I told her all about Imogen, and she listened with what she imagined was her dignified face.

Stephen chortled. 'Families. Guess there's no beating them.'

Jane, taking one look at Columba's stony expression, observed, 'You never know about those nearest to you. I remember a cousin of mine who . . .' She went off into an unusually rambling story for her, with which Columba dealt at first politely and then succinctly.

'Now,' she projected across the entire public restaurant in Charham Place, 'what does Imogen think she is achieving by this façade? Really, the girl is impossible. What will poor Flossie say when she hears?'

'I guess she'll be relieved not to have to pretend to her daughter any more,' Stephen said innocently.

'I presume, Stephen,' Columba said glacially, 'I may be permitted to know my own family?'

'But you don't,' I said bravely, 'and nor did I. That's the point. The good side of all this is that we can let John tell the full story in the biography now. Jasper has no hold over us. The book will be a sell-out.'

Columba did her Lady Bracknell. 'I will have no part in it. Do you imagine, Ellie, that I would be party to a tabloid sensation? I shall inform John that he will not have my collaboration.'

'But, Columba, even you,' I began unwisely, 'can't go back on it now. Nearly the whole family is in favour of it now, and I'm sure once Grandma Violet knows about Ted, she will be too.'

'Do you know my own mother better than I?' Columba said. 'Are you *aware* that it's her ninetieth birthday in less than a month's time?'

We were all aware of it, but it provided such minor difficulties compared with those of the biography that we had not thought much about it save to arrange the celebration.

'Is it to be wrecked?' Columba continued mournfully. 'Is my mother to have a heart attack through shock when Imogen tells her? How could you allow such a thing, Ellie?'

'Me?' Talk about long-range missiles. I thought I was safe on this one. 'It's nothing to do with me.'

'Of course it is. How typical of the younger generation to evade responsibility. Did I not act responsibly towards you when I pointed out your husband's probable parentage?'

'That's enough, Columba.' Stephen's sharp voice cut right across. It was the first time I had ever heard him use such a tone to anyone, let alone Columba. It worked, for she fell silent and just stared at him in amazement.

Stephen took full advantage. 'It's time you Flowerdews took stock of the situation. You've a chance of uniting over this biography, so why don't you do it? From what you've told us, you might get Ted back, even' – wild possibility here – 'Cecilia and Violet talking again.'

'The press . . .' Columba made a feeble protest.

'Forget the press, sweetheart,' Stephen said to her gently. 'Think of your family.'

Columba was very quiet for a moment, then said grandly, 'I shall. I shall invite Cecilia to the party. *And* Ted.' She turned to me. 'Where is he, Ellie?'

I only wish I knew.

It was quite a few days before I thought about going to see Imogen again. I had put the whole idea of the biography into the background while I thought about my greater problem, now boiling up again at home. Something had to be decided, Quinn said, and so far as he was concerned, it was he who had to leave my parents' house. It was, I saw, last-ditch time. Yet my brain seemed numb.

'When are you going to see Imogen?' Mum asked me at last, with Columba nagging her.

'I'll get round to it. There's plenty of time – he's not going to disappear again.'

Mum did a double take. I followed suit. We were both thinking of the same idle remark I'd made in Cornwall: what is it about our family that makes it so prone to sudden disappearances? We were on the same wavelength. Thank heavens for family blood.

I almost yelped at Mum: 'Did Richard get on well with Ted?'

'Very.' There was excitement in her voice. 'He admired his approach to life.'

'Do you think . . . ?'

'He might, though how . . . ?'

'I'll go now,' I said.

'I'll come too.'

'No. I'll go alone. Imogen will talk to me, but with you there she might feel inhibited and never give me Ted's address.'

Mum agreed reluctantly, though muttering that rumours of Imogen's inhibitions seemed to have been greatly exaggerated.

I rang Imogen first, in case she was out. This was unlikely, because evenings were her quality time with Cecilia, listening to Flowerdew memories.

'Why all the hurry, Ellie?' she asked as she let me in. Naturally I hadn't told her the reason for my visit.

'I need just five minutes, Imogen.'

'Come and talk to Aunt Cecilia first,' she said reproachfully.

That took care of an hour. I finally made the excuse to go to the kitchen with Imogen while she made Cecilia's cocoa. 'She always slips a tot of whisky into it – she thinks I don't know.' Imogen laughed, and I felt humbled at having underestimated Imogen all these years.

I threw myself on Imogen's mercy. I told her *all* about our predicament, and she was genuinely appalled. 'Oh, poor Aunt Margaret,' she said. 'I didn't know the half of it. Why didn't you tell me?'

'Same reason you didn't tell us about Uncle Ted.'

She considered this seriously. 'Yes, I see that. So how can I help now?'

'I think there's a chance, and so does Mum, that Richard Hart is staying with Ted. He's probably not done a runner for good, so he needs somewhere to stay for a while.'

She looked surprised. 'But why should he be with Father? He could have hired a cottage in the Orkneys. Gone to ground in a dive in Battersea. Leapt aboard Eurostar.'

'I don't know whether he has. It's pure hunch, because they used to get on so well and because they both see the need of escape. And you mentioned Ted went to Australia in the early eighties. Suppose he met Richard there? It was just an idea.' The more I talked about it, the weaker it sounded.

'It seems a very long shot to me.'

'But worth taking. Please, Imogen, tell me where Uncle Ted hangs out now. I won't pass it on, I swear. And, what's more, he could come to Violet's ninetieth party in July, and his whole story can be told in the biography. He might be ready for reconciliation. He'd love being the life and soul of the party.'

'I'm not sure he'd come if he was invited. You see, he'd be coming anyway – incognito, of course.'

'Well, tell me where he is anyway,' I almost howled at her.

'Oh, Ellie, I wish I could. But I don't know.'

'I don't believe you. I just don't.'

'I'm sorry, but it's true.'

'Then how do you let him know about these events? Oh, come on, Imogen. Think of poor Mum.'

She looked at me as if I were out of my mind. 'Have you forgotten? I told you. I use e-mail.'

Of course she had told me, but it just hadn't registered. E-mail! The curse of the twenty-first century. 'But don't you know where he lives? Surely he'd have mentioned it?'

'I'm afraid not,' Imogen replied courteously.

'Can I have his e-mail address then?'

How feeble an end to what I'd hoped was the clue to Richard's whereabouts – and to the saving of my marriage.

Sixteen

I almost expected Jane to greet me with 'Hello, stranger' when I appeared in the office. She is really remarkable. I abandon her in the middle of the summer wedding period, and however hot the pace, she keeps cool. Perhaps she actually likes working on her own, and I'm a mere distraction to be tolerated. I was beginning to think I didn't understand Jane. I could only presume that it's a by-product of the single life that allows such single-minded dedication. Then I remembered that long-standing occasional boyfriend, and I *knew* I didn't understand her.

I listened with one ear as she ran through the list of weddings, numbers and catering arrangements. It was hard trying to get myself back into work mode while every inch of me smarted at my personal failure to get any further with the quest I had so confidently undertaken. It was clear that Jane had everything under control here, so why couldn't I claim the same?

Jane had the museum to cope with too, though she had conceded that even she couldn't be in two places at once. A Mrs Plumtree was hired for the reception desk, and a theatre buff volunteer from the village threw himself eagerly into the role of guide and answerer of questions. Jane was left with all the paperwork though, and, since John had gone back to London, with the major decisions too.

I missed John; I wanted to howl out my anguish and frustration to him. Since he wasn't exactly a comfy person to be with, it was odd that in a storm such as I was in, he seemed a trusty harbour.

'How did it go?' Jane eventually came to the end of the important business.

I told her about our futile trip to Cornwall. 'I'm going to tackle the caterers this morning,' I ended up. 'It's the only route left.' Imogen had claimed she'd have to look up the e-mail address, but she hadn't come back to me, and when I rang, she was always out.

'The caterers?' Jane looked startled. 'What do they have to do with the Mighty Rich?'

I forgot I hadn't explained one vital element. I'd been so intent on 1969 and Woodstock, I omitted Uncle Ted – of *much* more importance to Jane. I hesitated, then reflected that she'd been so close to Flowerdews for so long she was entitled to share the family secrets. So I told her.

She laughed so much I was quite worried. Jane never normally laughs outright, especially at work, but today she did. Perhaps it was sheer delight at the thought that she might be instrumental in tracking down the great Edmund Flowerdew, bringing him back to life for the museum. He was currently restricted to a splendid array of photographs of his fifties' and sixties' performances, and two dates: birth and death. Ho-ho.

'I'll get the caterers for you,' she spluttered, still laughing after I'd explained our hunch. Jane isn't the sort of person to set store by hunches, but today it seemed anything went.

I gritted my teeth for a telephone campaign of prospective customers – not the best way to begin it – and left her to it. Jane had one last question as she picked up the phone. 'What name is he going under? It won't be Flowerdew, obviously.'

I could have wept in frustration. Of course it wouldn't be Flowerdew, so I'd have to ring Imogen yet again.

Imogen's sturdy comforting voice came over the telephone as though the revelation about her father had never taken place. Perhaps it was all an illusion on my part, I thought gloomily. Perhaps the world would turn back to normal, now that Imogen had relapsed into her sturdy-walking-boot image. I hopefully asked my question.

'Sorry, Ellie, I don't know.'

'You're joking.' I couldn't believe it.

'I'm not, Ellie.' Imogen was offended. 'I do not know my father's current *nom de plume*.'

Disaster. 'Well, at least you can give me that address,' I asked her resignedly. It was a last resort.

There was a slight pause, then reluctantly she spelled it out. It began – of course it would – 'hamletdaneesq'. 'Thanks, Imogen.' And thanks, Uncle Ted, I muttered vengefully to the unkind fates.

Jane was already busy on my behalf, waving one arm at me to indicate she had things under control. There were silences as she listened to the caterers talking at the other end of the line, then her even voice would begin again: 'Could you not even tell me . . .' She simply repeated this formula until at last they surrendered.

'They say,' she told me, 'they do take on temporary staff, from agencies scattered all over the south-east and London. There were half a dozen or so at the museum do. I told them he looked like Manuel in *Fawlty Towers* and they thought he was the one who came from an agency in Bath – I've got the number, and the name.'

'Macbeth Smith,' I suggested bitterly.

'No.' Jane looked surprised. 'A Frenchman called Jacques Ardennes.'

Well of course. Shakespeare's Jaques from the Forest of Arden, the dear old soul. 'I'll get you yet, Ted,' I vowed grimly.

Or would I? When I told the family of the Bath connection – and I still firmly include Quinn in the word 'family' – Mum was delighted. Quinn was less optimistic. 'You don't know for sure,' he pointed out, 'whether

Richard has flown to Ted as an escape route. It's merely a wild guess.'

'It's a possibility,' said Mum decidedly. 'I know both of them, remember.'

'Then how,' asked Quinn, determined to look on the black side, 'did Richard ever get in touch with Ted again?'

'I've no idea. It could have been a chance meeting in Australia; it could even have been that he kept in touch with Ted ever since he left England in '69, because he sensed in him a fellow runner.' I plucked this from the air.

'I don't like that idea, Ellie,' Dad growled. 'You mean Richard might have been keeping tabs on us through Ted? He—'

'The important thing,' Mum interrupted, 'is that we have a clue at least to where Ted is now. Did you ring the Bath caterers, Ellie?' She was getting quite excited.

'No. If I ring them, and he is alerted as a result, then we're in trouble. Same thing if we e-mail Ted direct.'

'True.' Mum frowned. 'We'll have to go there, Ellie.'

'I'm coming this time,' Quinn said.

'No,' I said reluctantly. 'Richard will recognise you straightaway.' How I longed for him to come.

'But I'll recognise *him* too. You may not – even you, Margaret.'

We squabbled amicably about this for a few minutes, then tossed for it. I won – if you could call it that. It was Mum and I again.

Quinn was obviously put out. I looked at the golden hairs on his lower arm, I looked at that mouth I loved so much – I wanted to hug him, then drag him upstairs to show him how much I wished he were coming. If anything strengthened me for the trip it was that thought. I was never going to be in a position to kiss that mouth again until we had this problem sorted out. We *would* do it. I was more and more convinced – I had to be – that we were on the right track.

We managed to get booked into a B. & B. on the outskirts

of the city, only a ten-minute stroll into the heart of Bath's busy tourist area. Our first appointment, however, was with the caterers, and that put paid to our optimism immediately. They were helpful enough, but puzzled, even suspicious. They had no Jacques Ardennes on their books. We described Uncle Ted as we had seen him last, and this brought forth no instant recognition as it had done with the Tonbridge caterers. As we could hardly demand to go through their entire temporary staff lists in search of Shakespearian pseudonyms, we were stumped.

'Perhaps Ted was wearing a false moustache at the museum do,' I said hollowly to Mum as we walked into the centre of the city, somewhat stunned at this early setback. 'All we can do now is e-mail Ted.'

'And Richard – if he's with him – will go straight back to Cornwall,' Mum pointed out. 'Perhaps Ted doesn't even work for this catering firm. Have you considered that?'

I hadn't. As a detective I was meant for some other profession.

'Let's have a coffee and think about it.' I suggested the universal antidote to bad news. I'd never been to Bath before, and Mum had only visited it once donkey's years ago, so we gravitated to the tourist centre round the Abbey. It was too early in the day for school parties, but there were tourists in plenty, either as individuals or in escorted groups and coach parties.

We sat at a table near the open square outside the magnificent Abbey, where the pace was hotting up for the day, with stalls being set up and entertainers embarking on their individual programmes. We agreed that e-mail was our only chance now. I'd brought my laptop with me, so we discussed without enthusiasm the wording of our message to send when we got back to our lodgings.

Outside the Roman Baths nearby there were several groups congregating round their leaders. One authoritarian courier was in the midst of his big speech for his little chicks; another smaller group was clustering round a gentleman in full eighteenth-century dress including wig; he was accompanied by another similarly clad gentleman playing Papageno's song from *The Magic Flute* on his own flute – equally magic, to my surprise. It was charming, and accounted for the group around him being silent as he played.

'The Pied Piper's come to town,' I remarked idly to Mum. I turned my attention back to Beau Nash, just as I became aware that she was no longer with me.

She was walking straight up to the Piper. I ran after her, just in time to hear her say:

'Hello, Richard.'

He didn't even look surprised to see her. He stopped playing – momentarily – smiled at her, and said, 'Hello, Margaret.'

So there we were, sitting in the Royal Victoria Park at midday with our very own Regency buck, all eating ice creams. At least Richard Hart wore his own hair. He had in fact offered to change first, but Mum refused to let him. Quite right. That was the last we'd see of him.

Beau Nash – having taken one look at his sister's face – eagerly volunteered to carry on the tour alone, with a hurried suggestion that we all meet for dinner at a restaurant that evening. No home address, that way.

'Splendid,' agreed Mum, 'provided I've talked to Richard first.'

Hence the park. The ice creams were my idea. I had tactfully volunteered to get them, so that the main contestants in this coming battle could get reacquainted. All appeared to be peaceful and even serene when I returned.

I looked at this man who had once been married to my mother, and who had once had half the youth of the Western world at his feet, and decided he might indeed be rather likeable. Mum seemed to have herself well in hand; Richard would – I guessed – stir no heartstrings now. The big discussion was still to come. I let them chat, about Bath, about her pottery, about Sussex, about Australia, the band, and thirty years of reassessment of each other. Eventually I joined in, and Richard looked at me fully for the first time.

'Ellie,' was all he said, but his gaze seemed to take all of me in, the emotional me, the physical, and my character. There was nothing sexy in it; it was a sort of impersonal, almost godlike, compassionate warmth. Yet this was the man who had caused so much grief with his irresponsibility. Nowt so strange as folk.

'Margaret said you met two of the band.'

So he knew about Colin's suicide. 'Yes, and I met your father and brother.'

His face didn't change a jot. 'I don't want to hear about them. Tell me about Mike and Bryan – and Cecilia.'

The last lick of ice cream, the last piece of wafer, and the courtesies were over. I told him, and he listened without comment. It was a useful exercise, because it was clear the running had to be by us.

'And now, Richard,' Mum at last threw the gauntlet well and truly down, 'tell us what *really* happened at Woodstock.'

'I told Quinn – I liked your husband, Ellie.'

'I like him too,' I rejoined. 'So I want to keep him, and I can't unless we know the whole story.'

'What whole story?'

I realised I would get nowhere, so I left it to Mum. She took Richard's hand and held it. 'Just tell me, Richard. I know there's more than you told Quinn. We need to know, so that I can kiss the past goodbye. By that I mean kiss Marcus goodbye.'

'I lost him, Margaret.'

'I know. I understand why you didn't come home. And I realise you don't know where Marcus is now, or even if he's alive.'

'No. It's been bad for me too, Margaret.'

'I know, my love. You're happy with Jessie, and I am with

Gerald. So let's go forward, not grieve over the question marks of the past. And if it remains a question mark, then we must share it, not be divided by it.'

Richard seemed to be swayed, but he glanced at me.

'Shall I go?' I asked awkwardly.

'No,' Mum replied for him. 'Richard, you don't know Ellie, but so much hangs for her as well as for me on what you tell us.'

If Mum were not still holding his hand, I think Richard might have got to his feet and run like hell. He looked scared, his eyes roving around as though seeking an escape. Then he looked down at his tightly held hand, and seemed to be making up his mind. I was beginning to tremble myself now. Which way would it go? How I wished I had Quinn here to hold my hand. If it wasn't that I would distract her, I'd grab Mum's – anything for contact. No, I told myself, be strong. You're doing this for Quinn.

'I did lose Marcus,' Richard said at last. It came out as a half-sigh. 'That's true. I lost him at Woodstock. You've no idea what it was like. The crowds, the noise, the music, the wonderful feeling of harmony, of being part of a great new world movement for peace. If you could have heard Jimi Hendrix, Ravi Shankar, Joan Baez, Janis Joplin – so many – crying out, you'd understand. I felt I'd been fumbling my way through my own stuff towards something that had already reached fulfilment in Woodstock. I needed something new. But after Woodstock it all started going wrong. Peace was being eaten up with violence and harshness. That's why I headed for Nepal—'

'Richard,' Mum interrupted gently.

He glanced at her. 'I had to explain. It wasn't just the pot and the lack of sleep, it was the whole mind-numbing experience – and on that Monday morning everyone, not just me, was still caught up in it. Reeling from Jimi Hendrix's *The Star-Spangled Banner*. We did the cleaning up – well, some anyway. We gathered our belongings and headed out to track down our vans, but we were still living inside that music.

'I had Marcus with me while I tried to find our van – I had the camper with me, the orange one, but there were hundreds of them. Marcus pulled away in the crowd when I stopped to have a few words with someone, and when I turned round, he'd vanished. Then I saw our van and guessed he had spotted it too. When I got to it, the door was slid open – none of us had bothered to lock up – and I could see Marcus curled up in the back already asleep. He was obviously tired out. Sorry Margaret, but I knew Woodstock was an experience he'd never forget.'

No, I almost said out loud as I thought of Quinn's nightmares. Dear God, what was coming next in Richard's story?

'So I drove off,' Richard continued, 'went straight to the docks, and seeing he was still dead to the world, I didn't disturb him. There was a ship ready to depart, so I did the paperwork, drove straight on, and it wasn't until we were well out to sea that I thought I'd better rouse him. Margaret, it wasn't Marcus. He was wearing Marcus's coat, but it wasn't him. It was the kid he'd made friends with during the festival.'

I was cold with apprehension. A spasm crossed Mum's face but she didn't flinch. 'So what did you do?'

'There was nothing I could do. I thought about getting the ship turned round and so on, and then I calmed down and began to think. You've no idea, Margaret, what I went through.'

'Why didn't you go back?' Almost a wail from Mum.

'I'll tell you. I thought it was for the best. I really did. There'd been another Volkswagen camper just the same parked by the side of ours – there were lots of them there, like I said. They drew up as we arrived at Woodstock, and we got friendly. They had this boy, the same age as Marcus, and they bonded too, so we stayed together day and night during the festival. That's why their kid wasn't scared when he woke up on the boat and found me. During the time I lost Marcus and was hunting for him, they'd reached their van and driven off. They wouldn't have gone knowingly without their kid, so I figured it just had to be that the two kids had run ahead together, mistaken the vans. They were so dog-tired they covered themselves with their coats and fell asleep. Problem was, they'd switched coats.'

Richard looked rather pleased with himself for this rational thinking, but Mum was losing her cool now. 'So what did you do, for heaven's sake? *Why* didn't you insist on going back?'

'Listen, Margaret, please,' he pleaded. 'I'm telling you as I saw it. These folks were American but said they lived in Paris. So they too would be heading back across the Atlantic. I knew they must have Marcus with them, so there was no point in my going back, was there?' he pleaded. 'I was out in the Atlantic by the time I found out.'

'I don't know,' moaned my mother.

'I'd had this row with Will Gossage,' Richard explained anxiously, 'at the last gig I did in Britain. He wanted me to do this French thing he'd fixed up. So I thought, why not take the kid I had in my van straight back to his parents?'

It sounded so logical at first, until I started thinking further. What about telegraphs, phones, wiring back to the New York police? Finding out about other ships? No. Richard being Richard – and having met him, I now understood what that meant – it was all clear in his mind. Marcus was in Paris, so he'd wait till he got there, pick Marcus up, and go home to Mum as though nothing had happened. But what *had* happened?

'Did you know where they lived?' Mum demanded.

'Only that it was in Paris.'

'What was their name?'

'Well, I—'

'Didn't know,' she finished bitterly.

'No one did, Margaret. Not at Woodstock. We didn't

258

even bother with forenames, let alone surnames. People
were people – we bonded, that was all.'

Great, I thought, and see where bonding got you.

'Once I got to Paris,' – it began to pour out now – 'I
thought it would be easy to find two American expats there
through the American Embassy; there were masses of US
organisations who could help, as well as the police.'

'And did it occur to you that they might have found out
they'd lost their son *before* they got on the boat?' Mum had
no sarcasm in her voice. She was just anxious to get the
whole story.

'Sure, but they would guess what had happened. They
knew I would be heading straight for the docks to get home
to you, so they wouldn't have lingered in the States either.'

I didn't know whether this was the best or the worst logic
I'd ever heard. Like Mum, I just wanted to get to the end.
Hope was rising, oh indeed it was – until I thought of this
crazy expat couple let loose in Paris with a child that didn't
belong to them. Mum saw the look on my face, and promptly
dropped Richard's hand to attend to her other little chick.

'Hold on, Ellie, we're getting there.'

The road to hell was what we were walking along though.
It might be paved with good intentions, but that was where
it was leading for Mum and for myself.

'I did a few gigs,' the happy wanderer continued, 'and
spent the rest of the time going round the organisations trying
to track this couple down. After all, I reasoned, there couldn't
be too many people who'd just come back from Woodstock
with a child who wasn't their own. I put out announcements
at my gigs, the Embassy and other organisations did all they
could, but nothing came back from any source. I couldn't
believe it, Margaret, truly.'

'What about the police?' The dynamite question.

'I couldn't,' he muttered. 'Not directly, anyway. You'd
find out. It was a last resort, so I had a better idea. I
was in a bad way, Margaret; I couldn't come back to you

without Marcus. I could stay on in Paris and hope I'd run into this couple, but I couldn't understand why *they* hadn't contacted the police or anyone about Marcus. There'd have been publicity if they had. I assumed they'd come back to Paris some time, but after two months, there was still no sign. The kid was getting restless, to say the least, and I wanted to get to Nepal. It was time for a new look at myself, so I had this idea. If I left the kid at an orphanage, they'd make all the enquiries I couldn't. They'd contact the police, his parents would pick him up, and the police would publicise Marcus. I only had to hang around a little longer doing another gig or two and it would turn out all right. Only it didn't. Still there was no word.'

Quinn! It must have been Quinn. My heart shouted with joy. Everything was coming up roses.

'The orphanage in Vincennes? You left him in the garden?'

'Yes.'

The relief poured out of me. 'Then that's my husband. Why on earth didn't you tell him that and save him all this worry?'

'I *did* tell him – all but the last bit.' Richard was genuinely aggrieved.

It didn't matter. I was safe. Quinn was mine – my husband for the rest of our lives.

And then I saw my mother's face.

By the time we arrived at the restaurant that evening, my mother had recovered sufficiently to face her brother as well as her ex-husband. 'After all,' she said bravely, 'I'm no worse off than I was this morning. Marcus is lost, and that's that. There's no tracing him now.' She tried to smile to show she meant it, but it was hard.

Fortunately the dinner took her mind off the subject of Marcus – Uncle Ted could be guaranteed to take one's mind off most things. It was a strange party: these figures from the past, Mum, and me. It was hard to believe, seeing the three of them together, that between them their lives could have covered so much drama. Uncle Ted looked like every girl's favourite uncle; there was no moustache this time, but a splendid crop of grey hair crowned a kindly face that almost had me charmed into wanting to marry him myself. He spoke so lovingly of Flossie, Joan and Patsy that it was easy to see why they still hankered after him.

Oh, I forgot to mention that there was one more person at the dinner party.

'My wife Katie,' Ted explained casually.

Mum and I took this on the chin. We couldn't very well enquire about the legalities of this marriage, especially since we both took to Katie. She was slim, dark, mid-fifties, and obviously devoted to Ted.

'She knows all about the Flowerdews and me – no need to hold back,' Ted roared at us. 'And about Les Girls.'

'And the little spell inside,' Katie added, 'though it's not something he cares to mention.'

'I can understand that,' Mum retorted. 'Are you proposing to tell all for the biography? You told Imogen you'd give John a truncated version of your interesting life.'

'Why not the lot?' Ted seemed surprised. 'The press can't get at me. They don't know my name. Or where I live.'

'Bath should help,' Mum pointed out.

'Who said I live here? Just doing the season, kid sister.'

I entered into the spirit of the occasion. 'Are you coming to Grandma Violet's ninetieth in July?' I asked politely.

'Wouldn't miss it for the world. Pity Katie can't come.'

'Why can't I?' she asked.

He looked at her thoughtfully. 'Well, why not indeed?' he roared at last. 'Maybe I've been separated too long from my loving family. Time to see my dear old Ma.'

'Joan and Patsy will be there, not to mention Flossie.' I tried to play fair.

'So?'

It was, I could see, going to be some party.

As we came out of the station at Crowborough we found that
Dad was there to meet us. I knew Mum had told him the news
over the telephone, but I had insisted that I would be the one
to tell Quinn.

I found him in the garden, prowling around, knowing I was
due back and trying to look nonchalant. I went straight up to
him, put my arms around him, and said:

'It's all right, Quinn. You're not my half-brother.'

That was all he needed. A howl of relief, of delight, of –
I'm glad to say – desire. Five minutes later we were in bed
– we could hardly indulge our reunion there and then on the
grass, in full view of the house.

Even then, a moment's reassurance was needed.

'Sure?'

'Yes,' I said. 'You're not my half-brother. Final answer.
Shall I tell you?'

'Later,' he ordered, *'please.'* Seeing that his hand was
where my interests were firmly at stake I was only too eager
to agree. Oh, the bliss. Not the mad passion of the day of
the museum opening, but the calm, exuberant knowledge
that there would be countless other days and countless other
nights on the path that led not to hell but to paradise.

Afterwards, his arm thrown across me, he remembered to
ask me for the details. He listened in the quietness of our
room as I poured out the whole story. 'It's true, then. Even I
believe it now,' he said after I'd finished. 'Just one thing.'

'Yes?'

'Who the hell *am* I?'

'My husband, that's all that matters.'

Was I right? Only time would tell. Could the past – having
been stirred up this far – be dropped so easily? And where
would we begin looking now? I could only gently reassure
Quinn that it didn't matter; he had two perfectly good
adoptive parents and that was more than a lot of people

262

had. It was time now to build our marriage – no more misunderstandings, no more mistrust. The road was open.

A *Note from Quinn*

Ellie was right, of course. There was no need for me to know my origins. The matter could be dropped forthwith.

Once that insidious serpent is stirred up, however, he is mighty difficult to ignore. When Ellie came to tell me in the garden that everything was coming up roses, I felt the panic slip away from me and leave me whole again – for the future, at least. But the past cannot be shaken off quite so quickly. Life does not ordain that every loose end should be tied, yet there is an urge that it should, that it is unfair to expect us to go through life and reach our deaths without ever knowing some of the answers.

When we joined Margaret and Gerald for dinner that evening, my lovely Ellie was shining brightly, but I watched her mother's face and knew she was thinking the same thing: it was not all over quite so quickly for us. Not for Margaret, not for me, for we both mourned those snatched away from us. I joined in the bubbling talk around the table, but all the time my brain was thinking furiously, trying to recall every detail of what Ellie had told me.

Gerald produced his speciality for dessert – pavlova with strawberries. I looked at the magnificent circular meringue with the hole in its middle. It seemed symbolic of Ellie and myself: bliss on the outside, but in the middle there was still a hole. Unless Margaret or Ellie had missed something out, there was an inconsistency in the story, a gap like that in the meringue before me. It could be filled with emptiness for ever, or it could be loaded with strawberries.

I knew which I preferred.

Seventeen

It was hard even to think of work as I struggled out of my blissfully reclaimed bed with Quinn next morning, but I had no choice. Jane had claimed her compensation for my being absent so much this summer by asking, very apologetically, if she might take a week's holiday, even though we usually try to leave our own breaks to September. (She promised faithfully that she would find a decent 'hotel' for my cat.)

Of course I agreed, while wondering whether I could ever get my mind round other people's marriages when the happiness of my own was so much in my mind. What's more, this was the week leading up to Grandma Violet's ninetieth. True, it wasn't being held at Charham Place, but even so, the amount of phone calls from Columba, who was organising it, were bound to be high. She was also using our caterers, which made it doubly exacting. It crossed my mind to wonder whether Uncle Ted was now engineering his waitering presence or whether he would arrive with a new persona – himself.

Quinn had explained he was in the middle of a project with a tight deadline, and asked if I minded if we hung on at Kingsgate House for ten days or so while he got it finished. Mum and Dad were delighted – Dad especially, since he was worried about how Mum was taking the realisation that the end of the road had come for picking up a trail to Marcus. To me, she appeared to be rallying remarkably well, but then I cottoned on to the fact that she wouldn't want to spoil my happiness – in which she shared of course, if only through pure relief that I was once more 'settled'.

I was rushed off my feet at work – not with new business, but with the thousand and one phone calls that the lead-up time to the wedding always generates. Fortunately, this is the part I enjoy, but even so, it left me little time for thinking of family matters. I half-expected to see John, as Jane wasn't here to oversee the museum, but he was obviously holding Columba's hand. The staff seemed perfectly capable of coping, however, even though Stephen wasn't around either. I knew he'd be over for the party, so I was slightly surprised he hadn't yet clocked in at Charham Place. The party was being held in Grandma's relatively large (for London) garden in Hampstead. The weather looked reasonably certain to be fine, but the usual marquee arrangements had been made just in case.

For once I was looking forward to a major Flowerdew gathering – one that included Cecilia. Everything that could go wrong had already done so, and even the biography looked set fair now. It seemed to me that unless someone was intent on throwing a spanner into the works, it would be a fun day. Anything was, of course, possible, but with Grandma Violet as the centrepiece, the usual gods of war would surely be restrained.

It wasn't for a day or two that I picked up the signals that Quinn was no longer sharing Cloud Nine with me. For some reason he had taken a parachute down a few thousand feet. The first night I told myself it was his work; the second night I was not so sure. There was an element of lip-service to our reunion – or was I getting over-sensitive to trouble? The lip-service I required had to be wholehearted, and so, when on the third night I found myself unexpectedly alone on the terrace with him after dinner, I nerved myself to ask the inevitable question: 'What's wrong, Quinn?'

He was startled – probably because I had noticed that

anything was wrong at all, I guessed. 'Wrong?' he answered warily.

So I knew I was right. 'Tell me, Quinn.'

'Sure you want to know?'

Getting worse. 'Yes.'

'I think – it's going round and round in my head – there's at least one gap or inconsistency in Richard's story.'

Worse than I thought. 'I expect you can't believe the truth,' I suggested hopefully. 'It takes time.'

'I can't be sure, but I think Richard told me he informed the police *in the States* about Marcus's disappearance. He must have done, otherwise why would I have asked Stephen to investigate there?'

My mind reeled. 'Perhaps you assumed he meant the States, Quinn. In fact it was Paris, and he must have meant they were alerted through the orphanage.'

He chided me gently. 'Not thinking, Ellie. The New York police had reports of my being missing, remember?'

'And Richard claims he didn't discover about the mistaken identity until he was on the boat.' Cloud Nine suddenly became very dark and rainy. I couldn't think straight. And then came the worse blow.

'And why, oh Ellie, why did I arrive at that orphanage saying my name was Quinn?'

That did it. My mind clarified like boiled butter. 'Right,' I announced briskly, 'let's deal with this. It all comes down to this: do we believe Richard was telling Mum the truth? We've both met him; we know Mum's opinion. The truth, and nothing but the truth. It's only the whole truth we're dealing with here.'

'A philosophical riddle, Ellie. Like the old chestnut, "Empedocles the Cretan said that all Cretan men are liars." If Richard *says* he was telling you the whole truth, how does that add up?'

I tried this one, and couldn't puzzle it out. 'I believe Richard,' I said simply. 'How about you?'

'I believe him too. Yet if we heard Richard's whole truth, where does that leave us? And suppose Richard's assumption that the other couple had Marcus was wrong?'

'I don't know, Quinn, but the main thing is, do you still have a doubt that you might be Marcus Quinn?'

'I ought to, but I don't.'

A great weight rolled off me – for a moment I thought we were right back at the beginning again, and I just couldn't have coped with that. Now it was easier. 'Then there has to be an answer to your questions. Now we've met Richard, he won't mind being tackled again. I'll e-mail Ted and drop a line to Richard's Cornish home.' (You won't be amazed to hear that he was ex-directory.) 'And as for Stephen,' – I glanced at my watch – 'we'll ring him now about the New York end.'

I spoke more confidently than I was feeling. We both dashed upstairs, Quinn to e-mail Ted on his computer line, and me to ring Stephen on the other line. The e-mail winged its way through cyberspace; my ringing tone ended in voice-mail. I left a message for Stephen to ring me urgently, and wrote a short note to Richard to post to Cornwall on the morrow. After that we went to bed and celebrated our oneness, emotionally as well as physically.

Twenty-four hours later neither e-mail nor voice-mail had been replied to. We both agreed that this time we would keep our enquiries to ourselves, in order not to upset Mum again. But the silence greeting our efforts continued.

We woke up on the Sunday morning of Grandma Violet's ninetieth none the wiser. No word from Stephen, none from Richard via Ted. At least, we comforted ourselves, we would be seeing Stephen at the party, and there was an odds-on chance Ted would be there too, if we kept our eyes skinned. I had expected to see John and Columba, as well as Stephen, at Charham Place before the birthday, but none of them turned up. I'd even been there on the

Saturday, since Jane was only returning from holiday that evening.

Moreover it was raining. I looked with dismay at the outfit I'd chosen, so suitable for a sunny July afternoon, and so ridiculous in the rain. Pale lemon indeed. I'd look like one too, in this rain.

'Wear it,' was my husband's advice.

I cheered up. Why not go into battle all flags flying, regardless of colour? And so I dressed up and felt better. Quinn – never keen on sartorial issues – produced a smart blazer, shirt and even a new tie, so you could tell it was a Real Occasion. Again we travelled separately from Mum and Dad, but not for the same reason as last time. Both our cars were packed with presents, since we'd chosen to give her rose bushes – as near violet in colour as we could manage – for her birthday.

The Flowerdew mansion was a red-brick, wisteria-covered early Victorian house and had a warmth about it that I always loved. I haven't said much so far about my grandmother, mainly because she hasn't played a direct role in this story, but also because we have little in common.

With Cecilia I know where I am. She is completely dotty and always has been, and is therefore tolerant of the world's little imperfections, especially as revealed in those dearest and nearest to her. Grandma Violet, on the other hand, is genuinely anxious to put the world's imperfections right, and *especially* as reflected in her descendants.

I always feel I am failing her in some way, probably because, like Mum, I have not carried the Flowerdew torch onto the stage. I like her – most people do – but her dedication to the Flowerdew cause is a bit much to take. She was still holding out on the biography, probably because she knew the truth about Uncle Ted. John could do without her co-operation, but it wouldn't look good.

For a start, it would give Jasper the whip hand. John would have to toe his every line, for otherwise Jasper would simply change sides. Jasper *and* Violet would be too formidable an opposition, and it had not gone unnoticed that Jasper was getting on remarkably well with Grandma at the museum opening. I hoped John was in good shape for battle.

As I hopped into our car, I thought about how all the Flowerdew family members and associates would be doing exactly the same thing around this time, all pointing their vehicles to one house. How would Joan and Patsy be feeling as they set off? How about the children? Would they be blessed with a real live father at the day's end? At very least, they must be taking this as an acknowledgement of their being part of the Flowerdew clan. Was Uncle Ted on his way with Katie? Columba and John would be getting ready to set out, and Stephen would be heading for Hampstead too. And how about Cecilia, clutching her surprise invitation? Would she accept her old enemy's olive branch, or spoil for a fight? Mum and Dad were looking forward to it, probably as an escape into problems not their own. And so was Quinn. It seemed an Armageddon where past scores might be fought out and an armistice arranged.

It was going to be a no-expense-spared occasion. I don't know who was footing the bill – Columba, I presumed. Violet had precious little money of her own, even though in the stateliness of the way she lived, she acted like the British Raj.

As we drove in, the sun obligingly came out and had a word with the puddles on the drive and the wet bedraggled grass. The word worked, for we saw no rain for the rest of the day.

The marquee was installed, and inside we could see caterers hard at work. A good number of guests had already arrived. Everything had been thought of. There was an ice-cream stall for the children, a first-aid post manned by St John's Ambulance, a croquet pitch for light exercise, a hamburger stall, a bouncy castle – and a large notice pointing the way to the house where a room had been devoted to a 'scrapbook' of

Flowerdew past. Not that the house wasn't that anyway, but this was for photographs and personal items never generally on display. John would have a field day.

Catering was still at coffee stage, since Violet was going to make a grand entrance from the house at twelve o'clock. A number of tables dotted the lawn – Cecilia had already staked out hers, as near to the centre table as she could.

We carted in our rose bushes and added them to the heap, then did a tour of the caterers to see whether Uncle Ted lurked amongst them. No sign, but that didn't mean he wasn't here. He'd be keeping out of our sight, at least until his mother came in.

The crowds were gathering now, and by an unspoken consensus we all drifted round being frightfully polite, and not getting down to serious issues. We all agreed that Violet looked marvellous for her age, that it was sad her husband had died so comparatively young, and that it was nice to see Cecilia here. Everyone chatted to Joan, Patsy, and their families – even Flossie. I heard Jasper trying to drop a spanner in the works; he was ignored, but seemed to take it in good part. Jane arrived with that after-holiday healthy look, closely followed by Columba and John, and, to my relief, Stephen.

Phew! I could hardly rush straight over with my questions, so Quinn and I held back until after Violet's arrival. That would be the starting pistol for the Flowerdew frolics. In fact Stephen disappeared again with Columba, so we were forced to contain our impatience anyway.

Promptly at twelve, Violet – with Stephen on one arm, Columba on the other, and her carer hovering anxiously behind – made her triumphant way into the garden. Corks popped, waiters scurried around with trays – efficiently, so no Uncle Ted, I guessed. Violet graciously acknowledged the cheering guests – well, you can guess the scene. The pistol had been fired and we were off.

I made a beeline for Stephen, Quinn hard on my heels. 'Didn't you get my message?' I demanded after the bare courtesies were over.

'No.' He looked surprised that anyone should want to contact him. 'Where did you leave it? Nothing wrong at the house, is there?'

'No,' I hastened to reassure him. 'It's about that phone call you made to the New York State police.' I explained the puzzle, and my heart sank as I could see him frowning. 'I hoped you might have got the wrong end of the stick.'

'I'm pretty good at sticks,' he replied mildly.

I suppose to be a millionaire you have to be, I thought, and fell back on line two: 'Could it be that the police just said there was a child missing at the time and you put the name in their mouths? It was you talking about Quinn, not them.'

He looked at me more kindly than I deserved. 'They *told* me the child was called Quinn.'

'Then Richard *was* lying,' I said hollowly, 'and if he was lying about that, he could have been lying about anything.'

Quinn put his arm round me. 'Don't give up, Ellie. We still haven't heard from Richard.'

'And we're not likely to,' I said bitterly, 'if he's strung us a heap of lies.'

'I truly don't think he would,' Quinn reassured me. 'Nor does your mother.'

'Then you think I'm lying? That my memory's going? You're entitled to think that, if you like,' Stephen informed us. He was quite nice about it, just adamant.

Knowing him, we couldn't believe that either.

'You know those jigsaws,' I said, 'where the pieces are so similar you're sometimes convinced you've got the right piece in place – until you get to the very end and the last pieces don't fit. You have to search for the wrong piece, hoick it out, the right one almost leaps into place, and the jigsaw's done. It's the same here: everyone is telling the truth but one piece has been fitted in wrongly.'

'Which is it, though?' asked Quinn.

'I wish I could help,' Stephen said wistfully, 'but I can't. Quinn is what the police said.'

We scoured the whole house and gardens for Uncle Ted. We accosted Grandma's housekeeper and her husband to see if they were actually Ted and Katie in disguise (they weren't), we cross-examined the caterers, tackled gardeners and stall owners, and were about to admit defeat when we ran into Imogen licking an ice cream with satisfaction.

'Have you seen your father here anywhere?' I asked hopefully.

'I doubt if he's coming. He hasn't told me anyway – not that he always does,' she conceded. 'I did send him an official invite by e-mail – Grandma doesn't know, of course.'

'If he does come, won't the shock be a bit much for her?'

'She's made of stern stuff.'

'True enough.'

'Ice creams,' yelled Quinn, looking at Imogen's ice cream.

Of course. We'd missed the ice-cream stall.

We doubled out of the marquee and checked the jovial ice-cream lady – who bore no relation to either Uncle Ted or Katie. So we had to buy ourselves ice creams to explain our presence. Very sophisticated.

Imogen strolled up to us as we licked away. 'By the way, Father sent a message to you. I don't know what it's about, but you may. He said, "The flute player didn't tell the New York police."' She looked at our flabbergasted faces. 'Is it important?'

'You could say so,' I said savagely. Seeing her crestfallen face, I immediately added, 'Not your fault, Imogen. Just ours, getting worked up again.'

'It must have been the other couple at Woodstock who told the New York police,' I said to Quinn when Imogen left us.

'Why should they tell the New York police about Marcus and not their own child? I suppose there has to be a logical explanation, but it beats me how we're going to find it.' We looked gloomily at the merry throng around us.

'We'll think about it later. Let's try to enjoy the party – it's only fair.'

If we threw ourselves with enough enthusiasm into the Flowerdew world, there was a chance we could temporarily forget the problems of Quinn and Ellie Connelly.

John appeared, and I saw Quinn's mental hackles rising. 'How's the biography going?' I asked brightly. I had rung Columba when it was obvious John was not going to show up in Charham, and asked her to tell John the news about Ted and his probable co-operation.

'I had your message. Is he here?'

'No sign of him yet. Imogen's sure he'll give it a miss after his overdose of family in Bath.'

'Perhaps he'll make a grand appearance later, to upstage Violet.'

'What as? The famous Fat Lady? I wouldn't put it past him. You should have seen him as Beau Nash.'

'I'm glad to hear about your success with the Mighty Rich,' John said. 'All's well then?'

'Yes,' Quinn answered curtly.

'Actually, no,' I said, determined to be truthful. I explained what was wrong now, concluding, 'It makes no major difference, since we do believe now that Quinn is not Marcus, but it would be so good to be able to tie up the loose ends. We can't explain how the police in New York knew about Quinn being missing.'

'Weird,' John frowned. 'Maybe the French police told them when Richard gave them the story.'

'Possible.' I clutched at this straw.

'My dear Watson,' Quinn said irritably, 'if you recall, Richard *didn't* tell the French police. The orphanage did. It was part of his master plan to flush out the couple from Woodstock. Then why, mastermind, did they—' Quinn

273

stopped short. 'The nuns gave the name Quinn to the police, as the only clue they had.'

'Guess that's right.' John wasn't smirking, but Quinn behaved as if he were.

'Now explain why I turned up at the orphanage calling myself Quinn. My parents . . .' He hesitated, and my heart bled for him. 'My adoptive parents can't have made that up, surely.'

'Maybe. They sometimes go to some lengths to cover up,' John replied.

Just as Quinn was about to snarl back, Columba arrived. If I thought my outfit was fancy, hers beat me to it. Bright mauve, silk trousers and tunic, most of it embroidered. Her green-streaked hair stuck out in contrast, and her lipstick shouted the odds over the lot. 'Darling,' she said to us all embracingly, though chiefly to John, 'I've been looking for you. It's time to make the announcement.'

'I thought Violet wasn't making her big speech till cake-cutting time,' I said.

'*Our* announcement, darling. So I need you there, John.'

She swept him off, and I gazed at Quinn in horror. 'You don't think she's going to announce her forthcoming marriage to John, do you? It would be so typical. It would be one way of ensuring that the biography *and* her mother get second place.'

'I wouldn't put it past' – Quinn paused, and finished sweetly – 'him.'

I laughed. 'You're prejudiced. In fact, I'd like to have John as my uncle.'

'All I can say is that they deserve each other.'

It was sunny enough for most people to have gravitated outside, even the two matriarchs. Fortunately Columba had thought of this possibility, and arranged a small dais with a microphone. 'For Violet,' she had murmured earlier when I noticed it, but it would do equally admirably for her.

I had to admit Columba looked stunning flanked by her

two admirers, John and Stephen. She made a glowing brief speech about the Flowerdews – though I noticed so far there was no mention of the biography – and explained that Violet would be making *the* speech later on. Then she 'shyly' told us she had a few words to say about a new member of the Flowerdew family. I froze. What would Jasper make of that? I need not have worried. She added, 'After our great delight in discovering two more whole families to carry on our tradition, I thought I could sneak one more in myself.'

Quinn squeezed my hand at this point. He practically had to hold me up too, when Columba continued: 'Darling Stephen and I are to be married.'

It was quite obvious that John was expecting this news, but not Stephen himself! He gazed around him as though not sure if he were still in jet lag. He didn't actually say, 'Wot me?' but it was written all over his face. Fortunately that expression was quickly replaced with one of sheer delight – poor sap.

Columba swooped on us after she had been through the mill of general congratulations. 'Darlings, won't it be nice to have me next door when you're back at the Lodge?' I thought I heard Quinn choke. 'I won't be there all the time, of course,' she continued. 'I shall keep up my career, but we'll have lots and lots of jolly times together.'

'Oh, good.' Quinn made a noble stab at enthusiasm, and I followed suit. After Columba and Stephen had passed on to the next round of congratulations, I said to John in relief, 'That was a near thing. I thought *you* were her candidate.'

He looked a little surprised. 'Did you? Oh no, I'm going to marry Jane. Wasn't that obvious?'

The problem with having crises in one's life is that they blind you to everyone else's lives. You become the axis of the whole world. Jane? John? Why should I find that so very staggering? They'd been thrown together a great deal this summer, and the more I thought about it, the more obtuse I seem to have been. The occasional boyfriend had been banished, and John had taken over. It explained why Jane was so reluctant for me to move in when I walked out on Quinn; it explained the success of the museum, why John had other plans for Christmas – and it explained the holiday, not to mention her good humour this summer.

It's just that I had it fixed in my head that Columba and he were an item, although, as I thought back, it could have been that John was simply amusing himself by encouraging this notion. Relief, and genuine pleasure for Jane, swept over me, and I told her so.

Quinn was more mixed in his reactions. He likes Jane. 'If she likes him, I suppose there must be more to the American cowboy than I thought,' he whispered grudgingly in my ear as John turned to grab a drink from a passing tray.

'How's the biography going?' I asked him quickly.

He grimaced. 'I was going to be tactful and leave it till after the cake-cutting ceremony, but your grandmother collared me. "Young man," she informed me, "I wish you to know that under no circumstances will I co-operate on this book, except, in my late husband's memory, to give you access to *his* memorabilia. Nothing else. Is that clear?" It was all too clear, and she meant it. It got worse. "When the time comes for the Flowerdew history to be written, it will be not by an American, but by a member of the Flowerdew family. I shall inform Jasper of my wishes." Great, isn't it?'

'Oh John. I'm so sorry. Are you going to wipe the dust of the Flowerdews off your feet?'

'I wiped one foot. The other's in the air till I've spoken to Jasper.'

'Who doesn't even know for sure his father's alive,' I said gloomily. 'As you said, John, great.'

I did my best, and I did it alone. It wasn't fair to drag Quinn in. Jasper was the key. We only had today to sort this out. If we left it to correspondence between the eighty or more Flowerdews gathered here today it would never get settled. No good speaking to Grandma Violet though, and it wasn't fair either. Jasper was a different matter.

'Hi,' he said as I strolled up, as though we'd been best cousin friends all our lives. 'Great show, isn't it?'

We murmured niceties for the briefest possible time. 'Could your enthusiasm to talk to me have anything to do with a biography?' he asked me, grinning.

'Yes, it could. I gather Grandma's fixed on you as biographer elect.'

'Terrific, isn't it? From bastard to heir apparent in one jump.'

'Are you going to do it?'

'Why not?'

'Do you want all the reasons, or just those that affect you?'

'Hard-hitting, Ellie. And you such a pretty little thing.'

'And you such an implausible villain.'

'Am I?'

'Where do you stand, Jasper? I guess your career comes first. Are you going to sacrifice your determination to do it on your own by irrevocably linking yourself to the Flowerdew name?'

'Ouch. I feel my Achilles heel going.'

'Well?'

'Truth?'

'Yes, please.'

'I don't know. She's only just sprung this on me. Your arrow very skilfully hit the mark. I'm not, *not* going to be a Flowerdew name parasite. I suppose I might wait till I become famous, and do it in the grandeur of my middle age.'

'So,' I said thoughtfully, 'since you've years to go – to middle age, of course, not to being famous – you could do your own book then, and no problem with John doing one now.'

'Aren't you forgetting something, Ellie?'

'Our darling Grandma Violet.'

*   *   *

The waiters had filled up every glass of champagne and disappeared. It was time for my grandmother to cut her cake in the marquee. She stood up without help, and despite my frustration I couldn't help admiring her. She had taken on at long last the aura of Flowerdew drama. Her speech was very short and to the point, but not relevant to this story, so I won't go into it. Except for the finale. The ninety candles on the huge cake were blown out with what appeared to be one breath, and we all duly sang. Then Grandma took the knife and cut the first slice. She put it on a plate herself. Slowly she walked over to Cecilia. 'This is for you, Cis.'

Cecilia – dressed as Aida today but playing herself for once – was totally upstaged. She gracefully got to her feet and kissed her sister-in-law. Violet walked back to the table for the next slice. She took the plate from the waiter, started to hand it to Columba, and then seemed to change her mind. How was she going to top her coup with Cecilia? I wondered. Violet looked round the tent, standing quite still. Suddenly she swayed a little, but before anyone could rush to her assistance, she recovered. She stood there, her head thrown back as if she were sniffing the spring air like Mole. How could she tell what had made this day so different from all the other family events? I have never worked it out, but it happened.

The guests were quite silent as she stood there. Then she called out:

'Ted! Come here this instant. I have some cake for you.'

Unbelievably, a St John's Ambulance man strolled up from the back of the tent towards the mother who thought she had not seen him for almost thirty years. There were a few muffled screams in the audience from Flossie, Joan and Patsy – the children who thought they had lacked a father all their lives took more time to cotton on.

My Grandmother Violet looked her errant son up and down in silence before finally speaking. 'Call yourself a Flowerdew?' she asked scathingly.

'No, Mother.' This grown man of nearly seventy was immediately reduced to jelly.

'Then it's time you did. Come back, son.'

Ted had enough of the public gaze. Gently he led his mother into the house, and no one followed them. He then of course vanished back into the cyberspace of his own making. He and his mother had, it transpired, come to some arrangement.

There was one step forward this time in that he said goodbye to *everyone*, and met all his children and partners again. He managed to convince them all that he'd be back to play an active role in their lives.

'I shan't, of course,' he told Mum. 'Too old to change my ways – besides, Katie might not like it.'

Maybe the police wouldn't either, but I knew his marital status was one question we were hardly likely to clarify for them. He promised faithfully to keep the same e-mail address – though not, I noticed, to stay in Bath – and handed it out to anyone who wanted it. Cyberspace is a safe place to hide.

He had, he told us, fulfilled one other mission: he had talked to his mother about the biography. He told her he couldn't care less what was written about him (so yes, he was about to leave Bath) and was in favour of it, and why shouldn't it be done now while Violet and Cecilia were still alive, rather than wait for Jasper?

Violet had refused, however. Ted could do what he liked, but she would not co-operate.

'She feels strongly about family,' Ted said apologetically. An understatement in my view.

The party was over. Columba invited us to Charham Place for dinner and an overnight stay. Somewhat reluctantly Mum, Dad, John, Jane and myself and Quinn agreed. John and Jane had their own reasons for hesitation; the rest of us were aware that our problems were still awaiting us back home and the sooner we faced them the better.

Harriet Hudson

I wonder how many of the world's problems get solved by sheer chance? In our case, we identified our wrong jigsaw piece purely by luck, although we should have thought of it, way, way back. Quinn later blamed himself for not fitting it in sooner. The important thing is that we did it now. Perhaps it was the champagne sharpening our wits rather than dulling them.

We were talking of John and Jane's coming wedding.

'Will you marry in England?' Mum asked.

'I don't think I'd want to be married anywhere else,' Jane said happily. 'I want Ellie to arrange it all.'

'Thanks very much,' I joked. 'Let me do all the work.'

'No, I'll give you a hand,' she replied seriously.

'I hope you're staying on when you're Mrs Curwen.'

Quinn had been talking to Mum and Dad and only caught the last of this. 'Yes?'

'Yes, what?' I answered.

'You were speaking to me.'

'No, I wasn't. I was speaking to Jane.'

'I heard you say Quinn.'

'Wrong.'

'Ellie said "when you're Mrs Curwen", Quinn,' Jane supported me.

And then we all realised. What's in a sound? We hear what we expect to hear. We all began to talk at once.

'They do sound alike.' Quinn was keeping excitement at bay. 'Do you think – no, too outrageous. How could everyone have mistaken it for so long?' Then a look of complete horror crossed his face as he croaked, 'John, didn't you once imply you were adopted?'

'Sure.' I don't think John was liking this any more than Quinn.

'And' – I was trying to keep the cork in the bottle before my brain exploded with possibilities – 'didn't you mention your adopted parents went to pop festivals?'

'Look—' Quinn began.

280

Mum stopped him. 'Go on, Ellie.'

'We know' – I fumbled my way through the dark tunnel – 'that you, Quinn, were the child that Richard took to France by mistake. Suppose when you got to the orphanage you were trying to say that your name was not Quinn, but *Curwen*.'

'I'd have told Richard too, then. He'd have known the name was Curwen.' Quinn was getting desperate with hope – or fear of failure. I didn't know which, but I had to go on.

'If he asked you your name and you said "Curwen" to him, Richard would have heard it as Quinn because of Marcus – you remember he used to call himself Quinn because he liked it better. So Richard thought you were only talking of Quinn because you'd been friendly with him at Woodstock. One hears what one expects.'

'But the New York police—' Stephen began.

'I bet your bottom dollar they did the same thing,' I rushed on excitedly. 'They said the missing child's name was Curwen, and you, Stephen, expecting to hear Quinn, heard it as such.'

'So that means . . .' Quinn tried to clear his head. 'That means I could be the child of John's parents – the Curwens – if, having failed to find Marcus's parents, they adopted him themselves.'

'Then who am I?' John was very pale. So was Mum.

'You're my son, Marcus,' she whispered.

And so it proved. The vans had been side by side at Woodstock, so that's where Richard had first met the Curwens. The children had simply got into the wrong vans. The lines to the States from Charham Place were red-hot that evening, with John rushing to get hold of his parents. Was he or was he not the child they had found in the van? He was, and they'd told the New York police immediately. But not realising that Richard lived in England as he has an Irish lilt to his voice, they left it at that. They probably thought he was an Irish immigrant to the States. The police in New York only had one *missing* child on the records because Marcus Quinn was not missing. Only Peter Curwen was.

There remained in that extraordinary dinner of rejoicing and confusion only one point to clear up. It was entirely fitting that it was Columba who raised it, congratulating herself on her wisdom in stirring all this up to begin with.

'I wonder why Richard went to France?'

'He told us the Curwens lived there,' I pointed out.

'But they never turned up. And they didn't live there anyway.'

We all looked at each other blankly, our brains befuddled by happiness, wine and the late hour.

It was Dad who triumphantly got there first. 'I think Columba can answer that.'

'Me?' She was taken aback. 'I wasn't there, Gerald. Truly.'

'Remember the time you got Margaret, Ellie and myself to rush over to Paris?'

'But that was years later, and anyway—' Columba stopped short. She laughed happily. 'My darlings, of course. The Curwens lived in Paris, Texas, not Paris, France.'

So Mum had her son restored to her, I had my wonderful husband back again, and Quinn had two more parents – and a brother-in-law.

Neither he nor John were too enthusiastic about it at first, until John observed that they had been friends as kids. Quinn saw his point and managed to laugh. All the same, when I sneaked a glance at Quinn's most recent work, the Rab-Hits' latest victim seemed to bear a suspicious resemblance to my brother John.

Even the biography had a happy ending. Grandma Violet was overcome with finding she had yet another grandson, and withdrew all her objections. 'After all,' she said, 'this American *is* one of the family.'